Freddie Tho

If
Nothin'
Don't
Happen

IF
NOTHIN'
DON'T
HAPPEN

by David M. Newell

Illustrated by Mark Livingston

ALFRED A. KNOPF   NEW YORK   1982

THIS IS A BORZOI BOOK
PUBLISHED BY ALFRED A. KNOPF, INC.

Copyright © 1974 by David M. Newell
All rights reserved under International and Pan-
American Copyright Conventions. Published in the
United States by Alfred A. Knopf, Inc., New York,
and simultaneously in Canada by Random House of
Canada Limited, Toronto. Distributed by Random
House, Inc., New York.

Library of Congress Cataloging in Publication Data:

Newell, David McCheyne, date.
    If nothin' don't happen.
    I. Title.
PZ4.N543If [PS3527.E83]   813'.5'2   74-7745
ISBN 0-394-49312-5

Manufactured in the United States of America
Published January 29, 1975
Reprinted Seven Times
Eighth Printing, March 1982

*To the memory of Charlie Dean, Uncle George Rawls
and other great old-time crackers
who supplied much of the material for this book
just by being themselves*

CONTENTS

If
Nothin'
Don't
Happen

INTRODUCTION

In these days of the four-letter word, Billy Driggers, who tells this story, avoids them. Oh, he knows them all, of course, and out among the net fishermen and the cowboys his language is rough as the next man's. But like your true Florida cracker he watches his language around womenfolks, preachers and polite society in general. That's the way Ma Driggers brought up her boys.

She was a good woman who loved her Creator, her Bible, her family and the world around her. She was an Epps from the North Carolina mountains, and her talk still bore traces of old England, much of which she passed along to her boys, Billy and Tarley. For instance, there is no set pattern for the use of the verb "to be." Billy might say, "It were a right cold day and I was a long way from home," using the different forms in the same sentence—whatever came easiest off his tongue and flowed the smoothest. And, after all, neither of the boys had "too much schoolin'," as they said.

Nor did Winton Epps, Ma's brother, but that didn't stop him from composing verse. About the family he wrote:

The Eppses and the Driggerses was rough and tough and crusty.
Their men was double-jointed and their womenfolks was lusty.
Their dogs could whip the other dogs, their horses run the fastest.
And when it come to drinkin' time, no Epps was ever lastest!

Uncle Wint would tell you what a good shot he was and then prove it. He'd offer to whip the other man in an argument and then do it. So when he'd tell a tale, as the kids say now, "You'd better believe it." I hope you do.

I

THE HAMMOCK

Uncle Winton had a mule one time that went into a trot and broke wind so loud it scared itself and ran away and turnt over the wagon and spilt a barrel of syrup that was worth fifty dollars even in them days. Uncle Wint couldn't afford to lose it, but he had to laugh at that dang mule anyhow. He could see the funny side of most anything. A feller's in real bad shape in this world if he can't laugh, specially at himself, because life is goin' to hand him a lot worse things than mule wind.

My name is Billy Driggers and Uncle Wint is my mother's brother, Winton Z. Epps. This here story is about him and me and my brother Tarley and all my folks and what happened to us as best I can remember it; not always in the order it happened, but just like it come to mind when I wrote it down. If I had a hound dog that strayed off on side trails like I do, I'd kill him, but one thing puts me in mind of another, so that's the way I have to tell it, whether it's about rattlesnakes, bobcats, a shootin' scrape, women, ordinary fights, how to cook ducks, or just some crazy happenin' that'll plain-out tickle the fire out of you.

Naturally, there's a lot about my brother Tarley, who's four years older than me and had to be the he coon around our place after the bad thing happened. Even when he were just a shirttail boy he were a scrappy little scaper and didn't take nothin' from nobody.

One of my earliest memories is of ridin' along in the ox-cart with Tarley when my daddy was carryin' a load of cane syrup to the commissary at Inglis. We met a feller in a big double wagon about a mile from the settlement. He reined up his team and Daddy finally talked old Buck, our ox, into stoppin'. There ain't no bridle or bit on a ox, so you drive him by talkin' to him and he'll handle pretty good if he's in the notion.

The feller in the big wagon said, "Howdy. My name's Lightfoot. I reckon you're Driggers—brother-in-law to Winton Epps, the feller that come down here from North Carolina and keeps goats."

"That's me," my daddy told him.

The feller pointed at me and Tarl with his pipe stem and asked, "Them your boys?"

"I reckon so," Daddy told him. "They was caught in my trap."

The feller laughed and said, "That biggest one there sure don't favor you!"

Daddy had black hair and a big black mustache, but Tarley favored Ma and had sandy hair, near 'bout red, and a freckled face.

"How old are you, boy?" the feller asked him.

"Who wants to know?" Tarl said.

"Why, I do."

"Well, how do you like the way you found out?" Tarl told him.

Before the feller could answer, Daddy slapped Tarley, popped the whip over old Buck and said, "Good-by, Mr. Lightfoot. Me and my boys ain't lookin' for no new acquaintances. And you, Tarley, mind your manners."

This is the way I remember my old man. He never said

more'n he had to and what he did say was short and most
always covered the ground. Maybe it were this habit of his that
caused the big trouble when it did come. Anyhow, he never
backed up from nothin', and my brother Tarley was a heap
like him.

From the very first, Tarley were tough. I don't mean bad
nor always on the prod nor nothin' like that. I just mean that
he could take whatever got dished out to him, most of the
time with a smile on his face. And when he got his mind
made up, there didn't nothin' change it even if it meant killin'
a man.

Us folks had moved up to the Hammock from the little
settlement out from Fort Myers where my daddy was borned.
When I speak of the Hammock, I'm talkin' about Gulf Hammock, a big piece of country which runs from Cedar Key
slap down to the Withlacoochee River. I mean *hammock* and
not *hummock,* which is what all Yankees will try to call it.
They'll tell you a hammock is a swingin' bed and of course
I know that. I've got one. But it's also a certain kind of woods
which I'll tell you about later on.

To the south of our place, across the river, was swamp and
hammock all the way down to Crystal River, about ten miles,
and to the east of us was flat piney woods and farther east
was sand hills. Scrub palmettos growed pretty thick in the
flatwoods, but out in the sand hills they was just here and
there in clumps and most of the trees was second-growth
pine and scrub oaks—what we call blackjacks and turkey
oaks. Where the palmettos, scrub oaks and scrub pines grow
real thick, we just call it scrub, and way on farther east is
what they call the Big Scrub, miles and miles and miles of it.
Some lady wrote up a book about some cousin of ourn over
there and a little old pet deer they raised, but I disremember
its name.

North of us, like I said, was hammock and swamp plumb
up to the Suwanee River. There's a high hammock and low
hammock and swamp, and I'll try to explain the difference.
High hammock has got mostly live oaks, red cedars, slash
pine, hickories, magnolias and cabbage palms, which we
mostly just call cabbages. High-hammock soil ain't as sandy

as scrub, but it ain't muddy and boggy like low hammock. Low hammock has sweet bay and red bay and black gum and sweet gum along with some magnolias and of course cabbages and palmettos. There ain't much difference when it comes to low hammock and swamp.

Where most of the trees are cypress trees, it's called a cypress strand or a cypress head. And what we call a bay head is a low, swampy place with bay trees a-growin' real thick. There ain't no worse place to try to go through, unless it's a mangrove swamp like down along the saltwater.

There's several kinds of scrub palmettos, including saw palmettos and needle palmettos. Either kind makes real rough goin' for a huntin' dog, because the stems of the saw palmettos will cut him and the spines of the needle palmettos will punch out his eyes if he ain't careful. You'll find gallberry bushes and huckleberry bushes growin' right with the palmettos in the flatwoods along the edge of the hammock. And the varmints use the flatwoods a heap when all them berries get ripe in the spring.

To the west of our place it's about six miles through the Hammock to the Gulf marsh. The country breaks up into rocky creeks and islands and shell mounds where there ain't nothin' growin' but a few cabbage palms, runty cedars and Spanish bayonets. There's a world of ducks come into these salt creeks and there's all kinds of fish in 'em—sheephead, snappers, mullet and plenty of trout and redfish in cool weather. Both varmints and people had plenty of good eatin' right handy.

Log Landing is near where the piney woods joins up with the Hammock, and our house were built out of cabbage logs set on end. The trunk of a cabbage palm will rot out pretty fast layin' on its side, but if it's stood up and capped over, it will last from now till then—and that's long enough.

We had a hundred and sixty acres, but only about half was cleared—enough for a garden, a cane patch, a couple of hog pens, a horse lot and a cow pen. We had about a hundred head of hogs and a couple of dozen range cows. All of our stock was marked in the ears with a crop and an under-bit in the right ear and two under-bits in the left. Everything was open range and both the hogs and cows ran wild in the Hammock and made their own livin'. We kept track of 'em with catch dogs, and I remember we had two of the best that ever made a track in the sand. Either one would catch and hold a cow or a steer till it were marked. They'd run under the steer's foreleg, grab his nose, set back and turn him end over end.

And when it comes to hogs, together they could handle the biggest, meanest old wild boar in the Hammock, and I've seen 'em hold one with tushes five inches long and weighin' a couple of hundred pounds. One would get on each side of him and catch him back of an ear and lay right to him so that he couldn't swing his head to reach either one. All the old man had to do were say, "Catch him," and they'd purely catch whatever he sent 'em after. A whole lot of our cattle and hog range in Florida is so thick and brushy that a feller can't hardly use a rope, and them old catch dogs was just the ticket. Of course they was pretty rough on the stock, and screw worms would often get into the places where the dogs had had hold of 'em, so after while folks quit usin' catch dogs altogether.

At first we had a mule and a milk cow, a couple of cow ponies and Buck, our old ox, for pullin' the cart and haulin' logs. Old Buck could pull more than ary two horses, specially in the low hammock where it were muddy and hard goin'. The old man got him mainly for haulin' up cabbage logs to build our house. It weren't no trouble then to find plenty of cabbage palms thirty or forty feet tall and near 'bout as straight as a pine tree. The logs are right light when they dry out, but they're sure heavy when they're green. But old Buck would walk off through the mud with one like it were nothin'.

And Buck paid his way when it come to grindin' cane, and we always made our own syrup. A meal ain't much without some hot biscuits and syrup, and ours was the best to be had. I remember how good that cold cane juice tasted when I got me a tin cup full where it run out the trough from the grinder.

The old ox were mighty good at plowin' too, though he were terrible slow, and we raised some of the best turnips and collards and black-eyed peas a feller could want. We'd dress out an acorn-fattened shoat and barbecue him in a rock pit while Ma were cookin' up a mess of peas and greens. Dessert were always hot biscuits and syrup. The old man liked to start his meal with a swig of 'shine and I recall his sayin' that some of it were so fresh and strong it would make you trot your oxen! And that must have been some kind of strong because I never seen nothin' that would make old Buck get out of a slow walk!

Daddy got our first cow from a old feller out in the flatwoods and I remember hearin' 'em talkin' trade.

"This here's a extra good cow," old man Findlay said.

"What do you want for her?" Daddy asked him.

"Fifty dollars," the old feller said. "And I keep the calf."

"That's a heap of money," Daddy told him. "How much milk does she give?"

"Well," old man Findlay said, "to be plumb honest about it, I don't rightly know—the calf has done the milkin'. But like I said, she's a dang good cow and I guarantee she'll give you all she's got!"

Daddy said, "A feller couldn't ask ary cow to do more'n that." So he taken a chance and bought her. It turned out to be a good deal because she were real gentle and gave enough milk for us to have plenty to drink and even make a little butter. Livin' was good and there weren't ary cloud in our sky—not that we could see then.

2

THE
BAD THING

About three miles upriver above Log Landing is what we call Gator Crawl Landing, or just Gator Crawl. This is about a hundred steps below where the commissary is at and got its name from the fact that it were a sandy bar breakin' into the river bank where 'gators used to like to crawl out and sun theirselves.

Most all of us who lived on the river used to run our boats in on Gator Crawl instead of tyin' up to the commissary dock. Of course if we was expectin' to bring back some horse feed or anything heavy like that, we'd go plumb up to the dock and tie up. But mostly we'd just run the bow of our boat in on the sandy beach and chunk an anchor up on the bank.

Well, some rich feller from Pennsylvania bought up near 'bout a whole section of land and when he had the survey made, it took in Gator Crawl. He were a-goin' to put in some fancy cattle and he built a fence around all his land, but left a gate on the east side where a sand road went from Gator Crawl up to the commissary. This road were so a feller could get from his boat to a wagon or a car.

The Yankee had a high wire gate put across the road and it were kept closed and a little shanty and a guard was put there. Everybody in the settlement got mad enough to bite a skunk about this gate because we'd all been a-goin' and a-comin' through there as long as we could remember. The word got around that any of us who lived around here could get a pass but couldn't go through without one. I knowed there would be trouble the first time my old man butted heads with that gate guard, and for quite a while Ma talked him out of goin' up there in his boat.

"Froney," he said, "My great-grandaddy dug these here west-coast rivers with his bowie knife and there ain't no man goin' to tell me when I can go and come. I'll take the wagon or ride a horse up to the store when it suits me, but the first time I take a notion to go in the boat, I'm a-goin! That's all there is to it!"

One day Dad and Tarley had been across the river checkin' up on a old sow that had turned up missin' and he run out of tobacco, so he just went on up to Gator Crawl, beached the boat and him and Tarley started up to the commissary. When they got to the gate it were locked and the guard come out and wrote 'em a pass. It seemed like the guard knowed my old man, but Dad didn't know the guard—some feller from Georgia. Anyhow, the feller said, "Here's your pass, Mr. Driggers."

There was three fellers comin' from the store who heard everything, and two of 'em backed up Tarley in tellin' what happened. One of the fellers were brother to the guard and the other two was commercial fishermen from Shell Island. They said that my old man just tore up the pass and throwed it down and him and Tarley walked on toward the store. When they come back, in about ten minutes, the gate were closed and the guard stepped out in front of 'em and said, "I told you that you had to have a pass to go through here."

Dad just laughed and started to open the gate, but the guard knocked him down from behind and then shot him in the back with his pistol. The bullet didn't break his back, but it paralyzed him so he couldn't stand up and he just dragged himself on all fours. Tarley run at the guard and he parted

Tarley's hair with the barrel of that pistol and put him to sleep. While this was goin' on, Dad managed to crawl to the boat and get his old long double-barrel out from under the bow deck. Then he propped himself across the bow of the boat and shot the guard. Three double-ought buckshot taken the feller right in the brisket and that chilled his chitlins!

Then the brother run and grabbed up the pistol and shot twice at Dad, missin' him the first time but hittin' him in the belly with the second shot. Then it were Dad's turn with the second barrel and he shot the brother down, breakin' his leg. Before Dad could find any more shells the feller crawled off out of range and by this time Dad were gettin' in pretty bad shape. One of them commercial fishermen testified that Dad got out his knife and said, "I'm a-goin' to let some of this blood out . . . I'm a-bleedin' to death inside." But he passed out before he could cut himself open, and they borrowed a team and wagon and started for the nearest hospital, which were at Ocala—more'n forty miles away and a five- or six-hour trip for the team. They taken Tarley with 'em because he still hadn't come to and they didn't know how bad he were hurt.

Daddy died on the way to the hospital, but Tarley woke up in time to hear him say, "Tell my brother-in-law, Winton Epps, to kill the next man that shuts that gate and keep killin' 'em as long as they shut it!" Them was the last words he ever spoke and Tarley never forgot 'em. He weren't but fourteen years old, but he come back home and told everybody what Daddy had said and promised that if anybody shut that gate again, he, Tarley Driggers, would personally shoot him that same day.

Later on he told me, "Billy, I ain't got no way to go up north a-lookin' for that Yankee who built the fence or for that Georgia cracker whose leg Daddy busted, but if either one of them polecats ever shows up around here I believe I'll just naturally be bound to shoot him!"

"Don't let Ma hear you talkin' that way," I told him. "You know she believes that vengeance belongs to the Lord."

"I know that," Tarl said. "But maybe He could spare me a little!"

Anyhow, from that day on, Tarley changed a heap. He were a man. And I'll say one thing: that gate ain't never been closed to this day!

Of course they had a inquest and the sheriff come down from the county seat, but there weren't no trial or nothin' because there weren't nobody to try. My dad and the guard was dead and the Georgia cracker with the broke leg had plumb disappeared, nobody knows how. But though we didn't know it then, we hadn't heard the last of the Yankee who hired the fence built or the other feller either.

Preacher Elliott helt the funeral for Daddy and it seemed like he were hard put to find somethin', to say, seein' as how Dad hardly ever set foot in the church. When he said, "The Lord has given and the Lord has taken away," Uncle Winton spoke right up and said, "Amen! That's as fair a proposition as I ever heered in my life."

I were only ten years old at the time of Daddy's funeral and I tried hard to be sad like I knowed I ought to be. I shut my eyes—or at least one of 'em—when Preacher Elliott prayed, and I helt tight to Ma's hand and I could feel her tremblin' a little. Dad hadn't been just exactly the feller she might have wanted him to be, but he'd worked hard and he hadn't been scared of nothin' that walked or crawled. "He were a man, boys," she would tell us, as if that were the most important thing could be said about a feller. And I reckon maybe it is.

"Like all men, he had his faults," Ma went on, "but I want you boys to remember one thing. The Book says, 'Honor thy father and thy mother that thy days may be long.' It don't say, 'Honor thy father if he done everything to suit you.' It just says to honor him because he's your daddy. So you boys remember that and honor his memory. I don't believe in fightin', but you fellers have my permission to climb onto anybody who low-rates the memory of your dad anytime, anywhere!" And me and Tarl never forgot that.

The Yankee who had bought the land and fenced off the river landin' and hired the guard was named McWirter and lived up in Pittsburgh. We found that out in the deed book over at Bronson. The guard who shot Daddy were named

Corson Lukins, and his brother, the one who got away with a broke leg, went by the name of Speck. Speck Lukins had more freckles than anybody I ever seen. He spent near about all his time net-fishin' for mullet at night, so I never could figure how come he had so many freckles. Anyhow, his skin were real white where it weren't orange-speckled and there wouldn't be no way to mistake him for nobody else.

"If ever I see him again, I'll cut down on him," Tarley said. "Time I lay eyes on him."

There weren't nothin' Ma could say to change him, even when she kept quotin' the Bible at him. Uncle Winton didn't help none, because he'd just say, "And if the boy misses, I won't." Then he surprised everybody by sayin', "That there Bible also says, 'Whoso sheddeth man's blood, by man shall his blood be shed.'"

"Sure," Ma told him, plumb surprised at his quotin' the Bible, "but that means the law—human law. It just don't mean *any* man."

"How do *you* know what man?" Uncle asked her. "If Tarl misses, *I'm* the man!"

"That ain't what the Book says," Ma told him.

"Well, it's what *I* say," Uncle said.

"But I ain't goin' to miss," Tarl told both of 'em, "so there ain't no use hasslin' about it no more."

The best Ma could get out of Tarl was a promise that he wouldn't go off up into Georgia lookin' for Lukins—if that's where he'd gone—or up north lookin' for McWirter. He did promise that much, but what happened later on changed his mind about a lot of things.

Uncle Winton, though, didn't promise nothin'. He is my own uncle and I think a heap of him, but I will have to say he had some funny ideas. Like his knife. He always carried a great big old pocket knife and kept it sharp enough to shave with. I'll grant you that a dull knife is no good, but Uncle was so proud of the edge on his that he was happy when he cut himself! I seen him cut his finger near 'bout off and he just smiled and said, "Boys, she's sharp enough to shave with!"

He's the only feller I ever seen who bragged on his knife when he cut himself. But I guess he knowed what he was doin', and I'd rather face a bear than have Uncle comin' at me with that knife. I hated to think of what would happen to Speck Lukins if Uncle ever got to him.

Like I said awhile ago, Lukins spent most of his time net-fishin', but folks said he were just like a Indian in the woods—a awful good hunter and a extra fine shot. Everybody who knowed him said he were meaner than a snake, specially when drinkin'. But nobody seemed to know just how bad hurt he'd been when he crawled off after the shootin' of Daddy. Somebody sure must of helped him off and carried him plumb out of the Hammock, but nobody would say who done it—if they knowed.

For a while after the shootin' Ma wouldn't hardly let me'n Tarl out of her sight and she didn't like for us to go back into the Hammock much either. "What if that feller is a-layin' out there somewhere nursin' his leg and just waitin' for a chance to bushwhack you boys?" she'd say. But we had to check up on our hogs now and then and we still had to have some game to eat, so it weren't long till us boys was huntin' again.

Of course we missed Daddy on our trips to the woods, but Uncle Winton spent a heap of time with us and nobody knowed more about huntin' than he did. And, like I said, no matter what happened, he could near about always see the funny side of it, specially if there was a mule in it!

3 OUR FIRST FIRE HUNT & UNCLE WINTON'S SOUL

Back in them days fire-huntin' weren't against the law, or if it were we didn't know about it. We'd ride out through the Hammock on a dark night, holdin' a pine-knot flambeau up over our heads and lookin' under its light for a deer's eyes. To make the flambeau we'd split a fat light'd pine knot into splinters. That fat pine is full of turpentine and will really burn. It's the best fire-lighter wood there is and some crackers call it "lighter'd" meaning lighter wood and others just call it "light'd" like I do.

You hear a lot of people talk about animals' eyes shinin', but it's only reflected light, and you don't never see it unless you are lookin' just right under the light of a flambeau or with a flashlight or in automobile headlights. Different animals' eyes shine different ways—a possum's eyes shine blood red, a coon's eyes shine green, a 'gator's eyes shine red and a wild-cat's or deer's eyes will shine a sort of golden red like a coal of fire.

I never will forget the first time Daddy had let me and

Tarley try our hand at night deer huntin'. We borrowed Uncle Winton's big old gray mule that were slow and gentle and we both got up on her and started out. Daddy let us take his old twelve-gauge hammer gun. It had a barrel so long that a feller had to go out on the front porch to turn around with it, and it were a far-knockin' weapon. When I were seven years old I seen Daddy kill a yearlin' bear eighty steps away with that gun.

Tarley, bein' the oldest, were a-goin' to do the shootin' while I helt the flambeau. For a long time we didn't see nothin' at all. The old mule went walkin' along, pickin' her way through the Hammock, over logs and 'round tree trunks, and we just about let her go where she wanted.

Fire-huntin' is just luck—that is, a feller don't know where the deer will be, but just keeps a-movin' and a-lookin' and a-hopin'. We'd been out about a half an hour and figgered we was about a mile or maybe a mile and a half back in the Hammock when all of a sudden we seen a whole bunch of eyes.

"A herd of 'em," Tarley whispered and reined up the old mule while I helt the light higher and could see what seemed to be eight or ten sets of eyes, all pretty close together.

Tarley slipped in a couple of number-one buckshot shells, cocked both barrels of that old pot iron and rared up in the stirrups and wadded it to 'em—*baloom! baloom!* When the gun fired, the old mule jumped and broke wind so loud it sounded like a third shot. I fell off, Tarley jumped off and all hell broke loose out in front of us. It weren't until then that we seen the fence and knowed what had happened. That dang mule had traveled in a circle, wantin' to get home, and Tarley had fired into Uncle's goats and killed five and crippled four more so that they had to be killed. It took us all day and until late the next night to finish skinnin' and butcherin' them goats, and I'm here to say that neither one of us would ever eat a piece of goat meat again if we was starvin' plumb to death.

Daddy had sure been mad, but he didn't whip us. He said he didn't believe in whippin' a boy for doin' somethin' wrong accident'ly. But if you ever did somethin' wrong on purpose and he caught you, he'd whip you till you begged like a pet coon.

One of the reasons we killed and crippled up so many goats were that Tarley had used them number-one buckshot because we didn't have no double-oughts. There's only nine double-oughts in a twelve-gauge shell—three layers of three. And there's sixteen number-one buckshot, almost twice as many, in a twelve-gauge shell. Any kind of buckshot is pretty chancy as far as tellin' just where the shots are goin' to go. You've got a better chance of hittin' a deer with number-one, but a double-ought will stop him better—if it hits him—and goats ain't no different!

Tarley were just enough older and bigger than me so that I got left out of a lot of things. I remember one time, when I were about ten years old, everybody goin' to a big frolic over to the Jacksons' place and I had to stay home and look after a neighbor's baby—a great big old blubber-headed baby about two years old that were the onliest child. They brought him and his cradle over to our house and explained to me that he had to be rocked to sleep. Then everybody rode off in their buggies and wagons and that baby began to beller. I made up my mind I weren't goin' to rock him but just let him beller and we'd see who gave out first. Well, I gave out first. He'd shut his eyes and open his mouth and squall till his face turned red. I couldn't stand it no more, so I went over to his cradle and said, "All right, young gentleman, you want to be rocked, so get ready to ride!" Then I rocked him. I mean I rocked him. I had him flyin' back and forth against the sides of that cradle so I don't believe he touched bottom for five minutes. When I stopped to rest he just laid there plumb still and I thought I'd killed him. Directly he opened one eye a little bit and looked at me real funny. I reached over to get hold of the cradle again and when I did he hollered bloody murder for sure. I jerked my hand back and he laid still. When I'd start to reach out he'd holler. What I mean is from that day on you didn't have to rock him to sleep—you didn't dare rock him at all! I heered his folks tellin' Ma later on that they just couldn't understand it.

We had one sorry old hound that would just stand at the back door beggin' for somethin' to eat and never got enough. I do believe a feller could just have wadded up a dish rag and throwed it out and he'd have swallered it before he knowed what it was. The evenin' I was watchin' the baby that dern dog kept whinin' and droolin' along with the baby hollerin' to be rocked and I got madder by the minute. We had a barrel of salt mullet in the breezeway and I decided to give that dog all he wanted to eat for once in his life. I tossed him three or four of them salt fish and then he went to the horse trough. Then he laid down under a orange tree. Pretty quick he went out to the horse trough and drank again and then come back and laid down under the orange tree. He didn't get settled till he was after another drink. By the time the folks got home he'd swelled up tighter'n a drum and liken to have died.

That evenin' cured three things—that dog from standin' at the door beggin', them people from askin' me to ever watch their baby again and the baby from havin' to be rocked in the cradle.

We never had no cradle, but I remember Ma rockin' me in her little old rockin' chair. And I remember my daddy singin' me to sleep, and Ma was always hummin' a little tune and had a right sweet voice. I loved to hear her, and when there weren't nobody around I done some singin' myself, but I'd of died before I'd let anybody hear me. Tarl never did care nothin' for music of no kind except hounds a-runnin', which he claimed were the sweetest music in the world.

One time when I were just a little scaper Ma taken me to some rich Yankee's house to hear some phonograph records. He was a feller who had bought a island and built a fancy home, and I remember a great big room where he had his phonograph. Quite a few of us folks from the settlement went there to hear the music that night, and I remember him playin' several songs by a feller named Caruso. That feller could really sing . . . seemed like five minutes before he'd have to catch a breath. I remember one real pretty piece he sung with some feller named Scotty, but I never did find out Scotty who. Anyhow, they both could really pour it out. If I could sing like that I'd get me up two or three weeks' rations and go off somewhere and camp and just sing to myself.

There were another piece called "Polly" somethin' or other and a place in it where Caruso sung without breathin' long enough to swim the Withlacoochee River underwater. I remember old man Johnson sayin' to the Yankee, "That sure was pretty. But, you know, I couldn't understand a dang word of it."

The Yankee feller just laughed and told him that Caruso always done his singin' in Eyetalian.

"Why?" old man Johnson asked him.

The Yankee told him that was the way the music was wrote.

"Well, Mr. Caruso can really put it out. I'll say that much."

"Yes," the Yankee told him, "he had a very powerful voice . . . in fact, he could sing into a drinking glass and crack it."

"I'll be dad-burned!" old man Johnson said. "That scoun'el couldn't have lived around me . . . I'd of killed him!"

Some of the tales the men told around the fireplace on winter nights was enough to make your hair stand up—shootin's, cuttin's and fights and all such as that. I remember when I were just a little bit of a skeester, settin' up and listenin' to 'em one night when Ma had gone to prayer meetin' and taken Tarley with her to drive the buggy. Daddy seen me settin' there and said, "Son, you're too young to listen to all this talk of killin's and such. Go on to bed."

When Daddy told us to go to bed, we went to bed and I mean right now. I went on down the hall to the room where me and Tarl slept and it sure did seem lonesome and dark. I got to thinkin' about wildcats and panthers and robbers and I just couldn't help cryin' some.

Uncle Wint must of heered me because he come in and set on the edge of my bed and said, "What's the matter, Billy boy?"

"Uncle Winton," I told him, "I'm scared."

"Scared of what?"

"Scared somethin' will get me."

"Nothin's goin' to get you," he told me. "Me and your daddy is right there down the hall."

"Yes, I know that," I told him, "and the good Lord's watchin' too, ain't He?"

Well, Uncle Winton weren't much on religion, but I reckon he didn't want to scare me no worser, so he nodded his head and said, "He sure is!"

"Yes, sir," I told him, "He's way up there in the sky and He can look right on down through the roof and the ceiling and see you settin' on this here bed talkin' to me, can't He?"

"That's right," Uncle said.

"Yes, sir," I told him. "I seen pictures in Sunday School. He's way up there in the sky with His arms spread out. If He'd put 'em down, He'd fall!"

For some reason or other, Uncle Winton got up and walked out of the room. I know now he was tryin' not to laugh and didn't want me to see. Him and Ma had some real serious talkin' about this religion business and, like I said, he didn't take much stock in it—or at least he let on that he didn't.

"Winton," Ma told him one time, "you can bet on the Chicago White Sox or a horse race out to Red Level or that freckledy-faced fighter Fitzsimmons or one of your sorry old potlickers to lead the pack in a bear chase and you can be wrong. But when it comes to what happens to your immortal soul after they put you in the ground, *you can't be wrong.*"

He'd just snort and walk off, specially when she'd speak about his favorite hounds as "sorry old potlickers." I don't think there were ary soul in that whole country who'd of dared say somethin' like that to Winton Epps about his dogs except his own sister. It were a lot of years later that I found out just how much stock he really took in what Ma said about his soul.

Uncle Wint hadn't never had much schoolin' and once in a while he'd get his words mixed up, and when he did, it were hard to put him straight. Like what he called his "epithets." He was always writin' 'em down for somebody's gravestone or to go on a marker for a dog that had died.

"You mean 'epitaphs,'" Ma told him one time when he had

just wrote one for old man McGreer, who was a mean old feller. "A epithet is somethin' bad you call a feller."

"Well then," Uncle said, "I'll guaran-dam-tee that's what this is." When Uncle really meant somethin' he'd guarantee it, and when he guaran-dam-teed it, you'd better believe him.

"Do you want to hear it?" he asked Ma.

"No," she told him.

"Well, by grannies, you're a-goin' to anyhow," he said and spoke it right out:

> The last remains of Mac McGreer,
> He lied in life and now lies here.
> He was a crooked, cheatin' dastard,
> A triple-dipped and third-class bastard.

"Where'd you ever hear 'dastard,' Winton?" Ma asked.

"I didn't hear it," Uncle told her. "I looked through half the dictionary for a word to rhyme with bastard. And it ain't no compliment neither."

"Pretty rough on poor Mr. McGreer," Ma said.

"He was rough on everybody else," Uncle said. "So dad-burned tight that every time he blinked his eyes his navel winked. And he were so crooked that they thought for a while they couldn't bury him layin' down but would have to screw him into the ground. He were the greediest feller I ever knowed in all my life and I do believe you could have set a coon trap in the seat of his britches and baited it with a nickel and caught his heart."

"Winton!" Ma said. "That's plumb vulgar. I'm surprised at you." But I seen a little twinkle in her eye and after Uncle left she told us boys, "You know, your uncle could have been a real poet with just a little schoolin'."

There were a time when Uncle Wint and Aunt Effie had some real hard sleddin'. Cold killed off his vegetables, cholera got into his hogs and he had to borrow a lot of money.

"It had me so worried, Billy," he told me one night when he were over to our house, "that I couldn't sleep at night."

"That'd be bad, Uncle Wint," I said. "What did you do?"

"I slept in the daytime," Uncle said. "A good nap after dinner will cure a lot of things."

"Well, if a feller didn't have to put up a struggle it would take all the interest out of life," Daddy said.

"I'd be glad to have it took out of mine," Uncle told him. "Five percent's too dern high." And he went to laughin'.

But even with his troubles Uncle Winton managed to scrape up a few dollars here and there and buy land. Every time he made a good crop or sold some beef or hogs he'd make a payment on a piece of land.

"Real estate is what they call it, boys," he told us, "and they ain't just whistlin' 'Dixie.' *Real* estate is what it is. Anything else is 'maginary estate. The land is there and will be there no matter what happens. Everybody is busy makin' more people, but nobody ain't makin' no more land. Your daddy left y'all a right pretty piece of ground here on the river, so hang on to it. I know your ma will."

"So long as I live and breathe," she told him, "this will be Driggers land kept for Jim Driggers' boys."

"That's the way to talk, Sis," Uncle told her. "An Epps don't back up from nobody or nothin'. And I'll be right on hand whenever y'all need me."

After he'd gone, Ma went into her room and shut the door, but if she cried about Daddy, we didn't hear her.

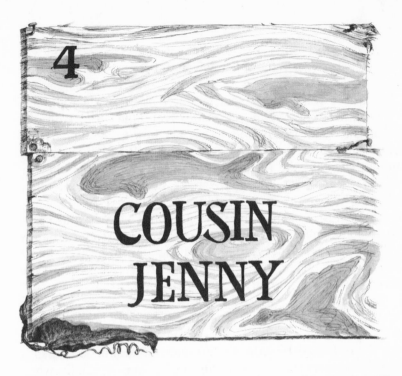

COUSIN JENNY

One thing I remember about my daddy was his singin'. The more 'shine he'd had, the better his voice got. He had a old gittar and when he felt real good he used to sing a Indian song. I can hear it just as plain today as if it was yesterday, but I can't remember the words to it. He called the song "Ogalalla" and I ain't never heard nobody sing it but my dad. I remember Tarley askin' him about it and what he answered.

"Son, my mammy learnt me that song and she learnt it from her daddy, whose name was O'Keefe. He was one of them Irishmen that come over here a long time ago to help build a railroad out west somewhere. The story was that there was about three hundred of them Irishmen and when they first come over they walked on all fours. But accordin' to your great-grandaddy, after they pushed them wheelbarrows around all day they was so stiff they couldn't bend over. And that's how he learnt to walk upright like a man! Of course, son, there ain't nothin' to make you believe this and I won't whip you if you don't!"

The only one of the O'Keefe family that we ever seen

down here in Florida were a big fat woman who Ma said was our cousin twice removed. I never did find out where she'd been removed from or why, but as far as I was concerned they didn't remove her soon enough or often enough. She come down not long after Daddy got killed and said she wanted to comfort Ma and advise her how to get along without a man in the house. This didn't set well with Tarl or with me either. And she made Tarl tell her all about the shootin' several times over and she'd shake her head and say they knowed how to take care of things like that out west.

She weighed near 'bout three hundred pounds and come from somewhere in Nebraska—out where Great-grandaddy O'Keefe had built that railroad. Her name were Jenny O'Keefe Bradley and her husband had died a year or two before she come down here and left her right smart insurance.

Well, Cousin Jenny were broader in the beam than the average mullet skiff and a-rarin' to go—anywhere, anytime or for anything. First off she rubbed Ma the wrong way by tryin' to change the kitchen around—"reorganizin'" it, she said. Ma never did like folks in her kitchen, specially when she were cookin', and it didn't take her long to get Cousin Jenny told about that. Then Cousin Jenny started in tryin' to teach her a lot of Yankee cookin' ideas—like cookin' pole beans with bakin' soda to make 'em nice and green, and leavin' out the fatback. I never tasted nothin' so tasteless in my natural life. Finally Ma run her out of the kitchen completely. Then Cousin Jenny turned her attention to me and Tarley and Uncle Winton—"the woodpile's runnin' low," "the well bucket's leakin'" or "the fence needs fixin'." She never let nobody rest, and I reckon her poor husband hadn't had much rest neither. She'd had him cremated and Uncle Winton said, "I'll bet she keeps the poor feller's ashes in a hourglass—and turns him every thirty minutes!"

Accordin' to her, he must of been a real he coon because she was always talkin' about him and all the things he could do. Whenever she seen anything around the place that needed doin' or fixin' she'd say, "My man wouldn't let somethin' like that go till next day. He'd fix it. Look at that weed patch. If that was Ed Bradley's he'd have had it growin' pretty flowers or vegetables and a nice fence around it. Why can't these boys clean it up?"

For some reason or other, Cousin Jenny and Uncle Winton butted heads the first time they met. Uncle never did take kindly to anybody tellin' him how to do nothin'. In fact, he told her so right quick one day when she went over to his house. The back screen door was stickin' a little at one corner when she opened it, and she said, "I'll tell you how to fix that screen door."

"Listen, Cousin Jenny," he said, "I don't let nobody tell me how to do nothin'."

"Nobody couldn't tell you how to do *nothin'*," she said. "You already know how to do *nothin'* better'n anybody I ever seen. Now, if Ed Bradley was here he'd fix that door. He was a topnotch carpenter. And he'd fix you some good stone steps that wouldn't rot out because he was a good stonemason too! I can't begin to tell you all the things he could do."

"Good!" said Uncle Winton and went on out of the house, slammin' that old door so hard it fell plumb off.

Not long after she got here, Cousin Jenny made me and Tarley take her down the river to see the Gulf. I guess the most water she ever seen before had been in a creek some-where, because when we rounded the bend and come in sight of the open water, she got right scared and made us stop the boat at Pelican Island, which lays right in the mouth of the river. It were a clear, cool day without much wind and the Gulf were as pretty a blue as you ever seen, just a-sparklin'.

"I'll be dogged if that ain't a sight in this world," Cousin Jenny said, "but what if that thing should get out of its banks?"

"Well, it does that once in a while," Tarley said, "and it ain't so pretty then."

"I reckon not," Cousin Jenny said. "That's the most water I ever seen to once in my whole life—and you don't see it all either, you just see what's on top!"

One thing I never could understand about women, most specially Yankee women, is how crazy they are to get tanned up. Even Cousin Jenny. When she come down it were late winter, and I guess she'd been stayin' inside out of the snow 'cause she had smooth white skin. Nothin' would do but that she had to get into a bathin' suit and go out in the boat "to get some sun." A feller didn't realize how much there were of Cousin Jenny and her pretty white skin until she come out in that bathin' suit. She laid down on the bow deck of our boat and Tarley had to stand up on the motor box to see where to go. I don't mean to say that Cousin Jenny weren't modest and proper, 'cause she were, and bathin' suits in them days amounted to somethin'—not like what they're wearin' now, just a couple of half dollars and a dollar bill.

Well, Cousin Jenny got some sun all right! In a hour and a half she looked like a fresh-boiled jumbo shrimp, and in a couple of days she peeled off and come out speckled as a mockin'-bird egg. But nothin' fazed that woman. After a few trips in the boat, she worried Tarley till he let her steer it, and she were comin' around the bend in Grassy Creek when we met another boat goin' out mullet fishin'. Cousin Jenny were standin' at the wheel of our boat, and she got excited and started turnin' the wheel the wrong way.

'Stead of swingin' starboard and passin' on the right, she swung the wheel hard over to port and cut right in front of the other boat. Tarley hollered at her, but it were too late! She didn't turn back to the right, but kept on to the left, and the more he hollered, the harder she turned. Like I said, she were a big strong woman and somethin' had to give! Naturally, it were the tiller rope. So the boat just rammed on into the saw grass, the mullet fishermen missed us by a whisker, and I'll bet Cousin Jenny heard words she never heard before, although I don't know. They say there is some rough characters out west too.

Well, Tarley went back astern and crawled up under the back seat to fix the tiller rope.

"What happened?" Cousin Jenny hollered.

"The tiller rope busted," Tarley said, grittin' his teeth.

"Where'bouts?" she hollered again.

"Right back here where I'm workin' on it," Tarley told her.

"Oh, I'm so glad," Cousin Jenny said. "I thought maybe I'd busted it!"

But though Cousin Jenny didn't know much about boats, she sure did know how to shoot ducks. A duck flyin' over her didn't have no more chance than a white shirt in a bear fight.

"Boys," she told us, "out where I live near Scottsbluff we got a creek that fills up with mallards as soon as the weather gets bitter and they come in from off them Canadian wheat fields. A big piece of that creek belongs to my first cousin once removed."

"Who got the creek after he were removed?" I asked her.

"You're a stupid kid," she said. "Just shut up and listen. This here creek is spring-fed and stays open when everything else freezes up fifty miles around. Have you ever seen a whole creek get up and fly off? Well, that's what it looks like when them mallards is there. And I want you to know they're big, heavy rascals, fattened on wheat and corn—not like these scrawny widgeons and pintails and such down here."

Uncle Winton was over to the house when she were doin' all this braggin' and it got too much for him.

"What are you talkin' about!" he snorted. "There ain't nothin' prettier than a big old pintail drake cuppin' his wings and showin' you that pretty white vest, settin' in to the deecoys."

"Shucks," Cousin Jenny said, "he's all neck. Out where I come from we'd just about as soon shoot a magpie. A dern sprig-tail hangs up there just like he's pasted onto the sky, waitin' to be shot. There ain't no way to miss him. The trouble with you, Winton Epps, is that you're just ignorant. All you know is what's in your own back yard. Why, I've had my hand farther in a paper bag than you've ever been away from home!"

"Is that right?" Uncle Wint said. And I could see he was gettin' a little bit hot. "Well, I'll just tell you what we'll do. Along about this time of year we have our Democrat Club meetin' and always serve a big wild-duck dinner. We'll just give you a gun and put you in a blind and see what you do with them pintails settin' so still up there in the sky."

"You do that!" Cousin Jenny said. "And you don't need to give me no gun—I brought my own dern gun."

"I'll bet it's a twenty-gauge or at best a sixteen," Uncle

Wint told her. "A poor little old puny gal like you couldn't stand up to a twelve."

"It's a twenty," Cousin Jenny told him, "and plenty big enough to kill your derned old pintails and widgeons and scaups."

"And what in the horrible hell is a scaup?" Uncle Winton asked her.

"It's a broadbill," she told him. "You got plenty of 'em down at the mouth of the river."

"She means bluebills, Uncle Wint," Tarley said.

"Well, why don't you say bluebills?" Uncle Wint said, spittin' on the floor, which he never does unless he's mad. "We don't eat them things around here because they eat snails and such and they're just too dang fishy. I tried to fix some bluebill gizzards for a giblet stew one time and they was so fishy you couldn't hardly stay in the boat with 'em. I doubt if a dad-burned pelican would have eat that stew."

"No wonder," Cousin Jenny said. "The poor scaups ain't got nothin' else to eat but snails. Out our way they're fat as butter from eatin' grain and they're just as good a table bird as any."

"Well, get yourself plenty of shells and be ready at four o'clock next Wednesday mornin'," Uncle said. "There'll be near 'bout a hundred fellers for that dinner and we've got to kill enough for everybody. This will be about our last crack at the ducks 'cause most of 'em are already startin' north."

Later on Uncle Wint told me that he wished she was one of the birds headin' north. "That woman aggravates me," he said. "Why do Yankees always have to have different names for fish and birds and everything else? It's bad enough for Yankees to call a brim a bluegill and a trout a bass and a salamander a gopher. Now we've got to have Yankee women tellin' us about bluebills being scaups. Well, we'll see what she does in the forks of Gator Creek when the pintails and widgeons come over."

But somethin' terrible happened that next Wednesday. Me and Tarley carried Uncle Wint and Cousin Jenny out to their stands—about a quarter apart—way before day and throwed out a few deecoys for each of 'em. Then we left 'em to go get us some oysters and they had to set there all day till the next tide come in and we could get back to 'em. When the water would get down to about a foot deep would be the time when the ducks would pile in there to feed on the eel grass. Pintails and widgeons and teals and Florida mallards like to feed in shallow water so they can just dip their heads down and get what they want. Bluebills can feed on the bottom in twenty feet of water and they don't go back into shallow, grassy creeks so much.

Where we had left Uncle Winton and Cousin Jenny the tide would go out and leave the whole country near 'bout plumb dry. There wouldn't be no way to get the boat back anywhere near 'em until late that evenin' when the tide come back in again. And there ain't no possible way to walk out because there's pot holes under that grass deep enough to drown a man a hundred years old.

Well, me and Tarley went on out to the oyster bars and loaded up the skiff with the prettiest ones you ever seen. Of course we taken along a bottle of ketchup and would eat a few now and then. I don't see how there could be any sweeter oysters than we had there. Tarley opened one that I do believe were four inches long.

After while Tarley said, "You know, Billy, I don't hear Uncle Winton and Cousin Jenny doin' much shootin'. But the Johnson boys seem to be bombardin' 'em." Three of the Johnson boys had went along in a couple of skiffs, but they'd turned south down into Cow Creek.

"I'd of figgered with this big tide our folks would be doin' better," I told him.

Later on me and Tarl went to sleep on the boat seats and the last thing I could remember was hearin' some pretty steady shootin' to the south and nothin' to the north. When the tide turned in and began swellin' in the creeks, we started workin' toward Uncle Winton in Crab Creek. Cousin Jenny were farther into the marsh on a point in the forks of Gator Creek, which were supposed to be the best blind in the whole country. When we rounded the bend we could see Uncle Winton standin' up in his blind and Tarley raised the pole and let the skiff drift.

"How many you got down?" he hollered to Uncle Wint.

Uncle Winton didn't say nothin'. Just stood there and motioned us to come on. And he weren't smilin'.

"Are you all right, Uncle Winton?" Tarley hollered.

"Just come on over here, boy," Uncle Wint said and his voice sounded right funny.

By this time we'd picked up two pintails, leavin' the saw-bill for the turtles. I pulled the deecoys into the skiff and wound up their anchor strings, and directly Tarley looked at me and said, "Do you know, Billy, I just thought of somethin'. I'll be derned if I don't believe I got them shells mixed up in the dark, and if I did, old Uncle Wint has been settin' there under them flyin' ducks all day with Cousin Jenny's twenty-gauges!"

"And Cousin Jenny with them big old twelves for her little twenty!" I said.

About that time Uncle Winton hollered, "Tarley Driggers, are you comin' over here or not?"

"I ain't just sure," Tarley answered him. "I'm afraid maybe I left you the wrong shells."

"Just come over here where I can reach that boat," Uncle said.

"What about Cousin Jenny?" Tarley hollered.

"She can stay out there all week as far as I'm concerned," Uncle Wint said. "If it wasn't for her and her dad-blasted pea-shooter I'd a had a boatload of the prettiest pintail drakes you ever seen. They just covered me up—ten and twenty and thirty in a bunch. Come on over here!"

"I'll be derned if I do," Tarley said. "Not till you promise. Daddy never whipped us for doin' wrong less'n we done it on purpose and you know we wouldn't a-dared do this to you—even if we'd of wanted to. And I'd rather face a old she 'gator on her nest than I would Cousin Jenny in that blind right now!"

"Never mind her—I'll take care of her. Just get me in that boat," Uncle Wint said, "and let's get out of here. I just spent ten of the most miserable hours I ever spent in my life and I want to get out of sight of this place. As to your Cousin

Jenny—I'm goin' to accuse her of doin' this on purpose just to keep me from showin' her up on her shootin'!"

We went and got Cousin Jenny and she didn't have ary duck. Uncle Winton had happened to have three shells in his coat to start with, but she hadn't fired a shot—just set there all day with a full case of twelve-gauge shells. When we first taken her aboard she were so mad she were shakin', but after while she started to open up.

"Shut up and set still!" Uncle Wint told her. "Every time you move you almost swamp this here boat. It's a dang good thing we ain't got a lot of ducks or we'd sink! Between you and the oysters there's about four hundred pounds more in this boat now than there ought to be."

The Johnson fellers had killed fifty-two good eatin' ducks and there was a hundred and six Democrats and one Republican at the dinner. The Republican were Cousin Jenny and she got the only whole duck, either because she were a woman or because she were a awful big woman and needed it. Of course, I better explain that all this happened a long time ago, and if there was any limit on ducks nobody knowed about it—or let on that he knowed about it if he did. Anyhow, my relatives sure didn't break any law that day.

Cousin Jenny were right worrisome in lots of ways, but I will say she could really shoot. Me and Tarley taken her out a few times just before she went home, and she could mortally knock them ducks out of the sky. We put her on a little grassy island they called Seven Cabbage durin' a real flight of canvasbacks goin' through. The wind were blowin' a gale out of the sou'west, puttin' a awful lot of water into the marsh and drivin' the canvasbacks inshore. Cousin Jenny had all the shootin' she wanted, and she had to admit that a big old canvasback drake were mighty fine and would stack up pretty dern well with them greenheads she was always a-braggin' about—either on the wing or on the table.

She skinned 'em and split 'em and broiled 'em over the coals and served 'em up with the meat still a little bit pink, and I want to tell you now that were some kind of good eatin'! Up to then none of us folks had ever eat a wild duck that hadn't been soaked in saltwater and parboiled and stuffed with apple or onion and then baked about two hours—"To take out the wild taste and the fishy taste," Ma said.

"Shucks," Cousin Jenny told her, "any fishy taste is in the skin, so throw that away. And if you don't want the wild taste, why kill 'em at all?"

Tarley spoke up and said, "I like 'em Ma's way and I like 'em Cousin Jenny's way."

"I like 'em best this new way," I said, "kind of rare, so it tastes near 'bout like a real tender, juicy little venison steak."

But Ma wouldn't even try 'em and neither would Uncle Wint.

"It's plumb heathenish," Ma said. Uncle never said nothin', but I figured he wouldn't eat none just to aggravate Cousin Jenny. He didn't like her ten cents' worth in commissary trade!

"Hit'd pleasure me to take that female duck huntin' twice and bring her back once!" he said. But he never had no chance because she left out for Nebraska and we ain't never heard from her or about her to this day.

When she left, Uncle said, "I sure am glad to see her go and I've a good will to take my shovel and dig up her tracks where she walked around in my yard and throw 'em over the fence! That woman's enough to give a feller nervous prostitution!"

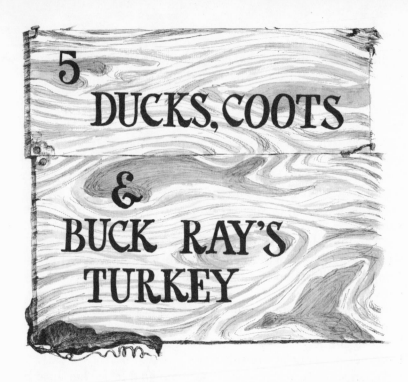

5
DUCKS, COOTS
&
BUCK RAY'S
TURKEY

Seein' Cousin Jenny shoot and eatin' them rare-cooked duck breasts sure made duck hunters out of me and Tarl, and we've done a heap of it since. Tarl could call 'em with his throat and learnt just what to say and when to say it, but there ain't nothin' to equal a live duck when it comes to bringin' birds in to a blind. One day Tarley picked up a crippled mallard hen with a busted wing and tied it up till it healed and she got tame as a dog. And it seemed like she could spot birds in the air a heap farther than a man could, and of course she could really talk the wild ones in.

She'd follow Tarl around the yard and when he'd go out in a skiff she'd hop in and ride along on the seat. A feller would of thought she'd of made a good deecoy and we tried anchorin' her out amongst the wooden ones. She didn't like this a dern bit and would squawk and flap till she near 'bout drowned, specially if she seen a hawk anywhere in the sky.

So Tarl would just take her along and let her sit on his knee in the blind or in the skiff. She'd keep watchin' the sky and could spot a flight of ducks half a mile off. She'd holler to 'em and here they'd come. Naturally, we called this old duck Susie and she sure were a big help. Sometimes, though, she'd spend most of the time sleepin' and Tarley would have to punch her with a reed to wake her up and make her talk.

"There's some ducks, Billy," Tarl would say. "Punch old Susie." I'd joog her with a stem of that sharp-pointed reed grass and she'd put out some quackin'!

About that time, though, the government decided every-body was havin' too much fun and killin' too many ducks, so live deecoys was out. I remember a couple of them Federal fellers comin' to us one day in Gator Creek. Old Susie had been doin' her stuff and we had been doin' ours. Tarl were always a good shot and that day I done better than usual. I believe the limit were ten apiece then and we'd picked up nineteen—one under the limit.

But it weren't limits so much these fellers was checkin' as it were usin' a live deecoy. They'd heard old Susie hollerin' and seen the ducks a-comin' to her.

Old Tarl tried to talk 'em out of it. "Shucks, fellers," he said, "I ain't usin' no live deecoy. This here's my pet and she's just a-settin' in the boat with me."

The Federal fellers scratched their heads and thought it over and finally one of 'em said, "All right this time, but don't bring no more pets when you go duck huntin' or we'll have to take you in and confiscate the pet."

Duck huntin' without Susie weren't near as much fun and a feller sure didn't get as good results—specially on a right still day when there weren't enough wind to move the wood blocks. Flyin' ducks look down and when they don't see no ripples nor action in the water from the deecoys, you can al-most hear 'em laughin' to theirselves and they just high-tail it away from there. Them wooden blocks look like just what they are—chunks of wood.

But a feller can rig up a long line and pass it through a ring in the anchor line of one of his deecoys and tie it to a screw eye on the underside of the bill and make the deecoy bob around to make some ripples in the calm water. This will help a whole lots, but there's one trouble with it. Some cracker slippin' around in the mist at daybreak will sure put a load of shot into your fancy-dancin' decoy! Most crackers will sure cut down on sittin' ducks, but I've seen old Tarl wave his gun and holler at one till it swam out of range before he'd shoot it on the water.

"Just as soon shoot one of Ma's chickens in the yard," he'd say. "I'll give any livin' thing a sportin' chance, Billy, except the varmint who shot Dad or the feller who hired him." So he'd always let a duck jump before he'd shoot.

I remember a Canadian feller named Jack Mayer who were a great duck hunter and knowed just about all there were to know about ducks—specially black ducks, which was the ones he hunted mostly up in New Brunswick. He claimed them black ducks was the smartest and scariest of all ducks and I reckon he's right. We don't get too many of 'em down here, but what we do get sure has sharp eyes. Well, Jack Mayer told about a greenhorn feller he taken out one time.

"I told that feller," Jack said, "that the most important thing in duck huntin' were to keep still and not be a-cranin' his neck around and lookin' up at the sky. A duck can see that white face for a country mile—which is a mile measured with a double wagon, throwin' in the tongue every time. So I told him, 'Keep your dern head down and set still! We're rigged out with the deecoys in front of us and the wind behind us, so if any ducks come, they'll circle overhead to check up on the spread, and if they decide everything looks right, they'll set their wings and come down over the blocks within good range. If they decide things don't look just right, they'll circle a time or two and then check out. So if they're comin', they're comin' and it sure don't help to keep lookin' up and cranin' your neck.'

"But in spite of everything, that feller kept a-twistin' and a-turnin' and lookin' up and each time I'd say, 'Keep your dang head down. Set still—don't move!' I'll bet I told him this twenty times. Finally, the feller said, 'Mr. Mayer, can ducks hear?' I told him, 'You're mighty right they can hear!' 'Then keep your dang mouth shut!' he told me."

Then Uncle Wint told a yarn about a greenhorn Yankee hunter that he were guidin' one time, but I didn't quite believe it.

"This feller didn't know turkey scratchin' from squirrel diggin' and even asked me how many kinds of deer we had in the Hammock—because in some of the tracks the hoofs was spread way apart and in others they was close together," Uncle said. "He didn't even know a walkin' track from a runnin' track. But he was a sport, I'll say that for him.

"He'd hunted a week and hadn't killed nothin', so we'd tied out a tame gobbler in the palmettos for him to shoot and led him around to where he could see it. Man! He got a gleam in his eye and started a-stalkin' that turkey. When he got to about thirty steps of it I told him, 'Shoot!' He didn't say nothin' or raise his gun—just kept a-stalkin'. 'Shoot!' I told him again. 'Shoot!' He stopped a second and whispered to me, 'I may not know much about huntin', but I do know that no real sportsman shoots a game bird on the ground. I'm waitin' for it to fly!' 'Well,' I told him, 'you'll have a dern long wait!' " Uncle always stopped the story right there and never would tell what happened after that, but I don't think it could of been too funny.

I heard some fellers played that same trick on old Buck Ray, one of the owners of a big spring over in the Ocala Forest. When he went to pick up the turkey, its wing fell down and there were a sign stuck under the wing—SEE SILVER SPRINGS! I just couldn't keep from tellin' this on old Buck because he's a extra good hunter and if anybody could tell a wild turkey from a tame one, he could—but that time he didn't. I've knowed him and his daddy before him a long time, so I reckon he won't be too mad with me for tellin' this on him. And old Allen Skaggs and John McCormick, the fellers who tied out the turkey, won't mind, I don't believe.

As far as shootin' a turkey on the ground is concerned, the time to shoot one is when you see it—on the ground, in a tree or any other dern way. I'd shoot one layin' on its back asleep if I could catch one that way. What a wild turkey can't see or hear can't be seen or heered. There ain't no such thing as takin' unfair advantage of one of them scapers.

Tarley got to be just about the best turkey hunter in the Hammock and he sure could call 'em. They's all manner of turkey yelpers, both homemade and store-boughten, and old

Tarl could use just about any of 'em. He'd cup the bowl of a old corncob pipe in his hands and suck wind through the stem or use the hollow wing bone of a turkey the same way. He could use a leaf between his thumbs or a cedar box with a hinged top or a cedar stick run through a corncob and scratched on a piece of slate. But he done best usin' his own throat and could sound like two or three different turkeys from real fine to real coarse—like a young-un, a full-grown hen or a old gobbler. Durin' gobblin' season, in early spring, he could get a old tom excited enough to tread a light'd knot. He'd yelp like a hen, gobble like a gobbler, beat his hat down in the leaves like birds a-scufflin', and if there were ary other gobbler within hearin' distance he'd come a-runnin'!

Of course, the main thing in huntin' turkeys is to keep well hid. Don't move nothin' but your eyeballs and move them easy. And don't do too much yelpin'. Turkeys yelp a little when they fly down from the roost in the mornin' to get together; and if a bunch gets scattered by a dog or a wildcat or a hunter, they'll answer a yelper pretty good. But any time you get an answer, you better not make a mis-lick with your cedar box or slate or whatever you're usin', because that old turkey is a-standin' out there really listenin' then and so your second call better be right. If he answers the second time, it's a good idea to shut up and let the turkey look for you, because he ain't near so apt to make a mistake as you are.

Tarley were just like a Indian in the woods and could set in one place without movin' for a hour at a time. I just can't do that. I get nervous or my hind end goes to sleep. So when we needed turkey, Tarl were the boy to get him. And he didn't want nobody along with him—includin' me.

We didn't have much choice of meat in the commissary—bacon and ham and now and again some fresh beef. Most folks in our neck of the woods did their own butcherin' and a heap of 'em cured their own ham and bacon. A feller couldn't hardly have a better variety of meat, though, than we could find in the woods or in the waters—turkeys, ducks, doves, quail, venison, squirrel, all kinds of fish, oysters and frogs.

Along with the ducks there was a heap of coots and marsh

hens, tender little good-eatin' birds that Yankees call rail birds. There's two or three kinds of 'em in the saltwater marsh and a littler one in the freshwater marshes. It ain't no bigger'n a jaybird, but the meat is the sweetest you ever tasted.

Down at the mouth of the river there's thousands of them white-billed, slaty-colored coots. They got short, pointed bills like chickens and their feet ain't webbed like a duck's, though they do have sort of flaps on their toes. They can fly, but they have a hard job gettin' off the water and have to run along on top to get a start. Once they get up, they fly pretty good and more'n once I've shot one soon in the mornin', thinkin' it were a duck goin' over. The breast meat of a coot ain't bad eatin' if you'll skin it before you fry it.

I know bald-headed eagles like 'em because I've set in my duck blind many a day and watched a old eagle divin' on a raft of coots. Man! They'll make a roar gettin' out from under him—sounds like a school of mullet showerin' when a shark or a porpoise gets into 'em. Generally, though, them old bald-headed eagles set around waitin' for a fish hawk to catch him a fish and then they'll take it away from him, divin' on him and makin' him drop it. Lots of times they'll catch that fish in the air when the osprey drops it. "Osprey" is just Yankee for fish hawk. One time I seen a real nervy fish hawk turn around and try his best to make the eagle drop the fish. I mean they done a piece of screechin'! They sound a little bit the same, but the eagle's got a louder, raspier, brassier screech.

Anyhow, back in the days when me and Tarl was growin' up, there weren't no reason to go hungry in the Hammock. The birds and varmints had acorns, cabbage berries, blue-berries, wild grapes, pine mast, and all kinds of buds and insects and worms. And us folks had our pick of whatever we wanted—fish, fowl or game. Of course we had all the beef and pork we wanted. And I want to tell you now that a young shoat fattened on water-oak acorns ain't bad to take. A feller can worry down a few mouthfuls of that even if he ain't hungry, specially if he's got plenty of grits and pokeberry greens or swamp cabbage to go along with it.

Some men like to cook and they tell me that the highest-paid cooks in the world are head cooks in them big-city hotels. Charlie Dean, the sheriff over to Inverness, sure could cook and he learnt a lot of it from a Spanish feller who had a big restaurant down in Tampa. He'd invite this feller to come up to his camp to go deer and turkey huntin', provided he'd bring along a lot of pots and kettles and seasonin' and stuff to show him about some of them Spanish and Cuban dishes.

Man, he could fix up Spanish-style spaghetti that would make you slap your grandma. It was some kind of good. Me and Tarl and Uncle Wint come into their camp one cold night after we'd killed a deer down on Bee Tree Slough, and they had a big pot of spaghetti cooked up. Of course we was starvin' hungry, but I know that was the best spaghetti sauce I ever eat in my life.

I ain't much of a cook myself, but I can make a pretty good fish chowder and I can fry oysters that everybody says is the very, very best. I learnt it from a lady who had a old hotel over in Dunnellon. She didn't mind tellin' me and I don't mind tellin' you. She'd just shake up a few oysters in a paper bag full of plain old Aunt Jemima pancake flour—just the dry flour, no batter or nothin'. Then you just drop 'em into real hot fat and they'll brown in about forty seconds. There won't be no big old gob of junk on 'em and they won't be tough and leathery—they'll be brown on the outside and tender and juicy on the inside, with none of that funny taste like they was cut out of somebody's old shoe.

Uncle Winton could tell some great tales about rations he'd eat on some of his trips, but he didn't do much cookin' if he could help it. Aunt Effie was a good cook and even made cheese out of that devilish goat's milk. She claimed it and the milk was good for your belly. Maybe for hers—but not for mine.

6 MUMPS, MIXED-UP MEDICINE & THE THREE MYSTERIES

Once in a while Ma would let us boys go off on a little camp hunt for a few days, and I remember when I was twelve years old I worried Tarley into takin' me along by promisin' to do the cookin'. Tarley were sixteen and the two other boys was a little bit older. I forget now just who was on that go-'round, but I know we didn't kill nothin' but squirrels.

We camped on a cedar ridge, near where Bee Tree Slough goes into a string of brackish-water ponds, close to the Gulf marsh. There was usually a lot of ducks in them ponds—big old greenhead mallards and what we call "black mallards." We'd slip along the edge of the ponds and jump-shoot 'em and they was some kind of good eatin', I want to tell you, when you baked 'em in a dutch oven or broiled the breasts over the coals.

The cabbage palms and hickories and magnolias and cedars and bays all growed pretty thick along the edge, and them ducks would have to climb near about straight up before they could level off. Even when he was only sixteen years old Tarley was one of the best shots I ever seen and

many's the time he'd drop a couple when they started
climbin' out. You'd hear them old ducks' wings start to beat
and you'd hear 'em hollerin' "Look out" in duck talk and
then you'd hear the old twelve-gauge.

But this day Tarley didn't have nothin' but a thirty-thirty
rifle because we was deer huntin'. One of the other boys had
a shotgun, but he couldn't hit them ducks to save his soul—
unless he'd catch 'em sittin' on the water. But for some reason
they was awful wild on this trip. Tarley was a wonderful rifle
shot and toward the end of our trip he killed one of them
black ducks with his thirty-thirty just at the top of its climb.
There wasn't much left of the breast meat, but we cooked it
anyhow.

There was plenty of deer and the dogs run big bucks
pretty close to all four of us, but you can't eat "pretty close"!
So we had to settle for squirrels and I tried my hand at makin'
up purloo the second night in camp. I was so give out I could
hardly drag around, but I'd promised Tarley to cook, so I flew
at it. I skinned out six or eight squirrels, cut 'em up and put
'em in a kettle with some water. When it got to boilin' good
I dumped in the rice and some salt and pepper and put on
the lid.

I hate to tell about that purloo. The rice would of made
good wallpaper paste—what weren't scorched—but the squirrels had only cooked long enough to make one of them hind
legs just like a piece of India rubber. You'd bite on it and
your jaws would bounce! Anyhow, Tarley cleaned up a big
plate of it and said, "Billy, that's plumb good! Give me some
more." I sure was proud and loaded up his plate again. When
I come back from puttin' the kettle back on the fire I seen
his plate was empty again and it wasn't until then that I
seen old Chief a-standin' under the camp table lookin' at
Tarley with the drool hangin' down a foot from each side
of his mouth. That dang brother of mine was feedin' that
purloo to that old red hound faster than I could serve it to
him! I thought I'd heard a funny noise while my back was
turned, and I guess I had—old Chief poppin' his lips when
Tarley helt the plate down to him! It didn't faze the dog and

what Tarl did eat didn't faze him, but I had a real stomped-down belly ache from just one plate.

My brother was tough and never had much the matter with him when he was young. Even when I had the measles he never taken it. But when he was about seventeen years old, I'll be derned if he didn't come down with the mumps. And he was a sick somebody, I mean! They settled on him and we had to get Doc Joyner to come out. He said he'd send some medicine out from town and for Tarley to stay in bed and lay real quiet.

Late that evenin' a boy fetched the medicine out horseback. Well, it turned out that the boy got the bottles mixed up and we give old Tarl two big doses before Ma noticed that the name on the bottle was "Mrs. Wiggins"! We found out later that Mrs. Wiggins was expectin' a young-un, and whatever was in that medicine liken to have killed Tarley. Still later we found out it hadn't been nothin' but flavored-up castor oil. And we never did find out if Mrs. Wiggins taken Tarley's medicine or what it done to her. But there weren't never nothin' about it in the *Chronicle*, so I reckon she made it all right.

The next time Tarley seen Doc Joyner he told him, "Anybody who'd tell a feller to stay in bed and lay quiet and then give him oil would take the ball away from a crippled tumble-bug and put him on the wrong road home!"

"I never had nothin' to do with that mix-up, Tarley Driggers, and you know it," Doc said. "That old boy who carried the medicine out to you couldn't read. I had done told him which bottle was which, but he forgot or didn't listen."

"Well," Tarley said, "I still got a half a bottle left and I've a good will to catch that old boy and give him the balance of it! That'll teach him to listen."

Uncle Winton was with us that day and he throwed in his two bits' worth: "A feller ought never to take nothin' out of a bottle less'n he reads what's on it."

When he said that, old Doc Joyner give me a great big wink. I guess he just couldn't figure Uncle Winton ever takin' time to read what was on ary bottle. Everybody knowed that

Winton Epps liked his whiskey and I remember Ma sayin' to my dad one time, "Poor Winton just don't have no will power when it comes to liquor."

"That ain't your brother's trouble," Daddy said. "He just ain't got no *won't* power!"

Uncle Winton went to every funeral around and done his best to comfort folks. Usually he had a little nip or two first to help him bear up and I remember one time a young gal had lost her husband and Uncle Winton set right down in the first row with her. While they was waitin' on Preacher Elliott she started cryin' and put her head over on Uncle Winton's shoulder and said, "Oh, Uncle Wint, there'll never be another man for me but John. I never want to see another man. I'll never love another man."

"There now, honey," Uncle said, puttin' his arm over her shoulder, "your comb will turn red again."

Dad and Uncle Winton had always been real close buddies, a heap more'n most brothers-in-law, and after Dad died Uncle would come by every few days to see how we was farin'. Aunt Effie didn't come often and we was sort of glad she didn't because she had a real sharp tongue and used it plenty. But we was always glad to see Uncle Wint and would go over to his house right often. I loved to be around him because he was always sayin' somethin' funny, like one time when we were buildin' a new barn and a piece of heart pine two-by-eight and twenty foot long fell and almost hit him.

"Billy," he said, spittin' tobacco juice, "if that plank had of fell on me I'd have laid there dead for God knows how long!"

Uncle Winton's daddy, old man Zeb Epps, had been a North Carolina mountain man and Uncle Wint said that he'd been rough as a cob—a great big old raw-boned, double-jointed feller with feet so big he got scared of his own track when he seen it in the snow. "He was a long-legged scaper and could just step over a three-wire fence," Uncle said. "They sure split him a long way before they tied the knot!"

"One time when I were just a shirttail boy," Uncle Wint told us, "there were a feller stealin' chickens and Daddy cleared all the chairs off the porch so he could see right down to the henhouse from his bed. Two or three nights later the feller came back and Daddy shot him. The feller hollered and fell over the fence.

" 'Did you hit him?' Mamma asked.

" 'Of course I hit him,' Daddy told her.

" 'Did you kill him?'

" 'I don't know.'

" 'Ain't you goin' out to look?'

" 'No,' said Daddy. 'If he's dead he'll be there in the mornin',' and he turned over and went to sleep.

" 'Winton,' Mamma told me, 'go out there and see if your daddy killed that man.'

"Well, I sure didn't want to, but I did and the feller weren't there. We heard next day that old Doc Angel was pickin' number-six shot out of Ab Walker for two hours and a half. We sure had some mighty ornery neighbors.

"Another time," Uncle Wint went on, "there was a feller stealin' corn out of the crib. He had cut him a hole between the logs on the back side where he couldn't be seen from the house. The hole was just big enough for him to reach his arm in and get a ear of corn. Daddy put a stop to that! He set him a coon trap inside the crib, and a few nights later the feller come back and reached in to get some corn. I wasn't home when this happened, but Daddy said the feller hollered like he was snake-bit when he grabbed the coon trap, but Dad just let him stand there the rest of the night. He couldn't get his left arm in to spring the trap and he couldn't get the trap out through the hole.

" 'When daylight come,' Daddy told me, 'I taken my shotgun and went out there and it was a feller I hadn't never seen before in my life. "I told him, Mister, I'm a-goin' to turn you loose and feed you a good breakfast and give you a sack of corn. And then you're goin' to get gone and if I ever see you around here again you're goin' to get shot." ' "

And that's just what'll happen to McWirter or Lukins if they ever show up down here, I thought to myself as Uncle went on.

"Our nearest neighbors was close enough so that on a clear night you could see the lights from their stills. The Revenue

officers come to our house two or three times and told
Daddy that he could help clean things up around there a heap
if he'd just tip 'em off a little.

" 'Things are just as clean now as I want 'em,' Daddy said.
'And I sure don't want my house burned down or my stock
shot up.' So he didn't tell 'em nothin'.

"I didn't visit around too much, and even when I went to
one of our neighbors' places I made it a point never to ask
about where the still were at or to go to it. Then I could
truthfully say I didn't know nothin' about no whiskey. Once
or twice I stayed over at old man Brown's overnight when the
boys would all get to drinkin' and there'd be a few fights."

"Weren't you scared to sleep there, Uncle Winton?" I asked
him.

"Well," he said, "I've slept in a lot of places and I've always
been there in the mornin'.'"

A few times I stayed over at Uncle's, like when somebody
were visitin' at our house. One night I remember there were
a terrible ruckus in the room where Uncle Winton and Aunt
Effie was sleepin'. I could hear 'em talkin' and directly Uncle
started laughin'. About that time I heered *Whap!* when Aunt
Effie slapped him. Then more laughin', then *Whap!* again.
After while they quieted down and I went to sleep.

Next mornin' when we was eatin' breakfast I seen Uncle
Wint a-lookin' down at his plate and tryin' not to laugh.
After a while Aunt Effie said, "Well, you just as well tell him
—I know he must of heered us." So he told me, or maybe I
better say they both told me. Aunt Effie said she woke up with
Uncle makin' a funny gurglin' sound with his mouth. He kept
it up and she thought somethin' ailed him, so she turned over
in bed just in time for him to spit right in her eye—full force.
And when Uncle Wint spit full force, it were somethin' to see.
Fellers said they'd seen him cut a dirt dauber's nest off a post
ten feet away. Anyhow, Aunt Effie hauled off and slapped
the fire out of him and when he woke up and asked her why
and she told him he had done spit in her eye, he went to
laughin' and she went to slappin'.

"You see, Billy," Uncle told me, "I were dreamin' that I
were standin' on the dock up at the commissary along with

the Morgan boys and old man Todd and another feller or two and we was havin' a contest to see who could spit the fartherest and I were just a-workin' up a real good gob, gettin' ready for my turn—which sure did come at the wrong time!" And he went to laughin' again.

Thinkin' about the commissary reminds me of another feller who picked the wrong time. Uncle Wint hadn't been feelin' very good that day, but he knowed just about everybody in the county and so the politicians figured he could sure help 'em and come election time they'd all be around sweet-talkin' him. The County Commissioners was elected to serve staggered terms, and a heap of times the candidates was already staggerin' before they was elected.

There were this one smooth-talkin' feller from up around Bronson who had already had a couple of run-ins with Uncle Winton over some cattle. He was kind of a ratfaced-lookin' feller with his eyes so close together that you could have run a pencil up his nose and punched out both his eyes. His name were Ray somethin' or other, and when he decided to run for Commissioner, one of the first things he done were to hunt up Uncle Winton. I had gone up to the store with Uncle and we was standin' by the meat counter when this feller walked up with a grin on his face like a mule eatin' briers and started to hand some of his campaign cards to Uncle.

"Good mornin', Winton," he said, "and how are you, Billy? Sure will appreciate your support, Winton, and I reckon you know I'll do anything I can for you anytime, just like I'll do for all the good people of this county."

"That's fine," Uncle told him, layin' the cards down on the counter. "You and me'll get along fine. But like the country gal said, 'Just don't try to put your hand in my bosom!' "

On our way home Uncle told me, "Billy, that feller might get elected, but I doubt it. He's just too abscessed with his own importance! He's got just a little too much sense for one man and not quite enough for two, and consequently he's a regular damn fool!"

Folks didn't often fool Uncle Winton. And, for that matter, nothin' didn't fool him much and he was always figurin' the whys and the wherefores. I remember his sayin' one time, "There's three things I don't understand all I know about. First, is how a cow can chaw a cud and swaller it and bring up another one and chaw it and swaller it and never get mixed up and bring up one she's already chawed. I've took fifty cows apart tryin' to find out. She's only got one throat and I just can't figger it. Second is how a derned old hound can hit a trail and know right off which way the deer, bear or varmint has gone. And the third is radio."

"Well," Tarl told him, "I can't help you none on the first and third, but I got some ideas about the hound trailin'."

"Let's hear 'em," Uncle told him.

"Of course hounds don't *always* know right off which way a trail is leadin'," Tarl said. "Once in a while even a old experienced dog will backtrack a little bit before he finds he's wrong."

"That's the truth," Uncle said. "And my daddy had a bear dog up in the mountains that would take the back trail for a little piece and I believe he'd of done it even if he'd of *seen* the bear goin' the other way."

"Why would he do somethin' like that?" I asked.

"Well," Uncle said, "I think he knowed there was just so many tracks between him and that bear and he loved the smell of 'em so much that he'd go back and collect up a few extra ones to start with."

"I'll believe that if you say so," Tarl told him, "but what we're talkin' about is how can a dog tell which way a critter's gone when he strikes its trail. Supposin' it's a runnin' deer that jumps over a fence and crosses a little old ten-acre field, say, and then goes into the woods on the other side. Maybe that deer run a hundred yards across that field and it sure didn't take him long to do it—maybe six or seven seconds. Let's say somethin' scairt that deer along about midnight and when the dog hits the trail it's seven o'clock in the mornin'. Supposin' the dog strikes the trail in the middle of that old field and that trail is seven hours old and there ain't but three or four seconds' difference in the age of the scent—to the left or to the right anywhere in that field—and yet the dog knows which way to turn."

"All right, I'll grant you that," Uncle said, "but *how* does he know?"

"Maybe it's like if you fell in the creek and walked on out through the marsh in your wet clothes. A feller could tell easy enough by lookin' at the grass which way you'd gone— which side of a clump of grass was wet where you'd brushed against it. Maybe that's the way it is with scent layin' on one side of the grass or leaves."

"Supposin' there ain't no grass or leaves?" Uncle asked him. "Suppose it's a fresh-mowed field or even a plowed field? I reckon you don't understand all you know about it neither."

"I reckon not," Tarl told him, "and I sure can't tell you nothin' about a cow's cud or a radio."

7 THE NERVOUS TICK

& THE TRAPPED TRAPPER

Uncle Winton told us boys to always be right careful when it come to gals and always see some clear track ahead before we made a move. He had done some travelin' when he was a young feller and I remember his tellin' us about a trip he made one time to St. Looey. He said there was the best-lookin' woman sittin' across from him that he had ever laid eyes on and when she looked around he winked at her.

"Boys," he said, "she just lifted her nose in the air and turnt and looked out the winder. Directly there come a feller about six four and near about three hundred pounds and set down by her. They talked a few seconds and then this big feller got up and come over to my seat and leant over and said, 'My wife tells me you winked at her.'

"Well, boys, I really done a fast piece of thinkin'. I looked up at that big feller and batted my left eye four or five times and said, 'Maybe she thought so, Mister. I'm sorry—an affliction.' And I batted that eye some more.

" 'Oh, I beg your pardon, sir,' the man said and went back over and set down by his wife.

"I was readin' a magazine and after while I looked up and seen 'em both just a-starin' at me. There wasn't nothin' to do but start battin' my eye and twitchin' my face again. I done that all the way to St. Looey and by the time I got back home I'd done got in the habit and had to see a doctor."

"I remember when you was a-doin' that, Uncle Winton," Tarl said. "I asked Doc Joyner what made you do it and he said it was just a nervous tick. I remember wonderin' what in the world kind of tick that could be. I'd had some bite me and make me nervous, all right. I guess a nervous tick was a real crawler that couldn't make up its mind where to dig in."

"I reckon so," Uncle said. "Anyhow, I overed it."

One day not long after that he stopped by our house and told Ma, "Sis, without mentionin' no names, I know a boy about the size and age of your Tarley who might bear watchin' 'round some of the neighbor gals. The other evenin' when I was turkey huntin' I slipped up on that young sprout and a gal a-settin' on a log just a-smoochin' up a storm. I mean he was a-kissin' that little old gal—sounded like six little coons a-nursin'! When they seen me they jumped up and started gatherin' light'd knots, lettin' on they was just pickin' up firewood. And they had a pile of knots picked up there in five minutes that would sweat a dang rat to run around!"

"I got a good idea about the boy," Ma said, "but who was the gal?"

"Now, Sis," Uncle Wint said, "I never told on you when you was a filly, and I ain't about to start besmirchin' the reputation of ary sweet young gal—particularly when her daddy's bigger than me and one of the best shots in the county!"

"I think I know who you're talkin' about," Ma said, settin' her mouth like she always done when she was aggravated, "but I'd never thought that little old brat was big enough to be studyin' such as that."

"When they can see out of a barrel they're big enough," Uncle said. "You better talk to Tarley . . . and Billy, too. That little scaper will be tomcattin' around before you know it."

Uncle didn't know I was listenin' through the kitchen door. And that ain't all he didn't know!

Well, Ma got me and Tarley told about gals the very next evenin' after school. She didn't tell us much we didn't know, but we was both right respectful, I thought. She was a mighty good woman and if every feller had a ma such as her there'd be a lots less meanness and a heap fewer fillies with woods colts.

Soon after that talkin'-to Ma give us there come a first cousin of hers from up in Georgia to visit us, Aunt Julie McGlumphy. Ma was a good Christian woman, but she weren't a caution to Aunt Julie, who spent a whole heap of time in her room a-prayin'. We didn't mind this until we heard her one evenin' askin' the Lord to protect His poor wild creatures. She didn't believe in huntin', and durin' the whole two weeks she were with us me'n Tarl didn't hardly kill nothin'. We never was so glad to see somebody leave.

I know there's some folks who don't believe in killin' *nothin'* and who won't eat nothin' but fruit and vegetables and nuts and such. That's all right. That's their privilege. But what gets me is for somebody to raise hell and put a chunk under it about hunters killin' game to eat while they theirselves is chompin' on a piece of chicken or bacon or beef.

I remember we eat a old hen we called Granny while Aunt Julie was here. This old hen was a regular pet and I sure did hate to kill her. But she'd got awful fat and weren't layin' no more, so Ma said, "Kill her and pick her for Sunday." And I will say she was some kind of good, stewed down and fixed out with dumplin's.

Aunt Julie set there at the table and preached a regular sermon about goin' out with a gun and shootin' doves and quail and such, all the time a-smackin' her lips over Granny's thigh and drumstick.

Finally Ma spoke up and said, "Well, Julie, you seem to be enjoyin' that chicken leg and it sure ain't alive. Somebody killed it, and if you'll get your Bible you'll find that when the Apostle Peter was a-prayin' one time the Lord let down a sheet from heaven full of all kinds of animals and reptiles and birds of the air and said, 'Rise, Peter, kill and eat.' That sheet might just as well have been a big old tablecloth and what was on it included gophers and turtles and frogs and all the different kinds of birds and critters the boys hunt for. So if the Lord told the Apostle to kill and eat, I ain't a-goin' to tell my boys not to!"

"Well, don't forget what Paul said," Aunt Julie told her. "He was an Apostle too and he said, 'If meat causes my brother to stumble, I'll eat no meat.' "

Ma gave a little snort and said, "Chicken is meat and you're eatin' it. And as far as makin' my brother stumble, eatin' meat ain't got nothin' to do with it. The only thing that'll make my brother stumble is corn liquor."

"I ain't talkin' about Winton Epps," Aunt Julie said, "and you know it! The Apostle meant that every man is your brother."

"Oh, I know that!" Ma said. "But I still say it's all right for my boys to kill wild game to eat—and you sure don't have to eat any if you don't want to!" And that ended the argument.

It's always bothered me a little bit to kill and butcher a pig or a calf that we've raised—or even a chicken—but I don't know any wild critters and they don't know me. If I don't get 'em, a hawk or a owl or a fox or a bobcat will. So when a turkey or a duck or a quail flies up I crack down on it without givin' it a thought. Of course, I hate to cripple game and try to kill it quick and clean if I can.

Ma paid us ten cents each for quail and doves, fifteen cents for squirrels and a quarter for cottontails. Swamp rabbits didn't count. Out of this we had to buy our own shells. Twelve-gauge was seventy-five cents a box then, and if I could get some doves bunched up in a tree and kill three or four at one shot, I felt like I could afford to try some wing shootin'. Tarley were always a better shot than me—with rifle, shotgun or pistol. He'd try all kinds of impossible shots, and if he missed one, nobody was surprised, and if he made one, he'd just let on that he expected to.

I had a trap line from the time I was ten years old and I salted away over two hundred dollars by the time I was thirteen. I'd get coons and possums and once in a while a otter, although them scapers is mighty sharp. And I got a few mink out in the marsh, but it were a long way to go.

Tarley never would trap and didn't even like to go with me to visit mine. "I hate it, Billy," he'd say. "I dream about that poor varmint a-hurtin' in that trap for eight—ten—twelve hours and it plumb sickens me. I'm bad as Aunt Julie."

Once in a while a bear would come down from Punkin Swamp to the north of us and go to catchin' our hogs. Uncle Wint said that a long time ago bears had got so plentiful he couldn't hardly raise no hogs or keep a beehive. He went to shootin' 'em and trappin' 'em until he thinned 'em out pretty good. Then the wild hogs got so plentiful and brave that they began breakin' down fences and rootin' up his garden till he couldn't raise nothin'.

"So, by grannies," Uncle Winton told us, "I taken a green bear hide that still had plenty of scent to it and I caught a big old black sow and I lashed that bear hide onto her real good and turnt her loose. The last time I seen that bunch of hogs she was tryin' to get with 'em and they was tryin' to keep her from gettin' with 'em!"

Uncle had a great big old steel trap made specially for bears. It weighed about forty pounds and had teeth two inches long. A feller had to set it with C-clamps. Uncle Wint set it in the bear's trail where it was comin' up out of the low hammock and put a wire around it and a sign sayin' BEAR TRAP, like the law required. Because if a man was to step into that thing it would sure break his leg and he'd be there from now on. Then, after Uncle got the trap set, he reached under one of them jaws and fixed a little stick about as big as a match under the pan so that a coon or some other small varmint wouldn't spring it.

I never will forget the night the bear got into that trap. It were at least a mile from the house, but we could hear that bear cryin' and bellerin' like it were just out in the horse lot. At first day me'n Tarley saddled our horses and tore out for Uncle Winton's. Then we all three went back to look for the bear. The trap had a toggle chain about ten feet long with a grapple anchor on the end, and when we come to the place where it had been set, it looked like lightnin' had struck in about four places. That bear had stood up and hammered that trap on tree trunks till the bark was skinned off six feet high. He'd tromped down and bit down bushes and saplin's big as your arm.

We found him about a quarter mile from there and the trail was easy to follow where the grapple had drug and hung up on bushes and logs. He was caught by the right front foot and were a-layin' down in the leaves makin' sort of a moanin' sound. Time he saw him, Tarley throwed up his thirty-thirty and shot him right between the eyes. Then he whirled his horse and left there at a lope without sayin' nothin' to nobody.

"What ails that boy?" Uncle wanted to know.

"He can't stand to see nothin' in a trap," I told him. "That's just the way he's always been."

"Well, I'll be John Browned," Uncle said. "Who'd ever of thought Jim Drigger's boy would be chickenhearted?"

"Don't forget he's your sister's boy, too," I told him. "And you know how Ma is about anything sufferin'."

"He don't mind shootin', but he can't stand trappin'. Now, ain't that sump'n!" Uncle said as we got down to skin the bear.

The job taken us about two hours because this bear were a big old feller. But it had a right nice coat for so early in the winter and Uncle wanted to save the head and the paws so he could carry the hide to a taxidermist feller to make a rug. I'd skinned a lot of varmints, but when it come to skinnin' out them bear paws and leavin' just the right toe joint to hold the claw it was some tricky. Seemed almost like them joints was put together with cotter keys.

While we was skinnin', Uncle Wint told me of some of his trappin' experiences.

"The worst thing ever happened to me was when I stepped in one of my own otter traps up on Spring Run. I had it set just underwater close to a big cypress tree and I set down on a tussock to try to get it off my foot. Well, I forgot I had a trap set on the tussock too and I set right on it! And I'm here to tell you that a feller with a otter trap on one foot and another on his butt is purely in one hell of a fix. I finally managed to cut me a saplin' and prized the one off my foot, but I had to walk three miles home with that one hangin' on my hind end, and every step was pure misery."

"I'll bet that really hurt," I told him.

"Not only that," Uncle said, "but somebody seen me walkin' in and passed the word around. Anyhow, your Aunt Effie finally got that trap off my butt without cripplin' me for life, and then she got mad and went to bed because I cussed a little. I couldn't get comfortable in no position, so I got my jug and eased the pain. Before I went to bed, I got me some Vaseline and cotton and adhesive tape and backed up to the mirror and patched my butt, which sure was sore. Then I had a couple more snorts and went to bed. By that time I wasn't hurtin' anywhere. Next mornin' your Aunt Effie says to me, 'Winton, you were drunk again last night,' and I said, 'No, I was not drunk . . . just easin' the pain.' She said, 'Well, if you weren't drunk, I'd sure like to know how come that grease and cotton and stuff got all over the mirror!'"

I got so tickled thinkin' about that I couldn't hardly hold my knife to keep on skinnin' the bear. At last, though, we got it skinned and I had to take the trap because my buckskin wasn't about to let us hang that bloody hide on him. So Uncle took the hide and a hindquarter of meat. While we was ridin' in, Uncle told me about another bear he'd caught— that time by a back foot.

"That'n drug the trap a half a mile through Punkin Swamp and it looked like a couple of horses had run away through the mud. But all of a sudden I just come to the end of the trail—there weren't no sign of nothin'. I went back quite a piece to see if the bear had doubled back, but he hadn't. All the tracks was headed the same way and so was the sign of the grapple. But it all come to a dead end—just disappeared into thin air. I taken off my hat and scratched my head and happened to look up. Well, by grannies, I were a-lookin' into the gappin' jaws of that bear and he was right over me with his forepaws stretched out to grab me. That was the awfulest-lookin' sight I ever seen in my life! Of course the bear were stiff and dead, but I jumped twenty feet out from under him before I realized it. The scoun'el had climbed a big tree and gone out on a limb and fell off and hung there by the hind foot, with the chain and anchor wropped around the limb, till he died."

I don't know if it were Uncle's stories or the sound of that poor old bear a-moanin' in our trap before Tarley shot him— but whatever it was, it just about cured me of trappin'. Up to then I had never give much thought to animals sufferin' and I always thought Tarl was a little chickenhearted about such as that. But I sure would hate to ever have to shoot a man, and Tarl was just the other way. Back in his mind he were just livin' for the day when he'd get his gunsights on the right feller.

That night after supper I said, "How come you to leave in such a hurry and leave us to skin the bear?"

"I guess I'm just chickenhearted about seein' something suffer," Tarl said.

"But you got it in the back of your mind to shoot a *man* someday—if you get the chance."

"That's different," Tarl said. "That poor old bear hadn't never done nothin' to me, but I got a bill to settle with the fellers who killed Daddy." And then he wouldn't talk about it no more.

I thought maybe he'd enjoy hearin' about the time Uncle sat in the otter trap, and he said he remembered it and that there was several people had seen Uncle Winton come a-hobblin' in with the otter trap clamped on his butt. Then somehow the word got around about how he had patched up his reflection. It must of been Aunt Effie told it on him because I know Tarl would never of dared do it and naturally Uncle wouldn't tell it on himself.

Tarl said one of the Johnson boys tried to joke Uncle Wint about it one day at the commissary,

"'Been doctorin' any mirrors lately, Mr. Epps?' he asked Uncle.

"'Horace, I'll just put your nose in the back of your head,' Uncle told him, 'and we'll see how *that* looks in a mirror!'

"'Well, *your* nose would look better on the back of your head,' Horace said."

Uncle had a big nose and for whatever reason the pores was large and there was a lot of red veins showin' in it.

"I thought he'd get mad at that," Tarl said. "But for some reason he just got tickled.

" 'Boy, what are you talkin' about? My nose is one of the prettiest things I've got,' Uncle told him.

" 'Well, I sure don't think it's very pretty,' Horace said.

" 'I'll have you know I've been offered two hundred dollars for this nose after I die—a feller wants it for a beehive!' "

Tarl said that sure did tickle old man Eichelberger, who was clerkin' in the commissary that day. He sure did love to laugh at somebody else, but didn't take very kindly to jokin' when the joke was on him. I remember a story they told on him about how countrified he was. They said a Yankee tourist lady come into the commissary in a big rush one day and asked the old man, "Do you have a rest room here?"

"No, ma'am," he told her, "but if you're tired there's a rockin' chair there on the porch!"

When he found out what she were really lookin' for he were some kind of embarrassed, so the next time a lady come in seemin' to be in a hurry he said, "Lookin' for the rest room, ma'am?"

This were a big old cracker gal in a homemade dress and she just looked at him like he had lost his mind and said, "Man, I ain't tired. Where's the can?"

8
OWLS, 'GATORS & RATTLESNAKES

Some of my earliest recollections are of the sounds that came from the woods after I'd gone to bed. Coons would get to fightin' and it weren't hard for a feller to imagine they was panthers screamin'. In the spring a couple of chuck-will's-widows would get to goin' and I never could figure out how they could draw their breath so fast. In all my life I never heered but one real northern whippoorwill. It didn't sound like our birds, but put the accent on the "will." Like this: "Whip-poor-*will,* whip-poor-*will,* whip-poor-*will.*" The ones we have down here holler, "*Chuck*-will's-*wid*ow, *chuck*-will's-*wid*ow, *chuck*-will's-*wid*ow." They tell me the Yankee birds looks like ours, but I ain't never seen one.

Mostly I remember the owls. The Hammock was full of 'em—the old hoot owl that's marked like a Plymouth Rock chicken and. says, "Who-cooks, who-cooks, who-cooks for you-all!" Two or three of them will get to fussin' and cacklin' like nothin' you ever heered, and once in a while one will let out a regular scream that will make your hair stand up. These fellers don't do much harm, catchin' mostly frogs and snakes and sometimes a cat squirrel.

Once in a while we'd hear the big old horned owls callin'—most specially on the first cold moonlight nights in the fall. Every year on the full moon in November or December we'd hear 'em and it's a wild, scary sort of a noise. It ain't so loud, but you can't tell just exactly where it's comin' from—near or far. It's a hard sound to describe, but it's sort of "Hoo, hoo-hoo-hoo . . . hoo-hoo." There's six notes to it. These owls are real rough on all kinds of small game, but we didn't often shoot 'em because we liked to hear 'em. Mostly they stay more in the piney woods than in the Hammock or swamp. They catch a heap of rabbits and squirrels, but also get plenty of woods rats and mice.

And if you can find where they're nestin', you'll find the ground under the tree is littered up with balls of fur and feathers they have puked up—feathers of all kinds of birds, includin' quail and doves and songbirds. When any little old bird goes to sleep around where them horned owls is at, it better be prepared not to wake up. Them big scoun'els sail through the air without makin' a sound and do their dirty work at night. Right at dusk, when most other birds are pickin' their roostin' places, horned owls are just startin' to hunt.

Then, of course, there's the little screech owls some folks call trembly owls. My Aunt Effie couldn't stand 'em and said when one hollers it's a sure sign of death and the only protection is to jump up and tie a knot in the sheet. I never did pay no mind to this kind of foolishness and always loved to hear the little fellers singin' their soft little notes.

We was always up and around at the break of day, along with all the birds. There'd be ducks flyin' over, goin' from the Gulf to the inland lakes and back again—woodpeckers and yaller-hammers and jaybirds and redbirds. Once in a while a big old "Lord God" would light on a dead light'd snag out by the hog pen and hammer that iron-hard wood till it would ring. This here woodpecker is two or three times as big as the ordinary kind and is sort of speckledy-black with a red top-knot. A long time ago there used to be a few big shiny black ones with red heads and white bills, but I ain't seen one of them since I were little.

Livin' off in the woods like we done, we just naturally got to know the birds and snakes and varmints and how they lived and what they ate and even how they mated. To see a couple of big alligators makin' love is somethin' a feller won't soon forget. And when a big old bull 'gator bellers on a cloudy evenin', it shakes the ground. There's still a lot of 'gators in some of the lakes and creeks, but nothin' like there was when me and Tarley was boys. It's too bad, too, because 'gators do a heap of good—eatin' snakes and turtles and diggin' out dens that hold water for the dry times—drinkin' places for all the varmints. Uncle Winton said the 'gators provide their-selves with "room service," which is what a city hotel calls it when they carry the rations right to your room.

But 'gator hides has always brought good money, and back when we was young we hunted 'em a whole lots. We had us a old lard-oil bull's-eye lantern that we strapped on our heads so we could look under the beam of it. We filled it with a mixture of half kerosene and half melted lard and it had a wick just like our kerosene lamps, only smaller.

The lens on the lantern were real thick glass and if you looked into it, it would near 'bout blind you. It didn't throw much light—at least not like a dry-cell battery flashlight—but it were a whole lot better 'cause it would reflect a 'gator's eye just as far without throwin' a lot of light on the water and grass. A heap of times a 'gator—specially a big one that's been shot at—won't hold for any kind of a light that shows up the grass and water too much around him. He'll just sink down and swim off.

A 'gator's awful hard to kill and I remember somethin' that happened one night when me and Tarley was way back in a deep old cypress lake at the head of a long chain of prairie lakes, out east about ten miles. We carried a little old homemade boat over there in the wagon and spent a week just 'gator huntin' at night and fishin' and sleepin' most of the daytime.

We'd take turns with the bull's-eye lantern, and on about the third night Tarley paddled me up to a little old 'gator 'bout

two feet long layin' in some water lettuce and I grabbed him by the back of the neck, tied him up and fastened him under the seat.

Well, about midnight Tarley shined a 'gator eye as big as a teacup and I eased the little old boat up almost to it. Tarley unhinged the top of its head with his thirty-thirty, knockin' out what few brains it had, and we towed it ashore. It sure were a big one, over three steps long. We built a fire and was plannin' to skin it right there, but the mosquitoes would have eat a feller up. They was so thick you could make a quick scoop with a pint cup and catch a quart!

"Let's get out of here," Tarley said, "before the devilish brassheads walk off with us!"

Somehow or other we forgot to do the most important thing in foolin' with a big "dead" 'gator—that's to cut the big cord at the base of his tail, 'cause even after he's supposed to be dead he'll switch that tail and knock a feller down or turn over a little boat like ours. The Larrigan boys had a big 'gator come to life in their boat one night and one of 'em got excited and shot it. While he were at it he shot a hole through the bottom of the boat that a catfish could swim through and sank the whole outfit in the middle of Lake Denham. They lost their gun and their light and had a awful time gettin' out of there 'cause the lake is plumb surrounded by a heavy sawgrass marsh and that stuff will cut you if you even look at it!

Our 'gator seemed to be plumb stone graveyard dead, and we just dragged him down and put him in the boat and got in and started back across the lake to our camp. There weren't much room in that little old twelve-foot boat with me and Tarley and that 'gator, I'll tell you. It had clouded over and got blacker than the inside of a cow by the time we got out in the middle of the lake.

Just about then that little 'gator I'd tied under the front seat decided he'd had enough of that boat-ridin' and he made a sudden scramble, slappin' me in the hip pocket with his tail. I had plumb forgot the little scaper and thought the big one had come alive, and it scared me so bad that I knocked a board loose in the bottom of that boat beatin' on the poor little 'gator. I had planned to take him back for a birthday present to Willene Rawls. But it happened so quick and scared me so bad that I killed him before I could stop.

"Don't worry about it," Tarley told me, "I don't hardly believe she'd care 'bout a live 'gator nohow."

It's funny what a feller will do when he's scared. I remember Sheriff Dean tellin' us 'bout the time he caught a rattlesnake alive one summer when he were workin' at the commissary. He kept it in a box in a big storeroom back of the office.

One evenin' he forgot to bring home a sack of grits and he were halfway home before he remembered. Well, by the time he got back to the commissary, it had got plumb dark, but he knowed every foot of the place and didn't bother to light a lamp.

"All of a sudden," he told us, "I stepped on a barrel hoop there in the dark and the dang thing flew up and hit me in the calf of the leg. It scared me so bad I could feel the poison goin' through my blood, and I lit a lamp and got me a hoe handle out of the rack and got my rattlesnake out of his box and beat him to death!"

I knowed just how he must of felt because of what happened to me when I was gatherin' eggs out in our barn one evenin' about first dark. The hens had been layin' in the manger and I reached my hand in to look for a egg and a settin' hen pecked me on the back of the hand. The only reason I didn't kill me a rattlesnake right then was because I just didn't have one handy!

I reckon the reason I got so scared were that just two or three days before Tarl had killed a little old baby diamondback, about a foot and half long, near the barn, so we was all on the watch for the rest of the litter. A snake that size ain't got as much poison as a big one, and of course his fangs ain't so long, but they tell me his poison is stronger than a big one's.

I ain't got a horror of snakes like I have for some other things—a dern spider, for instance. I just can't stand for a spider to get on me, specially one of them big old house spiders. Ma don't like to kill 'em because they catch roaches. That's another thing I can't stand—a dad-burned roach. I'll pick up a snake but not a roach—or a spider. A heap of folks think a snake is slimy and wouldn't pick one up for nothin', but it ain't. Its skin feels smooth and dry, just like a piece of oilcloth. But everybody's got their own ideas and likes and dislikes.

People are funny. A feller comes down here from the city and buys himself a few head of cows and right away he's a cattleman. Anybody with more'n one milk cow has to put on a big hat and cowboy boots. He sits in the saddle about like a sack of meal and I even heered tell of one feller who couldn't walk the day after his first ride because his shins was so sore from what he said were the beatin' of "them wooden things hangin' down on each side." Of course I don't believe that story because there couldn't be nobody that dumb.

I did see a Indian, though, that either didn't know enough to keep his feet in the stirrups or just weren't able to. Oh, I know Indians is supposed to be great riders and I reckon them western Indians are, but this here was a Seminole right out of the Glades and he didn't know no more about horseback ridin' than a wild hog knows about Sunday. There was a crew of fellers makin' a panther-huntin' movie and me and Tarl was helpin' 'em with our dogs. Where we was makin' the movies looked just like the Everglades and were supposed to *be* the Everglades.

They had two live panthers, a trim young female and a big pot-bellied old male with no more teeth than Uncle Winton when Uncle Hub got through with him. I'll tell you about that after while. The camera crew would switch them panthers around so that in the movie the dogs would be chasin' one and the next thing you knowed they'd be treed—but with the other panther. I reckon they figured folks would be so excited watchin' the picture there wouldn't nobody know the difference. I couldn't hardly believe that, but when I seen the movie at the picture show in Crystal about a year later I'll be dogged if I could tell them panthers apart—everything went so fast.

When we started the job, the boss of the crew said they'd ought to have a Indian in the picture, so they sent down to Everglades City and got 'em one. He had two names, as I remember: Frank Jimmy. They brought him and his dugout canoe up to the Hammock and I mean he could handle that dugout. The dern thing were about fifteen feet long and fifteen inches wide. If two fellers got in it, you didn't dare switch a cigarette from one side of your mouth to the other without tellin' the other feller or you'd flip bottom side up. But old Frank Jimmy would stand up in it and pole it through the water faster'n a man could walk.

But the panther-huntin' part of the picture called for horseback ridin' and that poor Indian suffered. I don't reckon he'd ever been on a horse in his life before, but he did manage to keep up and not fall off. It's a good thing, though, that they finished the ridin' part of the picture that day because old Frank Jimmy were a sore-butted Seminole when we got back to the camp.

Seminole Indians wear bright-colored shirts and cattlemen wear big hats and high-heeled boots and priests wear black shirts with their collars turned backwards and nowadays if a feller has a sports car he has to wear a little old silly-lookin' checked cap. Seems like everybody wants to get into some special outfit to show off who he is or what he is—ballplayers, cowboys, preachers or whatnot. When you come right down to it, though, it's like the drunk I heered about who were settin' up at the bar at Pappy's Last Resort. He looked at the big picture of the naked lady back of the bar and said, "Thash funny. My wife's got a outfit ezzactly like that!" So, underneath, people is just people—even Yankees.

9 GOSSIP & WARNIN'S & THE LAME DOG

Way back in the Hammock there lived an old couple who folks called Uncle Dan and Aunt Shug. I never did know if they had ary other name, but I'm here to say they was near 'bout the sloppiest folks I ever seen. One time when I were helpin' Uncle Wint hunt a lost dog we come by their place and went inside because it were a right cold December day. It seemed like Uncle Wint were a real old friend and him and Uncle Dan shaken hands and when Aunt Shug come in from the kitchen she hollered out, "Well, I'll be danged if'n it ain't old Winton Epps! How you doin', Winton?" And she give Uncle a big hug and kiss. I don't know how he stood it because she were a lookin' sight—long, straggly, tangled-up hair, no teeth and the saggin'est bosom you ever seen in your life.

"If I felt any better I'd have to take somethin'. Must be this cool weather. I whinnied a couple of times yesterday," Uncle said, sort of flippin' up one of them hound-ear bosoms. "You don't mind if I flip 'em up, do you, Shug?"

"Flip 'em up, Winton, if it gives me pneumonia," Aunt Shug

said, grinnin' till her nose near 'bout touched her chin. "I'm
so glad to see you that I'd even let you snap my pistol."

We stayed over for dinner, but I couldn't hardly eat nothin',
the place were so dirty. Aunt Shug mixed up biscuits and
helt the pan down and let the old sow lick it out when she got
through. There was also six or eight chickens peckin' around
in the kitchen and a big old fat house cat sleepin' right up
on the table where we was to eat.

To make things worse, Uncle Dan had been burnin' a hole
in a new huntin' horn and that purely makes a stink. The
horn must of come off a shorthorn bull because it were real
big around at the base and only about ten inches long. It
tapered down right fast to the point where Uncle Dan had
sawed it off and carved out a mouthpiece. He'd scraped it
down with some broken glass until it were real pretty and
smooth and then he'd heated a piece of heavy wire and burnt
a hole through the solid part into the hollow. This is what had
made the stink. Of course, just the scrapin's don't smell too
good theirselves, but the burnin' business is somethin' else.

He got the hole through just before it were time for us to
eat and said, "Winton, give her a blast and see how she
sounds."

Uncle Winton could really blow a cow horn until it frazzled
out at the end, and he put the pressure to that one until his
face turned red. The end was so big around and the horn was
so short that I'll bet you couldn't of heard it a quarter of a
mile.

"How does she sound to you?" Uncle Dan asked.

"About like a little boy breakin' wind in a gourd," Uncle
told him. "The dern thing's too short, Uncle Dan, and you'd
just as well throw it away and start over."

I don't think Uncle Dan appreciated that too much, and
just about then Aunt Shug called us to dinner, but I didn't
have much appetite. We had swamp cabbage and warmed-
over venison stew poured over the biscuits and for dessert
we had more biscuits with syrup.

While we was eatin', Uncle Dan said, "Winton, yesterday
evenin' I was out in the marsh checkin' on some mink traps

and there was some mullet fishermen in one of the creeks. They made a strike while I was there and I had a chance to see 'em and talk to 'em. One of 'em was a feller who used to work with Speck Lukins—just in case you're interested."

"Speck weren't with 'em or I reckon you'd said so, Dan," Uncle Winton said, layin' down his fork and squintin' his eyes.

"I didn't see him and I didn't ask where he was at. But if I was you or your nephew I wouldn't let myself get too far away from a gun. I hear Lukin's leg healed up and he can get around pretty good but he goes with a limp."

"How do you know all that, Dan," Uncle said, "if you didn't ask about him?"

"Well," Uncle Dan said, "after they pulled the net and was havin' some lunch, a dern coon walked out on a oyster bar across the creek, and when he seen the boat and the men he went a-rackin' back into the saw grass, and one of the fellers laughed and said, 'Look at that scoun'el rack . . . reminds me of the way Speck gets about.' That's all I heerd, Winton, but I just thought I'd pass the word."

Uncle Winton studied over this for quite a spell before he went to eatin' again, and when he'd sopped up the last of the syrup with a biscuit he said, "I'll be watchin' out, Dan, and you can pass *that* word. And Tarley Driggers is gettin' to be one of the best shots in this whole country—shotgun, rifle or pistol."

"I've heered about that boy. They tell me he can knock a flyin' duck out of the air with a rifle."

"He has done it," Uncle Wint said.

After we'd eat we went into the other room to look at some hog tushes out of a old boar Uncle Dan had killed a few days before and we set down a few minutes before we headed back to the river. The kitchen had been a pure mess and the rest of the house weren't much better—rusted-out steel traps, jugs, an old wore-out saddle, a half-finished cast net, old rubber boots and I don't know what all.

"Don't you ever clean up around here?" Uncle Winton asked.

"No," Uncle Dan said. "When it gets so bad I can't move around in it, I lay a new floor!"

I sure was glad to leave that place and I heard later that Aunt Shug really had caught pneumonia and near 'bout died, but I don't see how it could have been from just that short exposure.

Our lost dog had laid out somewhere and when we did find him he were poor as a snake and full of ticks. I'll bet I pulled fifty ticks off him and there was some in his ears and on his neck back of his head so that he had blind staggers so bad he could hardly get about. Ticks in a dog's ears or on the back of his head sure do mess up his balance. Old Rambler was wobblin' around like a drunk feller when we found him. Uncle fed him a bellyful of pot likker and greased him with lard and sulphur and he overed it. I do believe a hound dog can get well quicker'n anything in the world.

I told Ma what old Uncle Dan had said about the mullet fishermen and Speck Lukins, and she said, "Billy, I heered some of that same talk among the women. Mrs. Bellamy said she'd heered that Joe Turner's wife had said that a second cousin of Speck Lukins' first wife had told somebody that Speck were back in these parts and really carryin' a grudge. Well, he sure better lay it down and leave before your Uncle Winton meets up with him."

"Or Tarl either," I said.

"Oh, Billy," Ma said, "I just don't know what to do about that. In a way I can't blame Tarley, but Speck Lukins didn't shoot at your daddy until after your daddy had done killed his brother."

"But his brother shot Daddy first and started all the trouble," I told her.

"I know, I know," she said, "and it were terrible. I don't blame you nor Tarley nor Winton for feelin' like you do, but I just hate to think about any more shootin'. I just couldn't hardly stand it if either of you boys was to get killed. And killin' Speck Lukins won't bring your daddy back. I wish everybody would be willin' to let the Lord take His vengeance."

"Tarl's done promised he won't go off a-lookin' for Lukins or Mr. McWirter either, so if they'll just stay away from here nobody'll get hurt or killed," I told her, "and the Lord can have

His vengeance." But I weren't too easy about it and kept my twenty-two rifle handy by my bed.

Tarl always had his thirty-thirty on wall pegs by the head of his bed and he kept a shell in the barrel. "It's the 'unloaded' guns that kill folks accidental," he'd say. "Somebody'll pick up a gun and mess with it and . . . POW! 'Oh, I didn't know it were loaded,' they'll claim. Well, I'll tell you right now my gun is loaded and stays that way. Whenever a feller really needs a gun, a empty one won't do."

When I told Tarl about what Uncle Dan had said to Uncle Winton about the commercial fishermen, he didn't say nothin' for a long time—just set there studyin' it over. I reckon he were tryin' to figure why Uncle Winton hadn't already told him. Directly he said, "Billy, you don't suppose Uncle Wint wants first chance, do you?"

"You know Uncle as good as I do," I told him, and I had to laugh. "He wouldn't beat you to it no quicker'n he could."

"I do believe it," Tarl answered. "And he don't mean nothin' but the best. But I think I'll just take me a skiff and slip off a few days and do some checkin'."

So he taken his bedroll and his rifle and some rations and went on down the river in a skiff. Nobody didn't pay him no mind because he were always prowlin' and a heap of times he'd get him a deer just driftin' around in the creeks on the edge of the marsh. I sure wanted to go with him, but somebody had to help Ma look after the stock. It weren't that she minded stayin' alone, because she kept Daddy's old single-action forty-four forty hangin' in a belt on her bedpost and she sure knowed how to use it.

"Your daddy," she told us, "used to say God made guns and knives to make all men the same size, and I reckon that's true and applies to women as well as men. I know I ain't scared of nobody with that old hog-leg handy. I hope I don't never have to shoot at nobody, but if any feller comes a-prowlin' around here at night, he'll sure get ventilated. He's got robbery or some kind of meanness on his mind, and if he's a-carryin' a gun, he ought to be executed if he's caught."

I think she knowed what Tarl was up to the mornin' he left, but she didn't let on. Once when I passed her door I seen her down on her knees at her bed a-prayin', but that weren't nothin' specially unusual for her. She talked with the Lord a heap. I couldn't help but think of what would happen if that feller Speck Lukins were to bushwhack my brother, because that'd be the only way he could ever kill him. I thought about all I'd have to take care of if anything happened to Tarl, and it sure were something for a kid my age to think about.

Tarl come back in a couple of days with a bushel of fine oysters and a big old bull redfish that some commercial fishermen had give him. It weighed near 'bout twenty pounds and were long as a ax handle. When Ma seen it she said, "I'll just bake that gentleman in some grapefruit juice." That's all she said. She didn't ask Tarl nothin' and he didn't say nothin'. After he'd scaled off that redfish and we'd shucked out some oysters, he told me about his trip.

"Billy," he said, "I went on down the river to Blue Island and asked old man Dennison if he knowed where there was any outside fellers net-fishin'. He told me there was a crew camped back in on Mink Creek but he didn't know any of 'em. I stayed there at his place that night and went on up to Mink Creek yesterday mornin'. There was five fellers in the crew and they was camped on one of them little rocky cedar islands. They was fishin' at night and doin' pretty well, they said. Three of the fellers was there in camp and the other two had took in their catch to the fish house. Naturally I couldn't ask who the other two fellers was, so I just set around and talked and waited, stayin' pretty close to my boat where I'd pulled it up on the shore. I had my rifle hid in my bedroll, but handy to where I could get it right quick and easy in case Speck Lukins showed up.

"I told the fellers I was just doin' a little sneakin' around, deer huntin', and they said they was doin' a little deer huntin' theirselves—had a old blue-speckled hound that they said would run a deer long enough to give 'em a shot sometimes when it crossed the marsh between the islands. But the old feller were awful slow and lame in a hind leg from bein' caught in a otter trap one time."

Tarl stopped right there and eat a couple of them big oysters and then looked at me and laughed.

"Billy," he told me, "you know what that old hound's name were?"

"What?"

"Speck," he told me.

That night, after supper, Ma pinned him down about his trip. "I'm glad you're home, son," she said, "and I don't reckon there was no shootin' or I'd of done heard about it."

"No, there weren't no shootin'," Tarl told her, "but there sure might of been." Then he went on and told her the whole story.

"Well," Ma said when he'd finished, "suppose it had been Speck Lukins instead of Speck dog. Just what did you figger to do when the boat got back—just pull your rifle out and shoot the man in cold blood and then get killed yourself by the other fellers?"

"He had his rifle and them fellers only had shotguns," I said. "He could of backed off from the island out of range of the shotguns before he went to work with his rifle."

"And then what?" Ma wanted to know. "He'd of had to run from the law and them fellers too!"

All this time Tarl hadn't said nothin', so at last Ma spoke up again and said, "All right, son. What was you plannin' to do and how was you plannin' to do it?"

"I reckon I don't know," Tarl answered, shakin' his head. "All I knowed was that if I seen the feller who helped to kill Daddy, I meant to shoot him. I reckon I didn't think no further than that."

"You're a lot like your daddy," Ma said. "Slap, bang, dash and let the other feller get out of the way. But sometimes that'll get you killed. And like I told Billy, that feller Speck Lukins didn't start the trouble. He didn't even shoot at your daddy until after your daddy had killed his brother."

"Well, he shot at Dad and his brother killed Dad and that's enough for me," Tarl said and went on to our bedroom. When he got his mind made up, there weren't much anybody could say to him—not even Ma.

"Billy," she told me, "I don't ever want you boys to think I'm sidin' against your daddy about nothin' in this world. Not for one minute. I loved him and there won't never be another man for me, but he'd be with us right now if he'd been just a little more peacefuller."

I studied over what she had said a long time after I went to bed and I reckon it's true, but I could see where a feller could be so peaceful that he'd just get pushed around the rest of his life. It'd be just like if I was to go to school and that big old Roberts boy was to say, "Billy Driggers, I'm a-goin' to stomp on your foot and take your lunch!"

And I'd say, "Oh, no you ain't."

And he'd say, "Oh, yes I am."

And I'd say, "You don't dare."

And then he'd stomp my foot and grab my lunch. It wouldn't do me no good to say, "Don't you dare do that again," if I ever wanted to take another lunch to school or even go back to school. Sometimes a feller just has to draw the line and fight. I guess that goes for a whole country as well as just one man.

10 FISH & FISHERMEN FROM THE WITHLACOOCHEE TO SHARK RIVER & TAVERNIER

There weren't but the eight grades in our school in the settlement and if a feller wanted to go higher he'd of had to travel near 'bout twenty miles. I never did like school too much anyhow and couldn't of gone past the sixth grade if I'd wanted to, because after Daddy got killed we had some right hard times. Me and Tarl worked the farm and the stock and taken all sorts of odd jobs to make a little extra. I remember one summer when I had a chance to go down the coast with a commercial fishin' outfit and Ma finally let me go. We was to live on a big boat and tow four skiffs. I always did love any kind of fishin' and could handle a skiff better'n most grown men, so I figured I could get by even if I didn't know doodly-squat about net-fishin'.

There's always been a big squabble between sport fishermen and commercial fishermen, and the more I've learnt about it, the more I can understand each feller's side. The crew I worked with was all gill-net fishermen and I couldn't see where their operations done very much harm. We'd work mostly at night findin' a big school of mullet, runnin' the nets around 'em, and as we'd close the circle, we'd fram on the bottom or side of the skiff with a oar and make the mullet run so they'd hit the net and gill theirselves. The twine was small and when they'd stick their heads in the mesh it would slip behind their gills and there they'd be.

Of course we'd catch some game fish like redfish, trout and big old snooks. Most of the big redfish would bust through and them derned snooks would near 'bout always cut the net and go on through. They got sharp edges on their gill covers that cut like a razor.

I sure met up with some salty characters on that trip and I remember some of 'em. Old Oliver Blackburn and Ben Seale and Ben Dunn from around Sarasota and Uncle George Rawls and Mac Ringo and Pappy Turner and his folks from Nokomis. We laid over a few days there and I had a heap of fun, fishin' down at the mouth of Casey's Pass—just castin' for snooks. The train engineers' union was startin' a town there that they called Venice, but there weren't nothin' down at the Pass yet.

On the fallin' tide the snooks would just fill up the Pass—back fins and tails out of water—and would hit anything that moved. And when the tide turned in, the jacks and trout and redfish would do business. A feller just couldn't of had no faster action with a rod and reel. For a long time a snook weren't considered to be much of a food fish, but some feller found out that if you skin him instead of scalin' him, his meat is just as good or better'n a trout or redfish. At first they didn't bring much, but they sure was fun to catch.

I had a lot of fun with a shark line too, baitin' with a jack crevalle and slashin' it to make it bleed and them old sharks couldn't let it alone. The water went off deep from the cut bank and I didn't have to throw out over thirty feet or so. Then I'd tie the end of the rope to a cabbage-palm trunk and go on with my castin'. When I'd see that shark rope just a-surgin' from that cabbage trunk, I'd run back and lay down my castin' rod and grab the rope. And I remember them little towheaded Turner boys helpin' me pull in the sharks.

One night I strung about twenty snooks on the shark rope when I got through fishin', and was a-sloshin' 'em off the cut bank to wash the sand off 'em. One three- or four-pounder pulled loose and when I reached for him a big old ten-foot shark took him right out of my hand, you might say. It made a mighty splash and throwed water all over me and likened to have scared me to death. I've seen one of them big sharks cut a tarpon half-in-two as clean as if you'd sawed him with a crosscut saw, and if my hand had been six inches lower that's what would of happened to my arm.

The beach there at Venice and across the Pass at Nokomis is pretty as a feller will see anywhere and I sure did like to go swimmin' where I could walk on a nice sandy beach and not cut my feet on rocks or shells. I've always been a good swimmer, but after that shark took my snook that night I ain't too easy about bein' in deep saltwater. They tell me the books say that the kind of sharks we have along our coast won't attack a man, but maybe some of them big rascals ain't read the books.

I never will forget how scared I was one day when I was swimmin' out past the breakers in pretty deep water and a dad-burn shark sucker got after me. Near 'bout every shark we'd catch had one or two of them suckers stuck to him and I knowed the dern things was harmless, but when that one got after me and started slidin' that rough suction plate over my skin, I done everything but rise out of the water. Them shark suckers has got suction cups on top of their heads and they just clamp on to bigger fish like sharks, tarpon, jewfish and the like and hitchhike. Then when the shark or whatever starts to feed they turn loose and pick up the scraps.

It seemed like when this one got after me that the faster I would swim, the more excited it got. It went around my legs and under and across my bare belly and up past my neck and slid on down my back and it near about set me crazy. I don't know why because I knowed it couldn't hurt me, but I just couldn't stand the dern thing scrapin' agin me.

When folks found out how good snooks was to eat if they was skinned, some crews bought drag seines made of heavy tarred twine with a mesh so small a snook couldn't get his nose far enough into it to cut it. They'd take thousands of pounds of snooks at one haul and, of course, everything else

that happened to be there. It was them drag seines that
started most of the trouble between the sport fishermen and
the commercial fishermen. But there was a whole lots of commercial fishermen too who didn't like them big seines, and I
remember one feller sayin', "Me and my brother fished hard
all night and brought in about four hundred pounds of mullet
to the fish house and they'd just bought four thousand pounds
from a seine crew and couldn't handle no more. Said rather
than see us throw 'em away they'd give us two cents a pound.
Well, *we* just throwed 'em away!"

Most of the commercial fishermen I met up with had come
from families of fishin' folks. Their daddies and grandaddies
had been commercial fishermen, and I just don't know anybody who can be more independent in his thinkin' and his
actions. He's his own boss and will make or break, accordin'
to his own efforts and know-how. Mostly, they was fair-
minded men with an eye to the future, but I heered one feller
say, "To hell with the future. If I could catch every fish
that swims in the Gulf of Mexico tonight, I'd catch 'em and
sell 'em and put the money in my pocket and go into some
other line of business."

One of the worst things about them haul seines is how
they tear up the bottom. And, naturally, with a small mesh
they hold a heap of undersize fish, and when they pull the
net on the beach, them fish just lay there for the gulls and
buzzards to eat. I seen one time where a feller couldn't hardly
walk the beach without steppin' on undersize pompano—too
small to sell but just as dead as they'd ever be.

From Casey's Pass we worked on down the coast. Once in
a while we'd make a strike with our gill nets, thinkin' we'd
surrounded a big school of mullet, only to find out that we had
us a slew of ladyfish. Them ladyfish will gill just like mullets,
but they're full of bones and fit for nothin'. Ma always said
she'd rather try to eat a paper of pins. It'd take us a long time
to clear the net of them scoun'els when we got 'em. The
only thing I can say for a ladyfish is that it's a jumpin', fightin'
article on the end of a line whenever it latches on to a plug
or a spoon. I heard one old cracker say, "That's a well-named
fish. Hard as the devil to catch and not worth a dern after

you get it!" I were only fourteen years old at the time, so I didn't have much grounds for arguing about that.

Some people call a ladyfish a bonefish, but that's wrong. A bonefish is something plumb different. He don't *need* to jump! He just takes off. I never had hold of but one and that were toward the end of our trip when we went under the railroad trestle at Tavernier and out onto the ocean flats. Some feller told me to dig one of them herman crabs out of a conch shell and use him for bonefish bait. I found me one of them red rascals and put a chunk of him on a hook and cast it out. I were usin' the same little old steel castin' rod and reel that I always used and I had whipped down some pretty good snooks and redfish with it. Shucks! That dern bonefish picked up the herman crab and left out, huntin' more country. I'll swear the water weren't much over a foot deep and that fish headed for Africa, accordin' to my geography. I seen it when it picked up the bait and it didn't look to be over two feet long. But it felt like two hundred pounds shot out of a gun.

I hadn't wet down my reel first and when I put my thumb down on that dry line on the spool, it raised a blister big as a acorn. The line run off to where it was tied to the spool and popped like a twenty-two rifle.

"I sure ain't goin' to try to tell Uncle Winton nothin' about bonefish," I promised myself, "and maybe not even Tarl."

On our way back up the coast we stopped off at Flamingo, which weren't nothin' but a couple of shacks and some net spreads. I want to tell you right now that were a wild piece of country in them days, and I seen several big panther tracks when we went ashore on a little stretch of sandy beach on Cape Sable. I seen too where a bear had dug out a turtle nest.

I never will forget them big old black mangrove trees at the mouth of Shark River. I'll bet some of 'em was near 'bout a hundred feet tall and you could see 'em from a long way off. We done pretty well on the trip and had extra good luck off the mouths of some of them creeks that make into that big old bay. It's a good thing Aunt Effie ain't got as many mouths as Shark River, I thought to myself, or Uncle Winton wouldn't even have a chance to say "Howdy!"

We done real good, too, off of Lostmans River. That's a well-named place! A feller can go up into them islands and get so turned around he couldn't hit the ground with his hat —if there was any ground!

We laid over in a little place called Everglades and I heered a lot of talk about knifin' and shootin'. There was some real rough characters around there, I want you to know. A while before a couple of fellers had robbed a bank somewhere and come over there to Everglades and ordered one of them boat captains to take 'em to Cuba. I heered him tell it one night when he come aboard our boat. I forget his name, but he were a powerful-built feller and looked like a Indian. He said he let on like he was goin' to take 'em to Cuba without no trouble, but he were just waitin' his time.

After a while he told 'em he had bowel cramps and one of 'em took the wheel while he went to the head, which were way up forward in his boat. The other feller waited outside with a pistol and the captain said he went into the head and bolted the door real good. He had a loaded twelve-gauge shotgun standin' behind that door and he grabbed it and popped up through the hatch and shot and killed the feller at the wheel. The feller hollered when he fell and the second feller run back to the cockpit and the captain shot him. Then he took 'em both back and turned 'em in for the reward.

There was a lot of real old-time settlers around that place— Uncle Charley Boggess and Fonsy and Greg Lopez and the Wigginses. Folks said old Raleigh Wiggins knowed them islands and channels so well he showed the 'gators where to dig their dens!

I heered talk of a family of people named Lukins there at Everglades, but I seen 'em and none of 'em was light-skinned or freckled. I asked one of the boys if his folks had any relatives in Georgia and he said, "No," and that they had come there from Oklahoma and their grandaddy had been part Indian. They looked it too. So I reckon there must be other Lukinses after all, but them's the only ones I heered of on that whole trip.

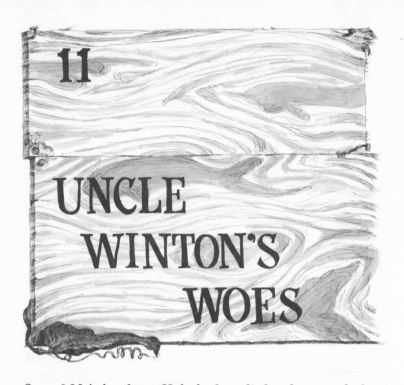

11

UNCLE WINTON'S WOES

One of Ma's brothers, Hub, had studied to be a tooth dentist and wound up in Georgia, where he wrote he were a-practicin'. I don't know how long he had to practice before he could be a real tooth dentist, but I do know he hadn't been at it long enough when Uncle Wint went up to him. There were always somethin' the matter with Uncle Wint, specially his teeth. A feller wouldn't think it to look at him, though, 'cause he had great big old strong-lookin' teeth. But they was always a-hurtin' him, and he claimed there weren't nothin' equaled a toothache for pure misery. I remember him tellin' me and Tarley a story about a feller ridin' through the country and he come upon another feller layin' in the ditch beside the road, just a-groanin' and a-rollin'.

"What ails you, friend?" the first feller asked, jumpin' down from his horse.

"Oh, my legs is broke, an' my left arm is broke, and I think several ribs is broke. My horse throwed me an' run off."

"Aw, shucks," said the first feller, "I thought maybe you had the toothache!" An' he rode off an' left him.

Well, anyhow, Uncle Wint said he had a plumb bellyful of achin' teeth, and he were goin' up to Uncle Hub's and get every dad-blamed one of 'em pulled out. Which he did. He were gone two or three weeks, and when me and Tarley seen him for the first time after he come back we liken to have split a gut. He said somethin' and then smiled at us, and Tarley said, "Uncle Winton, I'll be derned if you don't look just like a sheephead fish a-fixin' to nip off a fiddler crab."

Them store teeth Uncle Hub had made him was little and even and pearly white. He looked like he had a short ear of young corn wedged across his mouth. I thought at first he'd get mad, but he just nodded his head and said, "They look like the devil, don't they? And what's more, they hurt me in six different places. I've a good will to throw the dang things down the well." He didn't, but he might as well have, 'cause the next time we seen him were when he come over to our place to bring Ma some fresh guavas. The cold weather had nipped our bushes that winter, and he knowed Ma purely loved 'em.

Anyhow, he looked kind of funny, and after while Tarley said, "Uncle Winton, you ain't a-wearin' your teeth, I don't believe."

And Uncle Wint said, "You're dad-blamed right. I ain't a-wearin' 'em. And the next time you ask me I won't be a-wearin' 'em neither."

"What happened?" Tarley asked him. "Bust 'em on guava seeds?"

"Naw," Uncle told him. "They just kept a-naggin' me till I took 'em out and boiled 'em in a kettle to soften 'em up so I could sort of mold 'em to fit. And I did, too. But when the plagued things dried and cooled they was all ridged up and I couldn't stand 'em at all. So I got me a file and filed off the high spots. Only I filed too deep in one place and put a hole in 'em, so they wouldn't hold suction. So I patched 'em with a dab of roofin' cement and they helt all right, but after two weeks I could still taste that dang roofin' cement, so I just give up."

"Why, Winton, how in the world kin you eat?" Ma asked him.

"Oh, I get along about as good as a soft-shell turtle," he told her.

After he left, Tarley said not to worry none. "I seen a big old soft-shell—big as a washtub, and it snapped a broom handle right half-in-two," he told us. "So I reckon Uncle will make out."

Durin' the time Uncle didn't wear no teeth at all he were a bad-lookin' thing. He always wore a big old long mustache and without his teeth his chin near 'bout touched his nose, so he looked like he'd swallered a couple of minks and left their tails hangin' out of his mouth. I were in the commissary one day when he come in and some feller said, "If I was as ugly as you, I'd sue my mother and father for bringin' me into the world."

I thought Uncle would get mad about that, but he just gave a little laugh and said, "Well, I tried to, but they both swore they was just havin' fun and the judge threw the case out of court!" I guess Uncle knowed he weren't no beauty without ary teeth because it weren't too long after that that he went to another tooth dentist down in Tampa and had a new set of teeth made. They looked pretty good, but he liken to have shocked Aunt Effie to death when he first come back. He'd been into a arcade and bought him some trick celluloid teeth with great big tushes like a dog and slipped 'em over his new ones. When he said, "How you like 'em, Effie?" and grinned at her you could have knocked her eyes off with a stick! I mean he were a sight!

When Uncle finally got these teeth that felt just right, he sure was proud and took some kind of care of 'em. I remember goin' with him to look for some hogs up on Gun Barrel Creek, and we stretched a tarpolean in a little clearing where some fellers had been camped a-deer-huntin'. They'd nailed a old wood shell box up onto a black gum tree to keep stuff in, and Uncle Winton laid his teeth up on top of that box. He was afraid they'd get stepped on if he left 'em on the ground, or the hogs would root 'em up or somethin'.

Anyhow, next mornin' when I went to get the bacon out of the box there was a little old green tree toad nested down in Uncle's upper plate. It hopped out when I got to rummagin' around, but the natural suction of them teeth and its own feet too helt so that it almost taken the teeth with it. I never thought to tell Uncle about it till he complained about his teeth tastin' salty. Some hot coffee fixed that, though, and he never got sick nor nothin'. Uncle, I mean, not the toad!

It weren't long after that when he and the Beauforts and Hub Johnson and several other old fellers went off on a big deer hunt up to Georgia. Hub's daddy-in-law owned a big plantation where both deer and turkeys was thick as ants, to hear Hub tell it.

Anyhow, they all had to camp in a great big old log house and the first night they done a heap of plannin'. It takes plenty of liquor to plan right, accordin' to Uncle Wint, and they had two gallon jugs of Wiggins' 'shine. He made it smooth and strong enough to cock a cannon.

When Uncle Wint finally decided to turn in, about two o'clock in the mornin', he couldn't find ary cup or glass to put his teeth in, leastways one big enough, so he put 'em in the water bucket. Old man Jim Oaks went to get him a drink about three o'clock, and when he raised the dipper and seen them teeth a-grinnin' at him, it made him so mad he went around the camp and gathered up all the sets of teeth he could find in cups and glasses and dumped 'em in the water bucket along with Uncle Winton's. There was five sets of 'em. Then he mixed 'em well with the dipper and Hub told me it waked him up and sounded like somebody stirrin' a kettle of blue crabs.

There was a real ruckus next mornin' tryin' to sort out them teeth, and at first Uncle Wint swore he'd never wear his again, even if he did figure out which they was. Then, when everybody else had claimed their own, he took his and put 'em in a tin cup and poured it full of that new-made 'shine. He said if that didn't sterilize 'em, nothin' ever would! The fellers on the hunt all said that the very next mornin' the cup was plumb dry and Uncle Wint swore that them teeth had absorbed every drop.

"Wasn't you scared that whiskey would ruin them teeth?" I asked him when he got home.

"Boy, what are you talkin' about!" Uncle said. "Any teeth

of mine are used to good whiskey, and if they ain't, they soon will be."

I never seen a feller could have so many things ailin' him as my Uncle Wint. And he were the hairiest man I near 'bout ever seen too—not that that had anything to do with his ailin'. I just mention it because it's the first thing I think of when I think of my Uncle Winton—that black hair on his head and his mustache and his arms and his chest. Yes, and acrost his back too. He were purely a hairy old bear of a feller, if you ever seen him with his shirt off. I remember what he'd say when Tarley would ask him, "How you doin', Uncle Wint?"

"Terrible," he'd always say.

"What's ailin' you?" Tarley would ask.

"Everything," he would say. That would be his answer just as regular as a goose goes barefoot.

One time I remember he started right in afore he were hardly inside the yard gate. "Guess what's the matter with me now," he said.

"Ain't got no idea," Tarley told him.

"I got a tapeworm," Uncle Wint said. "I been to Doc Joyner and he told me. A tapeworm."

"Well, I'll bet you one thing," Tarley said. "I'll bet it ain't never drawed a sober breath in its life!"

Uncle Wint didn't like that very much and said so. A tapeworm, a real genuwine tapeworm, weren't no jokin' matter, he told us. So he didn't stay very long that time because he'd been takin' medicine.

It were about two months later we went over to Uncle Wint's to try to get him to go bear huntin' with us. A bear had tore up four of Ma's beehives and we didn't have no dogs that would tree him or hold him up. Uncle Wint had a yardful of cur dogs that would purely eat up anything he put 'em at. Well, this time we didn't have to ask Uncle Wint what ailed him. His leg were bandaged knee to hip, and he were limpin' around with a walkin' stick. "It's all because of that dang horse—that buckskin I got from Jim Royal last year."

"Throwed you, eh?" Tarley said, tryin' not to laugh, 'cause

Uncle Wint were supposed to be—and were—the best rider in the county.

"No, sir!" Uncle Wint said. Then he went on to tell us what happened.

It seemed like he had been roundin' up a bunch of woods cows down in the high palmettos Friday a week—which were the hottest day any of us could remember.

"Boys, I was hotter'n a hummin'bird layin' a goose egg!" Uncle said. He had got so hot that after he penned them cows he rode over to a little clearwater lake near there, stripped off his clothes and hung 'em on the saddle and went for a swim. Everything were fine until he come a-walkin' out. That horse never had seen Uncle naked before, so it just jerked the bridle over its head and run away—clothes and all. Of course, a feller couldn't really blame the horse, Uncle being so hairy and all.

It were about two miles home and there weren't nothing for Uncle Wint to do but walk it—buck naked. He didn't like that idea, so he got him a piece of grapevine and a couple of palmetto fans and tied 'em on front and rear. Well, when he got home and walked into the yard with them palmetto fans a-flappin' and him naked and all, that bunch of dogs really took to him. A great big old brindle catch dog, about half bull, bit him pretty bad too; and that's how come the bandage. You couldn't hardly blame the dogs, though, when they seen something like that a-comin'. Course it wouldn't probably have happened if Uncle Wint hadn't just been swimmin' and so didn't smell natural to the dogs. We sure didn't say nothin' about this then, though, because we was tryin' to get up a bear hunt and didn't want to make Uncle mad.

"Boys," he said, "I got some dogs here that'll natcherly work on a bear. I don't know about this big brindle that bit me, he's a new one, and I don't believe he's even ever heerd anybody say 'bear,' but he's big enough and mean enough and I believe he'll fight. We'll catch that bear or make him hunt more country. I'll bring the whole works over in a few days if nothin' don't happen!"

But like I said, it seemed as if somethin' was always happenin' to Uncle Winton. He got a little infection in his leg
where the dog bit him, but Doc Joyner cured that up all right.
Old Doc was pretty good and I never think of him but what
I remember the time Uncle Wint went to him years later
about a little old mole on his hip. This here mole weren't no
bigger than a grain of corn, but it was right where his belt
went 'round him, so that it worried him and sometimes got
right sore.

Well, old Doc Joyner had a nephew who was studyin' to be
a doctor hisself and he was in the office when Uncle Winton
come in. Both Doc Joyner and his nephew liked a snort now
and again, and that particular day were both times. It seemed
like Sam Joyner, the young feller, had killed a ten-point buck
that mornin' up 'round Otter Creek and they was kind of
celebratin'.

Uncle Winton told them about the mole and Doc agreed
that it had to come off of there and that he wouldn't be long
about gettin' it off. He was just a country doctor in a little old
country town, but he kept up pretty much with his business
and he had one of them electric needles. While he was
a-gettin' it all ready, his nephew Sam went to wash around
the place with alcohol and spilt a lot. Uncle Wint was a-layin'
on his side and the alcohol run down all over him. Then Sam
started to deaden the mole with something called Ethel somebody. Whatever it were, it were supposed to freeze the place
so it wouldn't hurt. Anyhow, about that time Doc Joyner
turned around and popped the electric needle to Uncle and
set him afire.

Well . . . they had a terrible time puttin' him out. They
grabbed some towels and went to beatin' on him, and Doc
Joyner said it were just like fightin' a brush fire. He said when
they got through, poor old Uncle Winton looked like a singed
chicken. But I'll tell you one thing: nobody in this family,
or in any other family 'round here, dared bring up the subject
'round Uncle Winton. I tried to joke him about it once by
sayin' it were too bad this hadn't happened before his horse
ran away that time he come out of the pond naked. Maybe
the horse wouldn't of run away.

"If you ever say anything like that again, boy," Uncle Wint said, "I'll slap you so hard your shirttail will fly up your back like a window shade!"

I remember another time when Uncle Winton went down to Tampa to get him a check-up and carried me with him. He had sort of a orangy-red rash on his back and neck and the doctor asked him, "Mr. Epps, have you ever had erysipelas?" and Uncle said, "No, sir, I ain't never had nary syphilis nor the clap neither." This got the doctor real tickled and he laughed so you could hear him all over the hospital. I didn't know what were so funny till I got home and told Ma what the doctor had really asked him and we looked it up. That rash were what the doctor called tinny verse color or somethin'. Uncle said that sounded worse than the "Old Joe," but the doc said it were just a skin rash caused by dirty livin' conditions and Uncle told him he had been sleepin' three to a bed up in the Hammock at old man Dan Yummer's place while he were up there hog huntin'.

A horse had kicked Uncle in the brisket and he told the doc about that too, so the doc said, "Well, let me check your sternum." So Uncle rolled over onto his face. That set off the doc to laughin' again. I never seen any doctor laugh so much.

"The horse kicked him in the brisket," I said. "Not in the butt."

"All right, young man," the doc said. "We'll check his brisket. Roll back over, Mr. Epps."

There were a bad bruise on Uncle's chest when the doctor got the hair parted to where he could see it, but no bones was broke. All the other tests was favorable. He didn't have no sign of TB or diabetes and his blood pressure were one-forty over eighty, whatever that means. The doctor give him a prescription for the rash and said, "Get this here prescription filled, rub it on and you'll be all right. And be careful where you set your sternum," and he went back into his office laughin'.

12

THE

BEAR

HUNT

In about a week, after his leg got healed and haired over, Uncle Wint come over to our place to go after that bear that had been tearin' up Ma's beehives. He had six or seven hounds and a whole collection of cur dogs and feists which he said would really take hold of a bear and knowed which end to go to. If a dog don't know which end of a bear to go to, he's a hurt dog.

Old man Shorter brought three dogs that he guaranteed would make a bear miserable and Jim Turner had a big old white-and-brindle cur dog that he said would catch anything he told it to catch. Up to that time he hadn't never told it to catch a bear, and after that hunt whenever anybody would ask Jim if his dog would run a bear he'd say, "Yes, sir! If the bear will keep up with him!"

We got that honey-robbin' bear the first mornin' in spite of the dogs catchin' and killin' a skunk. It seemed like every dad-blasted one of 'em was in on the job and that skunk sure sprayed it around. Skunk musk was so thick in the air it would smart your eyes. In spite of that they went to work and cold-trailed and jumped that bear just like nothin' had happened. It's sure a funny thing to me how a dog can get plastered by a skunk and in just a few minutes be able to cold-trail some other varmint. I can't figure out how he can smell anything because he stinks so strong hisself you can't get near him, but it don't seem to bother his huntin'.

Some people call the bears we have here in Florida hog bears, but they ain't nothing really but just ordinary black bears. Folks tell me that out west an old sow black bear might have brown or cinnamon-colored cubs, and one feller who had been out there huntin' told me he'd seen two black cubs and one brown one in the same litter, but I ain't never seen a Florida bear that were anything but black, and neither had Uncle Winton and he'd seen a heap of bears. This here one had just dug out a yellow jackets' nest and its belly was solid with both grown yellow jackets and grubs. A bear has a small belly for his size and this one's belly weren't much bigger than a man's head, but it must of had a couple of thousand yellow jackets in it and that sure must of been some kind of hot eatin'!

While everybody was in a bear-huntin' humor, we all moved over to the Sulphur Island scrubs and camped in a old, deserted homesteader's shack. Things wasn't too comfortable in that camp—there weren't no screens, and the weather had turned off warm, so the skeeters was really bad. Everybody had brought their own skeeter nets but old man Carlton Shorter.

"Carlton, these here brassheads are goin' to eat you up," Uncle Winton told him.

But old man Shorter just laughed and said, "Oh, I don't reckon. A skeeter comes through the window singin' 'mmm-mmmmmmmm,' but when he gets a good look at me, he goes back out the window singin' 'huh-uhhhhhhhh'!"

Well, I could believe that, all right. But it probably weren't the looks of old man Shorter that turned back the skeeters—them scapers go more by scent than sight.

Before we turned in, Uncle Winton brought in the coffeepot. "Here she be, boys," he said. "So hot you can't even point at it and strong enough to track a rabbit through!"

"Just the way I like it," old man Shorter told him. "Usually a feller could spear a fish twenty feet deep in your coffee!"

Everybody had some but me. I like it all right, but not at night; it don't keep me awake, but it makes my belly grumble and *that* keeps me awake. I told 'em so and Jim Turner said, "It ain't that the coffee keeps me awake so much as it is that it gets me awake. There just seems to be a heap more water in coffee than there used to be when I was a young feller!"

"It's funny what'll keep a feller awake," old man Shorter said. "My daddy was a big man and if he got a bunk that was too short for him and his feet stuck over and got cold, he'd dream about thunder. And he sure was scared to death of thunder! But that's all he was scared of."

That was the truth, all right. Everybody knowed that Carlton Shorter's daddy had been a big rough feller who liked to fight and who liked the gals.

"When the old man just couldn't sleep, he'd count women instead of sheep," Carlton said.

"That's an idea," Uncle Winton said. "But I always sleep good in a house like this even if it ain't much of a house. I don't rest too easy in a dad-burn tent, though—not since me and Jim Barnes had a rattlesnake join us.

"I remember old man George Rawls used to liven things up when we was workin' cattle on the Myakka flats. Somebody had give one of his grandchildren a little dancin'-man toy for Christmas. You wound it up with a key and when you set it down, the little man danced a regular jig on a little platform.

"Well, of course the kid busted it right away and it wouldn't stay wound up, and when there wasn't no dancin' man on the platform, that little spring would really whir. The thing was that it sounded more like a rattlesnake than a rattlesnake. And old man Rawls used to carry that old busted toy around in his saddlebags and at night, when everybody was in their bedrolls in the tent, he'd work the talk around to rattlesnakes.

" 'Boys,' he'd say, 'with all this high water, the snakes is really crawlin'. You've sure got to keep your eyes peeled.' And while he was talkin', he was windin' up that little old spring and reachin' way around behind some feller's pillow. When he'd turn it loose, they'd just about tear up the tent."

"I'd of killed that feller," said old man Shorter. And I believe he would, too. He was a wild old feller, a lot like his old man had been.

Several other hunters joined us at the camp—Horace Lassiter, Uncle Steve Kirkland and a preacher friend of theirs. With all the stories and planning for the hunt next day it must have been one o'clock in the mornin' before anybody got to sleep.

Uncle Winton rousted everybody out at four o'clock. He was always an early bird. I remember Aunt Effie sayin' one time when I was visitin' there, "I'm worried about your Uncle Winton, Billy. Somethin' must ail him 'cause he lay abed till sun-up!" Anyhow, he believed in getting an early start into the woods while the dew was still on the bushes so the dogs could trail good.

When he woke up old man Shorter, the old feller said, "What time is it?" And when Uncle Winton told him four o'clock, he hollered out, "What's the matter with you, Winton Epps? You afraid of gettin' bedsores? It sure don't take a feller long to spend the night in your camp!"

Uncle Wint let the preacher sleep till the last minutes and when he did wake him up he said, "Time to get up, Reverend. I'm cookin' eggs. How do you like yours?"

"What time is it now?" the preacher asked.

"Half past four," Uncle Wint told him.

"Hard-boiled, please," the preacher said. "About four hours!" But he were just funnin' and weren't no time pullin' on his pants and settin' down to eat right along with everybody else.

Some feller whose name I disremember rode into the camp just as day was beginnin' to lighten in the east, and Uncle hollered, "Where you been all forenoon?" He sure didn't let folks set around in the mornin'. "Many a big old buck has been missed and many a bear track has got cold while somebody set around in camp drinkin' a third cup of coffee," he'd say. "Let's get goin'!"

We had enough men to cover just about all the good stands along Sulphur Creek and Blackwater Creek both—from Sulphur Creek bridge to the Fish Hole and clean on over to Double Bridges, where Blackwater comes out of Seminole Swamp. It's a big piece of country and the only town anywhere close is called Cassia. Uncle Winton said Cassia was bigger than New York. "Course there ain't so many people, but it sure is bigger!"

The very first mornin' we found where the biggest kind of a bear had walked up out of Seminole Swamp, crossed the old sand road to Double Bridges and gone up into the scrub after acorns. We figgered he was somewhere up in that high scrub and we just about had him hemmed up. If he went east, headin' towards the St. Johns River Swamp, he'd have to cross the Fish Hole road; if he went back north, he'd have to come back across the Double Bridges road, and we didn't figger he'd head south 'cause he'd of had to cross Blackwater Creek and then he'd run into flatwoods and open piney woods, which a bear don't like. He likes to stay in the thickest place he can find. We knowed he wouldn't go west across Blackwater and beyond Double Bridges 'cause that was all open piney woods and blackjack-oak hills.

Before we turnt the dogs loose on the bear's trail, we put our standers all out in the likeliest spots, and then Uncle Winton put the whole kit and caboodle of dogs onto that fresh trail. The bear had walked on the dew and left the prints of his feet outlined in wet sand where he'd walked an old cross-tie that must have fell off a log cart when they was cuttin' ties on the edge of Seminole Swamp.

That devilish bear couldn't have been a quarter of a mile up in the scrub and the dogs didn't have to hardly trail him at all before they jumped him. You never heard such a fuss in your life as when that bunch of cur dogs and feists fell in with the hounds on that smokin' hot trail. They come a-boilin' down a little old draw, right in between Uncle Steve Kirkland and old man Shorter—just about the onliest place where anything could have got across the road without being seen by one of them two old-timers.

The bear went about half a mile back into the swamp

before the fightin' dogs made it so hot for him that he had to
back up to a tree and fight. He was a powerful big bear from
his tracks, and that first time he bayed up he killed one of the
hounds and put the fear of bears in Jim Turner's old big
white-and-brindle catch dog. It come runnin' back to Jim
with every hair turned the wrong way. It was glassy-eyed and
the hot water was runnin' out the sides of its mouth. Jim
swears that he had to get another feller to help pull that
dog's tail out from between its legs and that it never raised
its tail again the rest of its life—just carried it around like a
pump handle.

Several of the other fightin' dogs got cuffed around some,
and before any of us hunters could get to him, the bear
moved on north through the swamp. He bayed up two or
three times along the edge of Blackwater, but never would
go up a tree. Unless a feller has been through the middle of
that swamp, he just don't know what a real rough, bad place
is like. The ground is boggy and the saw palmettos are higher'n a man's head. Every tree is hung with bamboo briar
and there are a lot of blow-downs so that it's near 'bout
impossible to get through.

The bear picked the worst part of the swamp, headin'
north, and crossed the hard road near the bridge. Then he
followed Blackwater on around back of old man Beck's and
down into Hell Hole Bay. Uncle Bos Royal heard the chase
all the way up to his house above Blackwater and he saddled
up his horse and headed for Lake Norris.

The bear went on through across Bay Branch and when
he come out by the little old log bridge across Blackwater,
just where it comes out of Lake Norris, Uncle Bos was
waitin' for him with his old ten-gauge. He sure had figgered
right as to where that bear was headin', but then he'd killed
many a bear around Cassia and knowed their runs. Him and
his nephew Ernest Royal was the top bear hunters in that
whole country, and the only reason they hadn't gone into
camp with us was that they was on a deal to sell some land
that day. The feller was there and ready to talk business,
but when Uncle Bos heard them hounds a-bawlin' and them
feists a-yippin', he just had to go. "I told that feller I didn't

much want to sell the land nohow and when dogs were a-runnin' a bear, everything else had to wait!"

Anyhow, that chase wound up our bear hunt. We never did find two of the dogs and the rest was so stove up from the saw palmettos and briars that they could hardly walk. Some of 'em straggled back into our camp that night and Uncle Bos tied up the rest at his house. He rode over to our camp the next mornin' and me and Tarl and Uncle Winton and the preacher went back over to Lake Norris with him to help skin the bear. We all agreed to give the hide to the preacher. He sure was a nice feller and I wish I could remember his name.

I do remember that him and Tarl talked till way past midnight one night on the porch of the camp about the Lord, and I reckon Tarl must have told him about Dad and how he meant to shoot McWirter and Lukins on sight. Whatever was said, I don't reckon it had much effect on old Tarl. His mind was done made up.

Of all the bear dogs I ever seen, I reckon Uncle Winton's ol' Barrister was the best. The daddy of this dog had been the original ol' Barrister, a famous hound that old man Paul J. Rainey had brought down to Homosassa years ago from somewhere up in Mississippi, where he had his bear pack. Uncle Winton had been a guide on that hunt and he said that Rainey had thirty or forty dogs that would purely take a bear apart.

"No bear could stay on the ground when that bunch taken to him," Uncle said. "The two strike dogs that wouldn't run nothin' but a bear was ol' Barrister and ol' Brewster. Ol' Barrister were a big black-and-tan about one quarter bloodhound, with extra long ears and a wonderful nose for cold-trailin'. Ol' Brewster were blue-speckled and near 'bout as good.

"Where there were any moisture, like down in the swamp, that Barrister dog would work a trail ten or twelve hours old. And he had a voice that would raise goose pimples on a feller's goose pimples. He were a bear dog from his heart, but I'll tell you one thing: he didn't do no fightin'. He'd learnt about bears! When a bear were treed, ol' Barrister would set down fifty steps or more from the tree. He'd throw up his head and bark and grab a palmetto stem or a stick and growl and shake it and chew it up and raise all manner of hell. But that were the extent of his bear fightin'!

"Wherever Rainey would go, there'd be some feller with a hound or a feist or a cur or a catch dog that would run and fight a bear and Rainey would buy him, just about regardless of price. He wound up with a pack of dogs that was trouble for any bear anywhere. Later on, I read where he taken that same pack to Africa and gave them lions and leopards fits.

"While Rainey were down here he bought a couple of bull-and-cur catch dogs from the Dillard boys and tried to buy old Judy from me. But she were my strike dog and I wouldn't sell her. She come in season on that hunt and I bred her to ol' Barrister without tellin' nobody but ol' Barrister. And that's how come us to have this here Barrister. He were sure a good one and I don't know where a feller could find a better name for a bear dog."

Uncle Wint sure thought a heap of that dog. When the old feller died after gettin' mauled by a bear, Uncle buried him and put up a marker. He had a regular place where he buried his favorite dogs and sometimes he'd write a poem to cut on the marker. This time he wrote:

> Old Barrister is buried here—
> He wouldn't run a fox or deer—
> But when he hit the scent of bear—
> He'd squall until it raised your hair!

He carved all that out on a cypress board and it took him a long time, but he meant for it to last.

Right alongside was a marker for where he'd buried old Bull nine or ten years before. Bull was a catch dog that would purely work on a bear, hammin' one until it had to sit down and fight or climb a tree. You could still read what it said on the marker:

> There ain't no bear,
> Did ever dare
> To show his butt
> To this old mutt!

There was a great fox hunter named Jesse Letton over to Leesburg who had a dog named Auctioneer, and I thought that made a right good name for a big-mouthed hound. Speakin' of dogs' names, I remember a feller I hunted with once that had a dog he called Fewsuch, or somethin'. And when I asked him how come he named the dog that, he said, "I call him Fewsuch, son, 'cause there's just few such dang dogs as him!" This same feller had a dog named Moreover, which name he said come from the Bible. He said he'd read where it said, "Moreover the dog . . ." I never could find the place and even Ma couldn't.

Charlie Dean, the sheriff over to Inverness, were a great feller to hunt and always kept a bunch of dogs and he had one he called Travelin' Man. "He's bull and cur crossed and he's the most curious dog that ever lived," the sheriff told us. "If a new dog comes to town, old Travelin' Man somehow learns about it and pays a visit. I decided to have me a little fun, so I fixed him up a muzzle and mounted a big darnin' needle in the end of it. Well, sir, within three days there weren't ary dog in Inverness that would let my dog get within two blocks of him!"

"It was just touch and go," Tarley told him.

"That's what it was," the sheriff said, laughing. "That's just exactly what it was!"

13 THE BAD MAN, THE YANCY GAL & TARL'S BIG SURPRISE

One summer Tarley got a job cow huntin' with a big rancher back in the Myakka prairies, and he said that sure were a big lonesome country. Him and another cowboy had rounded up a bunch of young steers that hadn't seen nobody or nothin' for six months. He said they wasn't really mean but just wild as deer.

"We'd get 'em bunched and movin' and then somethin' would spook 'em and it were just like you'd turned over a old trunk full of roaches," Tarley said.

"We finally got 'em bunched again and into the pen. I started back for the cow camp, but my buddy decided to ride on in toward Nokomis, where he had a gal.

" 'I'll go see her while I got a chance,' he said. 'Only get to see her 'bout once a week.'

" 'That ain't very much,' I told him.

" 'No, but it will keep off fits!' my buddy said and rode off."

When Uncle Winton heard this he said, "I don't blame that old boy a bit. I've had a lot of smoochin' in my life and the worst I ever had was wonderful!"

"It were a right smart ride back to our cow camp," Tarley

continued, "and I was wonderin' whether I'd make it before the rain—a real frog-strangler makin' up to the southeast. The sky were about the color of a dead-ripe huckleberry, with some hot-lookin' lightnin' playin' around.

"When I seen that squall about to catch me, I hit my pony with the spurs and lit out for an old deserted two-story homesteader's place. It didn't have no doors and the windows was busted out, but I figgered it would give me some kind of shelter anyhow. The wind had freshened and the first big drops of rain was hittin' when I pulled up alongside the old ramshackle front porch. I jumped off my horse, tied him to a porch post and started inside. When I did, all hell broke loose upstairs.

"You've got to remember that this was way back out on the prairie and there weren't a livin' soul within ten miles. My horse pulled loose from the post and run away—or thought he did, but I was right alongside him, maybe a little bit ahead! I guess my hair must of stood straight up, because my hat started to come off and when I reached up to pull it back down I just stuck my hand right up in the roof of my mouth. I mean I were scared!

"Directly I got hold of the reins and into the saddle and by that time we was two hundred yards away. I looked back over my shoulder and seen about twenty goats comin' out of that house. I reckon they was scareder than me and the horse, because they took out right through the rain—and you know how a goat hates to get wet. They was livin' in that old house and of course a dern goat will go just as high as he can wherever he is, so they was all upstairs. When me and that pony arrived they all started down them stairs at once with the awfulest clatter you ever heered in your life.

"That turned out to be one of the heaviest rains I ever seen and there weren't nothin' to do but go back to the house and get in shelter. Why I hadn't smelt them goats when I first went in I don't know, but I sure smelt 'em for the next two hours, and the wetter things got, the worse it smelt and the more I thought about the time me and you shot up Uncle's goats and had to skin and butcher so many of 'em. By the time the rain stopped and I got saddled up and back to the camp it were plumb dark. Supper was over, but I couldn't have eat none nohow!"

This happened at the same camp where they had the trouble with the bad man. This feller were big and mean and had a awful reputation for fightin' all through Sarasota County, accordin' to Tarley, but he were a good cowhand when he were sober. He'd come into a camp, jump up and knock his heels together and holler out, "I can climb higher in a low pine and wade deeper in shallow water and shoot louder with less powder and get drunker on less whiskey than anybody in this county!"

Usually there weren't nobody took issue with any of them statements. They let this feller alone because he were very much of a man and would a little sooner fight than not. Well, this bad man had got a job with the outfit because they was short-handed, and when he brought his bedroll into the old house where they was camped, he spread it out alongside the cook's bedroll. Everybody were sleepin' on the floor wherever they could find space. This cook were a young feller named Willie Stevens and he didn't have too good sense. He were harelipped and he talked funny, but he could do a pretty good job of throwin' rations together. One of the cowboys went out in the kitchen and told him, "Willie, I see where that old bad feller has made up his bed next to yours, so keep your eye on him. He's terrible 'bout havin' fits in his sleep— clawed and bit one feller over in a camp near Arcadia so bad that the feller near 'bout died."

Willie didn't say nothin', but after supper he went over and sat down in the chimney corner with a whet rock and a butcher knife. Tarley said he were really puttin' a edge on that knife. He worked on it so long that after a while one of the boys asked him, "What you goin' to do with that knife, Willie?"

Willie cut his eyes over at the big bad man and said, "If that scoun'el has ary fit in this house tonight he'll never have nary 'nother one!"

Everybody laughed and the bad man wanted to know what went on. The boys told him and after while somebody seen him rollin' up his bedroll, fixin' to move.

"Where you goin'?" Tarley asked him.

"Out in the yard," the bad man said. "I wouldn't sleep alongside that crazy cook for two hundred otter hides. If I was to roll over in my sleep he'd cut my head off!" And he slept out in the yard every night.

This sure did tickle the cowboys and one of 'em said, "That cook ain't so crazy—he's got some cards. The ace may be gone, but the deuce is still there!"

Of course it wouldn't have done for Tarley and that bad feller to have butted heads. There weren't never nothin' real mean about Tarley, but it seemed like he just naturally enjoyed a good fight now and then—specially with some old braggin' loudmouth. I seen him fight one feller over near Red Level for over a hour—just because the feller said he could whip him. The feller were big and strong and knowed somethin' about boxin', all right. He'd knock Tarley down and old Tarl would just laugh and get right up. Once in a while Tarley would get through his guard, and when he did the big feller would go down. He told a feller afterward that when Tarley hit him it felt like a horse kickin' him. It were the longest and hardest fight I ever seen but one, and Tarley whipped him. I kept pullin' for Tarl all the time and one of the big feller's buddies hollered out, "You stay out of this, you little runty rooster, or I'll stomp you into the ground!"

"You'll never do it," I told him. But do you know, I lied about that! He did stomp me and would of hurt me bad if a couple of the Butler boys hadn't of pulled him off of me. Even after I were twenty years old and full-growed I only weighed one hundred and sixty pounds and stood four or five inches lesser'n Tarley. I weren't scary or nothin', but just never did pack as much meat and muscle as my brother.

When Tarley were only eighteen years old he stood six two and weighed two twenty-two and were as strong as a bull yearlin'. All the gals in our part of the county was crazy about him, but he stayed too busy huntin' and fishin' to pay 'em any mind—most of the time. He were only in the seventh grade because for a long time we didn't have no schoolteacher and he didn't get a very good start. When we was just little scapers we did have one buzzard-necked feller with a Adam's apple big as a orange, but he didn't stay long. Daddy run him off when he'd only been there a month—said he weren't goin' to have nobody teachin' his boys to spell possum with a "o" and 'tater with a "p."

The seventh grade had a lady teacher and she had her hands full with them old Gulf Hammock cracker boys. Most of 'em was about thirteen years old and a heap smaller than Tarley, and it sure did hack old Tarl to be the biggest and oldest in his class. None of the boys dared to make fun of him to his face, but the gals would laugh at some of his answers and he'd just get up and leave the room and go to the outhouse. And he'd stay there. The teacher couldn't get none of the boys to go out there and tell him to come in and she didn't dare go out there herself. I remember Tarl tellin' somebody years later that the reason he didn't have much education were on account of spendin' too much time out back!

Like I said, Tarley didn't pay much mind to the gals, but there were one big old redheaded country gal who lived out near Bee Ridge that he taken a shine to. And maybe that's too weak a way of describin' it.

"Brother," he told me, "I want that old Yancy gal worse'n any hen ever wanted to set and I'm goin' to make a date with her one of these moonlight nights."

Well, that's just what he done. They'd planned that she would slip out after the old folks got to sleep one night and Tarley went out there and hid under the edge of the porch. The Yancys lived on a farm with no near neighbors, in a great big frame house with a front porch about three feet off the ground. Old Tarley hid there all cramped up for about two hours. He said that between the excitement and the cold wind blowin' under that porch, he were a-shiverin' like a wet bird dog when the screen door squeaked and out she come in a long white nightgown. Well, she walked over to the edge of the porch and Tarley stood up and took a-hold of her to help her down. But it weren't her. It were the old man! And Tarley said it were such a surprise that he just throwed him right out in the yard, and when he did, old man Yancy went to hollerin', "Help! Murder! Robbers!" And Tarl really caught air.

The next day old man Yancy went to town and reported to the sheriff that some feller had attacked him and that if he hadn't fought him off the feller would of stole everything he had. I wouldn't tell this story if old man Yancy were still alive and if Lilly Mae hadn't married a Yankee and left the county. Tarley said he'd had only one worse surprise in his life, and I were along with him that time, so I'll tell about it.

There was a bunch of turkeys usin' along the edge of Fox Scrub, near where it joins up with the Hammock and Black-water Swamp. The low-bush acorns was ripe and them turkeys was givin' 'em a fit. One evenin' we roosted 'em on the edge of the swamp where there was three or four big old bald cypress that some way or other hadn't been cut out of there. Turkeys love to roost over water—maybe because it makes it harder for somethin' to slip up on 'em and maybe because it's just that they like to hear their droppin's hit the water, like some folks say. Anyhow, me and Tarley figured they was in them cypresses and we'd be back there in the mornin' when they flew down from the roost, or even before, so we could maybe outline 'em against the sky.

Well, there'd been a winter rain and the wind went around into the northwest about midnight and it really turned cold. We set down at the base of a great big old live oak, not more'n thirty steps from the first cypress. The roots of the live oak spread out so they fitted a feller almost like a chair, and we'd of been pretty comfortable if it hadn't been so dad-blasted cold. We hadn't been there more than fifteen minutes till my toes was so cold I could of snapped 'em off like sody crackers.

'Bout the time there were a little streak of light in the east Tarl turned 'round to me and said, "Cut that out." I were tryin' to figure what ailed him when he said it again: "Brother, quit it!" Then he reached down under him and let out a screech a feller could hear plumb to Gun Barrel Creek. Then he went to clawin' and hollerin' like nothin' you ever heard.

"Rattlesnake!" he hollered. "Rattlesnake! Rattlesnake!"

I don't believe I'll ever get over that, it scared me so bad. Of course the turkeys took off, but by this time we weren't thinkin' about turkeys. Tarley had been sittin' right down on the coil of a six-foot diamondback that were almost froze solid. It had kind of burrowed down in the leaves and after Tarley set on it awhile it thawed out and started a-tryin' to crawl off. Tarley felt it and thought I were a-ticklin' him—why, I don't know. I guess he didn't either, but when he reached under him and felt that rattlesnake he went to clawin' it like a crazy man until he had rattlesnake scales under all his fingernails. And if you think a feller can't jump six feet high and twenty feet wide from a sittin' position, you just ain't never set down on a rattlesnake! And Tarl said it were almost as bad a surprise as when he went to help Lilly Mae down from the porch!

14
THE
BIRD HORSE

Tarley always said there was only four real pretty things in the world—a big green tree full of ripe tangerines, a little speckled pointer puppy, a big shiny black stud horse, and the fourth and prettiest of all, a redheaded woman. Even that go-'round he'd had with old man Yancy over his Lilly Mae didn't cure him of likin' redheads. But while he were tryin' to find just the right one, he managed to latch on to the next prettiest thing in the world, which were a black stallion he seen at a rodeo.

This horse were the meanest thing I near 'bout ever laid eyes on, and the only man who could handle him were a little old runty feller who traveled with the show. He'd ride out at the end of the show, sag down in the saddle and the horse would sort of kneel down. They called this act "The End of the Trail" and they'd play a little sweet music on their fiddles and jew's harps to end the performance. Well, the little runty cowboy got his neck broke tryin' to bulldog a wild old steer and there weren't nobody else could handle that black stud. But Tarley always did have a way with dogs and horses, and for some reason that horse let Tarley handle him. So he wound up buyin' the critter for a song and brought him on home.

Along about that time there come a judge from somewhere up in Kentucky who brought his bird dogs down to Crystal River to go huntin'. He were a great quail hunter and he had five or six of the prettiest pointers anybody ever seen. Then he started lookin' for a good woods pony to hunt on and Tarley heard about it.

"I'm goin' to have me a little fun," Tarley told me. "Saddle up your buckskin and come along."

We hunted up this judge and made a date to go with him. "I got the best huntin' horse here that ever hit the woods," Tarley told him. "Wait till you see him. And I know where there's plenty of birds, too."

Well, I couldn't quite figure what was in Tarley's mind, but for the next two or three mornin's he were up and gone way before day. He'd ride back in for breakfast about ten o'clock and the third mornin' he told me what he'd been doin'. The time to locate quail is just at the crack of day and Tarley had been ridin' an old woods road through the flatwoods every mornin' just as the sky begun to lighten up. When he'd hear a covey gettin' together, he'd blaze a pine saplin' and ride on. A covey of birds will near 'bout always roost in their own territory, which ain't too big—sometimes no more'n a few acres. They're pretty regular in their habits and a feller can find 'em in 'bout the same places at certain times of the day.

Bobwhite quail don't hardly ever holler "Bobwhite" except in the spring and summer when they're matin' and nestin', and then it's only the cock birds say it. The rest of the year they make all kinds of little whistles and clucks, but the main thing you hear is the get-together call of a covey that's been scattered just before goin' to roost, or soon in the mornin' when they first start to move out from where they're roostin'. They roost down in the grass, in a circle, with their tails pointed into the center, as you can tell by their droppin's, so each one is set to take off in a hurry if he has to.

If there's ary salamander mounds anywhere quail are usin', you'll see the birds' tracks on 'em—they love to stand up on 'em to look around, I reckon. What we call a salamander is sort of like a big old brown mole that digs tunnels and throws the sand out into little hills a foot high or so. You'll see 'em all over the sand-hill country.

A Yankee tried to tell me a salamander were some kind of gopher, but what us fellers call a gopher is just a old land turtle. That same feller tried to tell me that a salamander were some kind of lizard or sump'n. But I quit tryin' to figger out Yankees a long time ago. I'll have to admit, though, that sometimes they're right.

Different hunters have different ideas about when's the best time for dogs to find birds. Some like the early mornin', but I like it from four o'clock to dusky, specially if it's cool and still. By then the birds has moved around feedin' and made plenty of scent. In the mornin's, particularly if it's right chilly, they don't stir too much till the sun gets up, so there ain't much trail to follow. In the middle of the day is the worst time. That's when they're "noonin' "—settin' around in a oak thicket or dustin' in a sandy spot. Tarley said he had blazed sixteen saplin's during the three mornin's, but that a couple of 'em might of been for the same covey.

When the day came for us to go a-huntin' with the judge, I rode my buckskin, Tarley rode old Satan, which were a dern good name for him, and the judge rode a old, broken-down, swayback mare that just went around lookin' for gopher holes to step in and tripped over every log. Well, it weren't long before a couple of them fast, stylish pointers of the judge's found 'em a covey of birds. One of 'em slammed into the prettiest point you ever seen and the other one froze up too. Tarley rode up behind 'em and when he got about twenty feet from the lead dog that black stud horse dropped down on one knee and put his nose in the wire grass, and the judge said, "Careful there, you'll flush the birds. What in the world ails that horse?"

"What do you mean, what ails him?" Tarley said. "He loves the smell of them quail just as much as the dogs and he's just a-backin' them pointers!"

All you had to do was press a little stick down against that stallion's shoulder and he'd go into his "End of the

Trail" act. And that's just what Tarley had done! I never will forget the expression on the judge's face, and I believe he'd of paid Tarley five hundred dollars for that horse then and there just to show off to his friends. The only trouble was that when the birds got up and the judge started shootin', old Satan took off and no rodeo bronc ever went higher or broke in two faster. Tarley come unglued about the fourth jump and just missed buttin' his head into an old black light'd stump that sure would have scattered his brains. That little act put a crimp in any deal for a huntin' horse. And it took me an hour to catch that devilish stallion.

Tarley tried hitchin' him to the buggy not long after that and, to everybody's surprise, he behaved pretty well. "I believe the scoun'el has been drove before," Tarley said. "He sure looks good and steps along real smart." So in a day or two he hitched him up and took Preacher Jones's daughter out to the commissary to buy some stuff for her ma.

"That was some trip!" Tarley told me when he got back. "We was goin' along in that lane between Dad Easley's pasture and the old Johnson place when we run up on a mare in the lane. Old Satan raised up his head and snorted and whinnied and started for her. I jerked back on my lines and one of 'em broke and I fell out of the buggy. There weren't nothin' I could do but stand there, and Lulie Jane just helt on to the buggy for dear life. Afterward I fixed the line and got back in the buggy and we drove on for almost a half a mile without sayin' nothin'. Then Lulie Jane said, 'Mr. Driggers, your horse sure is mean to fight!'"

When a stallion gets his mind on somethin', he's hard to control, all right, and an old jackass is even worse. Uncle Winton used to tell a story about a farmer and his boy who taken a mare over to old man Jorks's place for service. The old man had a big old jack which had daddied some fine mules, but he charged twenty-five dollars stud fee and that was a big price back in them times. Well, the farmer and his boy put the mare in the lot next to where the jack was and went in to see old man Jorks.

"We got a mare in season out there and we want us a mule colt," said the farmer.

"All right," old man Jorks told him, "that'll be twenty-five dollars."

"I ain't got twenty-five dollars," the farmer said. "I can give you five dollars now and five dollars a month."

"No," old man Jorks told him, "it's a cash deal or nothin'.'"

"Well then," the farmer said, "we'll just have to go on home, I reckon."

They all walked out to the lot and when the boy started to lead the mare away Uncle swore that the old jack reared up on the rail fence and hollered out, "Truuuust him . . . truuuust him . . . he'll pay—he'll pay—he'll pay!" And that's all I can ever think of to this day when I hear a donkey brayin'.

I think Tarl had a idea he might raise some colts from Satan, but a feller who brought a big wagonload of freight into the commissary left his big old draft horses overnight in our pasture. Me and Tarl was out huntin' and Ma forgot about that stallion bein' out there when she told the feller he could put up his team at our place. Anyhow, them horses must of weighed sixteen hundred or more and their feet was big as dinner plates. Ma said when Satan seen 'em he laid back his ears and bared his teeth and made a charge. When he rared up to strike at one, it just humped its back and kicked him full force in the neck right close up under his jawbone and must of busted somethin' because he died a few days later. Like the preacher's gal said, Satan sure was mean to fight.

Tarley told me that Preacher Jones spoke to him about what happened with Lulie Jane, but didn't seem to be too mad. He were a pretty good feller and I never will forget one time when me and Tarl was comin' by his house just as he was a-fixin' to leave for church, all dressed up in his frock coat with the family a-waitin' in the surrey. But his calf had got out of the lot and he was tryin' to get it back in. It had been rainin' and that calf lot was a pure sure-enough mess. Preacher Jones had the calf by the ears and was backin' up, pullin' as hard as he could, and the calf was bracin' against him with its eyes walled up in its head. All of a sudden the calf decided to go and Preacher Jones went flat on his back with the calf down on top of him. But the old man never turned loose his holt of the calf's ears and he finally wallowed around and got a-straddle of it. Then he started beatin' that calf's head down in the mud and each time he'd say, "If it wasn't for the love of God in my heart"—*wham!*—"and the salvation of my soul"—*wham!*—"I'd beat your dad-blasted, blankety-blank brains out!"

Like I said, Preacher Jones was a pretty good feller and done quite a bit of huntin' when he had the chance. He was a great turkey hunter and later on he got to be quite a bird hunter and bought him a Model T so he could cover more country. He had a Yankee friend from Maine who used to come down and board with him for a month or so every winter and they'd go bird huntin' near 'bout every day that there weren't a funeral or a weddin' or a service of some kind.

The Yankee feller was a good shot, but all he talked about was huntin' woodcock upcountry. We don't have but dern few of them birds down here, so I don't know much about 'em. They're bigger'n a snipe and got big black eyes. From what I hear, they travel mostly at night when they're migratin', and this Yankee hunter sure did a heap of braggin' on what a fine bird a woodcock were and how much better to eat than a quail and how much sportier to shoot and so on and so on! He'd brought down with him a great big old black-and-white English setter that must of weighed seventy-five pounds. Tarl guided this feller one day and rode in the back seat of the car with that setter.

"Billy," he told me, "that dog charged back and forth from side to side of that car, steppin' on me and slobberin' on me until I wanted to kill him. He'd been cooped up in a crate for near 'bout a week and he were really rarin' to go. The preacher and his friend from Maine was a-settin' in the front seat and every little while that Yankee would whirl around and holler, '*Charge!*' at the dog. Instead of sayin', 'Lay down and be quiet!' he'd holler, '*Charge!*' when the dog were already chargin' as hard as he knowed how to.

"After the hunt I asked Preacher Jones what the feller meant by tellin' his dog to charge and he just laughed and said, 'That's just his Yankee way of tellin' the dog to lay down and shut up.' That beat me. I sure don't know how them dern Yankees ever won the war."

15 PANTHER CATS, INDIANS & THE HERMIT IN THE BIG CYPRESS SWAMP

Back in the old days there used to be panthers all over Florida, accordin' to the old-timers, but most of 'em was to be found in what they call the Big Cypress Swamp, east of Fort Myers, Bonita Springs and Naples. They called this country the Big Cypress not because the cypress trees theirselves was so big—though some of them old bald cypress was plenty big enough—but because it was a big swamp of cypress strands and cypress heads and saw-grass marsh—about six or seven hundred square miles of it. Whatever real big cypress trees are left are way back in the heavy strands. A strand is a long stretch of cypress timber and can be from a hundred yards to a mile wide and several miles long, like big Fahkahatchee Strand. A cypress head is just a little old island of cypress timber settin' out in the flat piney woods or the marsh and might be only a acre or two in size.

The first time me and Tarl was ever in the Big Cypress we got one big old male panther and saw sign of several more. This'n had killed a black boar hog with tushes about four inches long, whetted sharp on the edge. In spite of them tushes, the panther had killed that hog without gettin' scratched and had covered it all up with dead grass, sticks and pine straw. It made a pile two feet high and about five feet long and we guessed the hog would of weighed two hundred anyhow.

Where the panther had made his first dash in the mud along the edge of a cypress strand to where he'd caught and finished killin' the hog weren't over fifty yards. The sign was easy to read there in the mud, and the panther tracks was spraddled out, showin' the claws, like they do when they're runnin'. Just like a bobcat or a house cat, a panther don't show its claws when it's just a-walkin', only when it's a-grabbin' at something. They tell me there's a cat over in Africa that's got feet like a dog and don't draw in its claws like other cats. I reckon that's why it's called a cheater.

From what old-time panther hunters tell me, males average about a hundred and twenty-five pounds and females about eighty. This'n we killed weighed a hundred forty-six and was near 'bout eight feet from the tip of his nose to the tip of his tail. He run almost a hour ahead of five good dogs and, accordin' to the old-timers, this was unusual. A panther is short-winded and will most always tree right quick.

We seen quite a bit of panther sign and several old kills of deer, which is their favorite food when they can get it. They will kill calves and colts, though, and sometimes a grown horse. If livin' gets tough, they'll eat coons, small 'gators, wild turkeys, cranes or anything else they can catch, and they'll near 'bout always cover it up with grass and trash to hide it from the buzzards and to keep off the flies. If they make a kill in an open place, they'll drag it into thick cover way back in the cypress. They'll lie up pretty close to their kill and eat on it till it gets plumb rank—then they'll leave it and kill again. Where we was huntin' was in a game refuge and deer was plentiful. The Indians and old-timers figured that each panther would account for about a deer a week.

You hear a lot of stories about panthers screamin', and I know for a fact that they do because I seen and heard one do it right while I was a-lookin' at it in a zoo. But I wouldn't say they go around screamin' like a "woman in distress," which is how a lot of folks describe it. I've always been kind to women, so I wouldn't know about that, and I wouldn't say that panthers holler like we say turkeys gobble and hogs grunt and dogs bark. I talked to some real old-timers and Indians who have lived in the woods and who say they never heard a panther make a sound but to growl and spit and snarl at dogs when they had it bayed or treed.

Bill and Les Piper had four or five panthers in cages at their place in Bonita Springs and I watched 'em a heap. They'd meow just like a big old house cat, and sometimes they'd make high whistlin' sounds that a feller would swear was made by some kind of bird. It ain't a whistle, really, because they make it with their mouths open and way down in their throats. But it's near 'bout as high-pitched as a whistle. And once in a while they'll do this so loud that a feller could call it a scream.

There's a heap of talk about panthers jumpin' on people. I do know they'll follow a feller, either afoot or on horseback, because I've seen their tracks where they followed my tracks. I reckon there's cases of their attackin' a man, but they're pretty rare and I ain't never met anybody who knows it for a fact. I sure never seen anybody who'd been jumped on.

Uncle Wint said that once he helped catch one alive near a place called Deep Slough back of Bonita Springs. He climbed right up to it and flipped a rope on it and it never offered to jump on him—just spit and growled. It's a good thing these big old yellow cats is not too nervy because they're big enough and strong enough so that a man wouldn't stand a chance if one was to jump him.

In all of our huntin' we never seen where a panther had jumped on anything from a tree—always sneaked up and made a dash. And a whole lot of the kills we seen was big old buck deer—not just runts or sickly ones like some people claim.

When Uncle Winton's folks first come to Florida and he was a young feller, he worked for a rancher down at Immokalee on the edge of the Big Cypress. There was a heap of panthers down there in them days and one time the catch dogs bayed up a big old boar panther back in sort of a cave in the riverbank. Uncle Wint said he didn't have a gun with him—which is hard for me to believe—and he had to do something right now because the dogs was gettin' cut up and any minute the panther might catch and kill one. A big panther will catch a dog back of the ears with his claws and pull him up and bite him through the head.

But Uncle did have a big old jackknife and he cut him a willow pole and lashed that knife on the end of it with one of his bootlaces and made him a lance!

"And by grannies," he told us, "I just jooged that cat to death." He did, too, because I remember seein' the hide when I was just a little feller and it was full of holes. It stretched out over eight feet and was the color of a deer.

"People keep talkin' about *black* panthers," Uncle Wint told us. "Some of 'em is a little darker and browner than others, same as a deer is darker in the winter, but there ain't no *black* ones—not down here in our country anyhow." He said the feller at the big museum in Chicago explained to him about cats; said our Florida panthers was the same animals that folks called cougars and mountain lions and I forget what-all in other parts of the country. And he said what folks called black panthers was really black leopards that just happened to be black and not spotted. They come from Africa and India, he said.

Here in Florida our panthers cover a lot of ground when they're huntin'. The old toms specially have a regular beat they travel, visitin' their lady friends and nearly always stoppin' by their old kills where they have sign heaps—which is where they cover up their doin's. An old tom will usually take from six to eight days to make his round and if you see his tracks crossin' a mud flat, you're more'n apt to see 'em again in 'bout a week, always headed the same way. He just makes a big circle.

Most of the work for dogs in panther huntin' is in trailin'. Like I said, they're short-winded cats and usually don't run far or long before takin' a tree. But the dogs might have to cold-trail one for a good many miles before they jump him, specially if he ain't made a kill and just keeps travelin'. We cold-trailed one all day one time and jumped it about five o'clock that evening on the edge of a cypress head. It didn't

run over a hundred yards down through the leather fern
until it went up a runty cypress which was about five feet
through at the base but not very tall. The panther stopped
on a low limb, not over fifteen feet off the ground, and by
the time we'd tied our horses and got there our dogs was
near 'bout crazy.

There was a blow-down log a-layin' right under that cypress
and them dogs was puttin' on a regular circus act—runnin'
up that log, jumpin' up at the panther, fallin' off in the ferns
and then gettin' back in the procession again. The panther
was a real snuffy old tom and he would snarl and spit and
slap at each dog when it jumped at him. I'm tellin' you it was
some kind of excitin'!

Tarl told me to shoot and said, "Billy, kill him graveyard
dead. If he falls out onto them dogs crippled, it'll be just too
bad!"

So I put a thirty-thirty in the burr of his ear and that
fixed his clock. It wasn't till I went to shoot that I realized
I was wearin' a wood bracelet. While we'd been a-lopin' our
horses when the trail got hot, a stirrup leather busted on my
saddle and I just reached down and slipped the stirrup over
my left arm. After that there wasn't no time to lay it down.
Like most hunters, I get real stirred up when them hounds
go to cryin' on a smokin'-hot scent. And, of course, when
they're after a panther my hackles just stand straight up.
It's a wonder I remembered to tie my horse!

Some of the biggest cypress trees we seen on our hunts
down in that country was in Corkscrew Swamp—the biggest
trees I ever seen in my life. A heap of them old ironhead
cranes come into Corkscrew Swamp to nest—them big old
white fellers with black tips on their wings and black heads
and curved bills. The Yankees call them wood ibexes, I
believe, but they're just ironheads to me.

There's some funny names for places back in that country
—Table Camp, the old Ward Camp, Curry Camp, Rowdy
Camp and Big Rowdy Camp. They say Rowdy Camp was
named when a bunch of old-time hunters got to drinkin' and
a-fightin' and then moved over a couple of miles and did some
more drinkin' and fightin' and called that place Big Rowdy.

Curry Camp was named for some old-time settlers in toward Immokalee, and Ward Camp is named after an old feller who hunted panthers down there for many years and killed a heap of 'em. Table Camp got its name from a cypress-slab camp table that some hunters built and it must have stood there over twenty years. Part of it was still up when we camped there.

One day we trailed a panther way back east through the saw-grass marsh of the Everglades and came out onto a pine island where there was an old feller camped all by hisself. I reckon you'd call him a hermit. He had him a shack built up, roofed over and sided up with palmetto fans, somethin' like a Indian chickee. There weren't nothin' but a dirt floor and the only furniture was an old stump to set on. He seemed mighty glad to see us and said he hadn't even seen an Indian for three months or more. It was too late to try to get back to our camp that night, so we tied up the dogs and stayed over with the old feller. He had some venison and I do believe that was the toughest meat I ever tried to chew.

"I know it's tough," the old feller said, "but like my Grandma McCain used to say, 'Tain't as tough as none!' "

After we'd eat and talked a while, the old feller said, "Well, I know you boys is tired, so I reckon we'll turn in." Then he reached up to the rafters and pulled down a old dried cowhide and threw it down on the ground. "Here," he said, "you boys take the bed—I'll rough it!"

That was a miserable night and the skeeters was as bad as I ever seen. Me and Tarley kept slappin' 'em and finally the old man said, "I wish you fellers would quit killin' them critters . . . they's all that keeps this whole country from bein' took over by Miami Yankees!"

We tried to pick up the panther's trail next mornin', but the dogs never could straighten it out, so we headed back west to our camp. It weren't too far east of that hermit's camp to the reservation where the Seminole Indians have their big corn dance, and Uncle Winton claimed he was just about the onliest white man ever to see one.

"Some of them Indians could make whiskey that was almost too strong even for me," he told us, "and everybody had a few snorts. Then all the bucks made up a circle and started a-dancin' around the fire. That was back when the menfolks wore them bright-colored dresses down to their knees, so I just taken off my pants and let my shirttail hang down and joined in the dance.

"They'd all take two or three short hops and then a big hop and they was a-gruntin' and singin' like nothin' you ever heered. I done my best to join in, but after two or three circles the old chief come up to me and tapped me on the shoulder and said, 'Sit down! Shirttail too short . . . jump too high . . . show hoswassee all time . . . no can dance . . . sit down!' "

Uncle knowed quite a few Seminole words and said that my Great-grandaddy O'Keefe had knowed a lot of Indian talk.

"He lived out west with them Indians," Uncle said. "The Crowsfeet and the Blackheads and the Comanches and the Shy Anns, a tribe of women Indians, I reckon."

"That would be where he'd stay, all right," Aunt Effie put in. "If'n he were anything like his progeny."

When I got home I looked up that word and all it meant was just the reverse of ancestor. It meant me and Tarl, I guess, and didn't mean nothin' bad at all, which were unusual for Aunt Effie.

16 THE BIG RUCKUS & TARL FALLS IN LOVE

There were a family of people named Henry who moved into the old Ellison homestead and I don't believe there's ever been a rougher outfit in this country than them Henrys—if anything, they was even worser than old man Ellison and everybody knowed how bad he were. Just before he'd jump on a feller he'd holler out, "I'm goin' to climb up on your weatherboardin' and tear down your shingles!" And he'd do it too! But one day he found a feller who were meaner'n he were and after that the Henrys moved in.

Well, the Henrys had two sons—both big, rough, strong fellers—one named Goin and the other named Gaynus. And there were a big old rawboned, blondheaded daughter who could stand flat-footed and jump over a four-rail fence.

Goin Henry were, I do believe, the strongest man I ever seen exceptin' maybe Mose Baldree. Goin were about two ax handles long and must of weighed close to two fifty. One time I seen him pick up the front end of a old Buick automobile while a feller put a block under it. That's how strong he were.

Gaynus were just about as strong in the body, but he were sort of weak in the head—just did have sense enough to keep out of the fire! Uncle Wint said that he barely had walkin'-around sense and that described him pretty good. "That feller don't know nothin'," Uncle said. "In fact, he not only don't know nothin', he don't even suspect nothin'. I reckon his bread weren't quite done when they taken him out of the oven!"

Any friend of Goin's were a friend of Gaynus's and nobody better say nothin' against old Goin where Gaynus could hear it. All you had to say were, "Old So-and-so done your brother Goin a dirty trick," and Gaynus wouldn't even wait to hear what the dirty trick were. He'd just hunt up old So-and-so and stomp him into the ground.

Some of the boys thought it would be a good joke to see Gaynus Henry tangle with Tarley—so they pointed out Tarley to Gaynus one day in the settlement and said, "You see that feller? Well, he's been a-talkin' about your brother Goin and says he's a-goin' to whip him the first chance he gets!"

Old Gaynus didn't say nothin', but just walked up to Tarley and hit him the hardest lick I ever seen a man take—right in the face. There hadn't been no warnin' and Tarley went down like a beef hit with a sledge. But he weren't out and he rolled back up onto his hands and knees and shook his head and got up. Right then I knowed there were goin' to be a real fight, so I just stepped into Pop's Hardware and picked a ax out of the rack and I told them fellers, "All right, boys, you wanted a fight and you've got it . . . and it better be a fair one!"

Ray Larkin started to say something, but I told him, "Shut up or I'll cut your dad-burned head off and chunk it at your dead butt!"

Gaynus were stronger than Tarley, but Tarley were quicker. Gaynus kept tryin' to close with him and a couple of times he did and they went to the ground. Both times Tarley tore loose and got back to his feet and went to poppin' him with short jolts that weren't doin' Gaynus a bit of good.

They'd been a-fightin' for a half hour at least and was both about give out when here comes the rest of the Henry family in their big double wagon. Old man Henry tied the team and him and Goin joined the crowd, but Mrs. Henry and the gal stayed in the wagon.

"What's goin' on here?" old man Henry asked me, I reckon because I had the ax and kind of had folks backed off.

"Mr. Henry," I told him, "I don't know you nor none of your family, but neither me nor none of my family has got any reason to fight you. Some of these here smart-alecky boys told your boy Gaynus that my brother Tarley were goin' around braggin' about how he were a-plannin' to whip Goin Henry and that's just a dang lie! My brother Tarley's much of a man, but he don't go 'round braggin'."

"Did your brother say he could whip me?" Goin Henry asked, kind of bristlin' up.

"Not that I know of," I told him, "but if he did, he can do it."

"I'll be derned if that's so," Goin said. "He can't even whip Gaynus."

"I'll be derned if that's so either," I told him. "If you'll just look!"

Tarley had put Gaynus down and he were stayin' down. Well, old man Henry and Goin toted Gaynus to the wagon and then old man Henry come back and asked me again what had started the ruckus. I told him, and old man Henry made a little speech to the crowd. When he got through there weren't no doubt in their minds about what he would do to anybody who took advantage of Gaynus another time.

Tarley couldn't hardly talk, his mouth were so cut and swoll up, but he told him, "I'm sorry about this, Mr. Henry. I were just walkin' along the street when your boy stepped up and popped it to me without sayin' word one."

"I'm sorry too," Mr. Henry said. "Gaynus is easy took in and he's right touchy about his brother."

So we shook hands and went over to the wagon and shook hands with Gaynus and apologized to old lady Henry and the gal, whose name turned out to be Loofy. She were a-settin' there moppin' off Gaynus's face and she looked at Tarley like she'd like to chew him up and spit him out!

Well, I taken the ax back to the hardware store and me and Tarley started home.

"Goin and Gaynus and Loofy," Tarley said, "if that ain't the derndest mess of names I ever heered in my life. But you know, that old gal ain't too bad to look at!"

Later on when we got to know them Henrys better we found out that "Loofy" were just a little old pet name her brother had give her tryin' to say "Lucy." We found out too that "Goin" come from "Burgoyne," but we never did find out about "Gaynus." Tarley asked him how to spell it and he thought a while and then he said, "I don't reckon it's ever been spelt!"

After that fight with Gaynus Henry, Tarley found he had got hisself quite a name as a fighter. But he didn't go around lookin' for trouble like some fellers do. Near 'bout every time a feller gets a name as a fighter there's some other feller decides to test him, specially after a few snorts. There were one little old wiry feller from Crystal River who liked his liquor and figured hisself a real bad man. We heered that he were goin' around tellin' folks that Tarley Driggers weren't nothin' but just another cracker boy and that God made guns and knives to make all men the same size.

Well, when this got to Uncle Winton, Uncle went to this feller's house, and what I mean, he went up on his front porch and he rung his bell.

"Son," he told him, "I hear talk of your pickin' a fight with my nephew Tarley Driggers, and if you want to try him bare knuckles, that's all right with me. Tarley Driggers could squirrel-hunt all day with you in the seat of his britches and wouldn't even know you was there! But if you're talkin' about guns and knives, like I hear tell, that's a different story. If you got any ideas about bushwhackin' my nephew, let me tell you right now that the day you do you'll die before the sun goes down!"

Accordin' to Uncle Winton, the feller didn't make no answer, so I guess they just left it that way. Anyhow, there weren't never no trouble out of that feller.

"Gossip is one thing," Uncle told me later when we was

talkin' about it, "but threats is another. Threats ought to be took care of right now, but gossip is like when a dog starts a-barkin' at somethin' he thinks he heard in the night. And then the neighbor's dog starts a-barkin' and pretty soon all the dogs in the settlement is barkin' and there ain't none of 'em knows why but one—and he ain't sure!"

Every now and then me'n Tarl would pleasure our ma and go to church with her, and one Sunday not long after, derned if all them Henry folks didn't come a-marchin' in too. Gaynus still had some purple showin' around one eye, but both him and Tarl was near about plumb healed up from their go-'round.

The Henrys was all dressed up and I will have to say that the gal, Loofy, was what Uncle Wint would call a luscious lump—if'n he was out of Aunt Effie's hearin'! Her hair was the color of new cane syrup—sort of red-gold and all shiny and soft-lookin'. She had a high, full bosom and the white dress she was wearin' didn't do nothin' to hide it. She was a big, rangy, long-legged heifer and a feller could almost hear Tarl's mouth waterin' when he looked at her. They all set down in a pew just three rows in front of us and I'll bet Tarley didn't take his eyes off of her the whole time we was there.

Ma had read us in the Bible where it said if a man looked at a woman and lusted after her, he had committed adultery in his heart, so I guess Tarl just set there and committed it as hard as he could for a solid hour. To give him credit, though, he wasn't just lustin', but was actually fallin' in love with that Henry gal.

"Ain't she the sweetest, prettiest thing you ever seen, Billy?" he asked me on the way home in the buggy. I agreed with him, all right, but I didn't want to be too strong about it. Tarley was five inches taller than me and forty pounds heavier. Loofy Henry was about my height—five nine—and I guessed her at about one fifty. She was a armful, all right, if a feller liked 'em big and strong. I might have teased Tarl about her some, but I didn't want to say nothin' in front of Ma.

After church we had said howdy to the Henrys, but that

was about all. They didn't stand around and visit, but went and got into their big wagon and drove off. The men had been friendly enough, but that gal had sure kept her nose in the air.

"That Henry girl has a fine face," Ma said as we was drivin' along. "She's still cool because of that fight, but she'll thaw out. We must get up a fishin' picnic and ask 'em along."

"That'd be fine," Tarl said. "Let's do it Saturday."

"We'll go out to the redfish hole," Ma said. "With this cold snap they ought to be in there—and some trout and snappers too." Next day, Monday, Ma reminded me of it again.

"I'll ride over there and ask 'em this evenin'," I said.

"Good," Ma said. "That might be bettern' Tarl goin', 'count of the fight."

I could see Tarley didn't like this too much, but there weren't much he could say.

That evenin' after we had fed the stock I saddled a horse and rode out to the old Ellison place, where the Henrys lived. They hadn't lived there very long, but they sure had things lookin' better. The orange trees was hoed and pruned and the yard was raked clean of leaves and pine straw. Old man Ellison had got so old and puny that he couldn't do enough work to pad a crutch and the place had gone downhill for a long time. It was good to see it comin' back. There was a real old lady settin' in a rocker on the porch. She had wrinkles that would have helt four days of rain and I figured she was Loofy's grandma.

"Good evenin', ma'am," I said. "Is Miss Loofy around?"

"Nope," the old granny said. "Her 'n Goin has gone hog huntin'. But they ought to be back directly. Tie your horse and set and tell me about your honesty. It won't take a minute." I didn't much like that, but I guess she didn't mean nothin' because she was right friendly after we got to talkin' and I told her who I was.

"So you're the brother of the young feller who whupped Gaynus," she said. "Well, I'm Gramma Henry and in a way I'm glad old Gaynus got his come-uppance. He ain't too bright, but he had kind of got to thinkin' he was the he coon in the woods. Now he knows he ain't and he'll be careful about jumpin' onto strangers. Your brother must be much of a man. Leastways that's what Loofy says."

"I'm glad to hear that," I told the old lady, "and I know Tarley will be too. He sort of taken a shine to Loofy."

"Well, I do say!" the old lady cackled. "Ain't that sump'n! I ain't seen your brother, but I hear he's a great big old double-jointed buck and you know our Loofy ain't no shy little house wren. They'd make a pair, all right, and I hope I can see 'em together."

"If I know my brother," I told her, "that'll happen right soon."

About that time we seen Loofy and Goin comin' up through the orange grove. They had two or three old bull-and-cur catch dogs with 'em and Goin was a-totin' a shoat that would of weighed thirty or forty pounds anyhow, just as easy as if it was a cat squirrel.

"This here's Billy Driggers," the old granny said. "Reckon you remember him—or anyhow his brother."

"I reckon we do," Goin said, but Loofy didn't say nothin'. Just walked on into the house. Watchin' her walk in them tight boy's pants was just like watchin' a couple of shoats a-fightin' under a blanket.

After while I said, "My ma knows where there's a redfish hole on out in the marsh at the edge of the Hammock where there's some right good fishin' durin' a cold snap. And seein' as how we've got a cold snap right now, she sent me over to ask you folks to go with us and have a fish fry out there on Saturday."

"Can you get there with a wagon?" Goin asked.

"Not hardly, after a heavy rain like we just had ahead of this cold snap," I told him. "We'd better go 'round by boat and we ought to leave early to catch the tide right. Them creeks go almost dry on a low tide."

"Can I go?" Gramma Henry piped up. "I sure do like to tear up my face with fish bones. And there ain't nothin' better'n a slab of redfish cooked over the coals—specially if they's mangrove or buttonwood coals."

"Yes, ma'am," I told her. "You sure can go and all you got to do is set in the boat and ride. We'll take our boat and I

know Tarl can get Uncle Winton's boat. That'll take care of the
whole crowd. I reckon Mr. Henry and Gaynus will want to go
too. Of course, we got to leave early like I said."

"That'll suit my old man just fine," Goin said. "His in-
somnia has been comin' down on him about four o'clock every
mornin' anyhow. He called me this mornin' at half past four
and hollered, 'Get up! It's Monday mornin', tomorrow'll be
Tuesday and the next day Wednesday and ain't nothin' done
yet!' "

"Where's your old man now?" I asked him.

"Him and Gaynus took the team to haul up some firewood."

While we was talkin', old man Henry and Gaynus drove
in and I told 'em about the fish fry. Mister Henry said he'd
be glad to go and Gaynus said he'd do anything you could
get him to do, so it looked like we was all set. But I hadn't asked
anybody about Loofy.

"What about the girl?" I asked Mr. Henry.

"If it's got anything to do with fishin', she'll go. I ain't
never seen a boy like to fish any more'n that gal and she sure
loves to eat 'em too. But just to make sure I'll ask her," and
he went on in the house.

Me and Gaynus was standing in the shade of a big live
oak and it was right chilly, so I said to him, "Let's stand out
in the sun where it ain't so dern cold."

We stepped out into the sun and Gaynus said that there
had been a Yankee feller visitin' 'em for a few days during the
cold snap and that he sure didn't appreciate havin' to go out to
the outhouse them cold nights. "I felt sorry for the feller,"
Gaynus said, "so I got him a coffee can to take to his room.
I was just gettin' to sleep when he come down the hall and
knocked on my door and asked if I didn't have nothin' bigger
than that coffee can. Said it gave him cloisterphobia . . . whatever that is."

I was just fixin' to go on home when Loofy come back
out on the porch. She had done washed up and put on a dress
and she sure was prettied up.

"Daddy says we're all a-goin' fishin' Saturday," she said.
"I got me a new castin' rod and reel and I can't hardly wait.
I mortally love to fish—just any kind of fishin'. Why, I even

love to set and watch a little old bottle cork pop under when a shiner grabs a little bitty piece of dough bait."

That was the first words I'd ever heard that gal speak and they was music to my ears because I purely love fishin' myself and none of my family but Ma cared a dern about it. I was glad to hear Loofy say she was crazy about fishin' and I liked the way she said it. She was a big, bouncy gal, but she spoke real soft and easy. I don't mean deep, like she was in a holler log, but just real soft and sweet-like. I could see old Tarl was really goin' to go for this'n.

I'd got so busy sizin' her up that I'd plumb forgot her ma, so I said, "How about your mother, Miss Loofy? Does she like to catch fish?"

"Not her," Loofy said. "But she'll sure eat her share."

"She's a-goin' along, all right, I reckon," I said.

"Well, she ain't here right now, but I'm sure she'll go. She taken our visitor over to town to catch the train, but she'll be back most any time now. Maybe you could stay and eat supper and ask her yourself. We're goin' to have squirrel purloo and rice."

I wanted to stay, all right, but my horse was gettin' restless and tryin' to paw up a orange tree, so I thanked her and went on home. And I don't mind sayin' I began countin' the time till Saturday.

17 THE PICNIC
& THE SPLINTER
& THE
BOAR HOG

About three o'clock Friday evenin' we had another rain and the wind went around into the nor'west toward mornin' and it faired off and really got cold. Everybody showed up, though, for the trip to the fishin' hole but Goin Henry.

"That scoun'el has been gettin' sorrier and sorrier," old man Henry said while we was unloadin' the lunch baskets and stuff from their wagon down onto our dock. "He's been a-layin' around in bed until sun-up lately. Well, without him there'll be more fish for my girl to catch. And you just watch her catch 'em."

Loofy had her new rod and reel along and she was a-scurryin' around, carryin' and loadin' stuff, strong as a man.

"Ain't she sump'n?" Tarl whispered to me. "I bet if a feller would start lovin' her, she'd cut more capers than a monkey on a twenty-foot grapevine." I agreed with him, all right, but somehow or another I didn't like him sayin' it. It didn't seem quite respectful toward Miss Loofy.

Well, at last we got everybody loaded into the two boats, nine of us altogether. As usual, Tarl's catch dog, old Bull, had sneaked aboard our boat. Uncle Winton went along to run his boat, but Aunt Effie didn't go. It seemed like she didn't much want him to go either and had told him so because he was still mad when he got to our dock.

"That woman," he said, "is a woman of few words, but she uses 'em a lot!"

To rile him still more, his boat engine didn't want to start. It was a old single-cylinder jump-spark rig and a feller had to open a petcock and prime it with some gasoline. On a cold mornin' Uncle would talk to it and say, "Come on, old engine, good old engine," while he was a-primin' it. Then he'd crank and crank and then he'd prime her again and crank some more. Each time he'd turn her over, the arm would spring the points and the piston would make a funny noise in the cylinder and Uncle would say, "Dad blast your sorry soul . . . I buy you good cylinder oil and good gasoline and you go 'phu-uph-hoo' at me!" But once he got her started, she'd just keep a-chuggin' along all day.

Mr. Henry kept lookin' at the sky and it seemed like he was a little nervous about startin'. That cold wind was blowin' dead fans off of them tall cabbages down at the landin', and at last Mr. Henry said, "This weather don't look too good to me to be goin' out on that Gulf. Maybe we'd better put off our picnic."

Tarl spoke up and said, "It'll be all right, Mr. Henry. It's going to be cold and windy till we get to the fishin' hole, but after the sun gets up it won't be bad and we can build us a nice campfire. We got everything all packed and everybody's here. Seems like we ought to go. What do you think, Uncle Winton?"

Uncle looked at the sky and spit in the river. "Well, I always say it's better to be ready and not go than to go and not be ready. But I don't really believe there's reason *not* to go. These here boats are used to that Gulf and me and the boys and even my sister, Froney Driggers, know them channels and can go to that fish hole just as straight as a martin to his gourd!"

"Let's go, Daddy," Miss Loofy said. "There ain't nothin' to be scared about if Mr. Epps says so."

"That ain't exactly what I said, young lady," Uncle Winton told her. "Any time you go out on that old Gulf you'd better be scared of it. Maybe I better just say respectful of it. Big salt-water ain't nothin' to take lightly no time. Can you swim, Mr. Henry?"

"Just like a ax head, Mr. Epps," he said.

"Don't worry about Pa," Gaynus said. "Me'n Loofy can swim like otters. Anything was to happen, we'd get Pa out." Later on I seen both of 'em swim and that Loofy was somethin' to see in a bathin' suit, both in and out of the water. She was graceful as a otter, all right, but old Gaynus was more like a manatee, the way he wallered around.

"If we're a-goin' we better get started," Tarl said. "This tide is floodin' right now."

We cut off from the main river at Grassy Creek and went on through to the Gulf. Boy, it were cold when we hit that open sweep and started up the coast and my teeth were chit-terin' like the bill of a mad owl. We had to throttle down to almost nothin', takin' the waves head on and even then the bow spray was whippin' back pretty strong. We jumped several good bunches of canvasbacks and one real big bunch of sprig-tails off the mouth of Salt Creek. It sure was pretty to see them old sprigs climb up into that nor'west wind, hang up there for a little piece and then drop off and go barrelin' downwind, ninety or nothin'. Most always canvasbacks have to run a little piece on top of the water, like coots, to take off. But not that day! That wind would pick 'em up time they took two steps. Then them flat-headed scoun'els would really carry the mail.

Even at high tide we had to fight a lot of oyster bars in Demory Creek on the way to the pothole, but we finally made it and poled the boats up through the saw grass to where we could jump out on the rocky ground at what we called "the walk-over." Then it were about two hundred steps to the hole where we was goin' to fish. It were a little boggy right where we landed, so I toted Ma a few steps and Tarl picked up Gramma Henry and set her down on good dry ground. Maybe he was a-figurin' on a chance to tote Loofy, but she was half-way across to the pothole by the time he set the old lady down.

We had us a bucket of good, big, fresh shrimp and business began to pick up just as soon as we went to fishin'. Like I said, cold weather puts the fish into the rivers and creeks. The Gulf is shallow a long ways out and the fish are hunting warmer water. First crack out of the box I caught me about a eight-pound redfish and that scaper really cut a flutter around that pothole. It ain't much over an acre big and the creek comes into it underground and goes out underground. A feller don't dare let a fish go back under them rocks or he'll get his line cut.

I mean that Loofy Henry could use that little castin' rod. It's hard to cast a shrimp without snappin' him off, but she laid it out there just as easy and right where she wanted it. The first fish she got was about a three-pound trout and the next one was a redfish about the size of mine. It weren't no time at all till we had us enough for dinner. Even Tarley caught one when Miss Loofy made him try. She caught the most—five trout and four redfish—and she caught her last three trout on a little old wobbly spoon. She could make it dip and dodge like a scared shiner and it were somethin' pretty to watch her workin' it.

We filled up on trout and redfish and hush puppies for dinner and I mean that was good eatin'. Ma always could make the best hush puppies I ever put in my mouth—a little chopped onion mixed in with two parts of cornmeal and one part of flour, a little baking powder and a little salt and pepper mixed into a good thick batter with buttermilk and a egg or two, and then spooned off into a big old dutch oven full of boilin' hot fat. Each spoonful would make a gob about the size of a turtle egg, and when the underside would cook, it would roll over and the topside would cook.

After we'd eat we set around and talked awhile and then went back to fishin' to get some to carry home. Almost a quarter from where we had eat dinner the creek comes out again above ground and makes another little old pothole. The fishin' ain't really as good as it is in the big pothole, but I think Tarl just wanted to get Miss Loofy off to himself.

They went on over there to try it and old Bull went along with 'em. They'd hardly had time to get there before we heard old Bull a-barkin' and Tarl a-hollerin' for me to bring the ax. Man, I lit out. I didn't know whether he'd been 'gator-caught, snake-bit or what. It was open marsh most of the way and I seen Tarley about the same time I heard a boar hog woofin' and gruntin' and poppin' his teeth. Old Bull had him back of the ear and Tarl had him by the hind legs and was givin' him a battle. He was a rusty-black rascal, about a hundred and fifty or sixty pounds, with tushes four inches long, and I knowed Tarl needed some help right quick. That razorback was tryin' to get his head turned back to slash Tarl and Tarl was tryin' to kick his front legs out from under him to throw him.

I had a chunk of rope in my pocket that I'd figured on usin' for a fish stringer and I got it out and untangled it while I was runnin'. First thing I done when I got to Tarl was to jam that ax head into that old boar's mouth and let him bite down on it, which he did and popped his big tushes right off. Then he weren't near so dangerous and we finally got him down and tied up and persuaded old Bull to hush up and stand back. I'll swear that old piney-woods rooter's head was near 'bout as long as his body. He could have stuck his nose two feet in the ground and then been lookin' right straight at you!

Tarl taken out his knife to put Daddy's mark on his ears. "I think I'll just change the channel of this feller's thoughts too while I'm at it," he said.

"Not while Miss Loofy's around," I told him. Then I looked for her and seen her settin' on a rock lookin' at her hand and she was right on the edge of cryin'.

"What's the matter?" I hollered.

"I got me a big old splinter under my fingernail," she called out, "and I can't get it out . . . it's way down in there."

"Shucks," Tarl said. "She oughtn't to be studyin' no little old sore finger. If this hog had a got to her, he'd a cut her down. I never seen a more vicious one in my natch'l life and I couldn't a helt him another two minutes to save my soul. Ain't no time to be cryin' over a little splinter."

"You know good and well there ain't nothin' hurts worser than a splinter down under your fingernail," I said and walked

off and left him. When I got over to Miss Loofy she showed
me the finger—the middle one on her right hand—and she'd
got it when she went to grab up a old snag to try to fight
off that hog. She had tried to get it out with her own knife,
but the splinter had broke off and the point was way down
under the nail where a feller just couldn't get to it without it
really hurtin'.

"Now, Miss Loofy," I told her, "I'm goin' to take that
splinter out for you and I ain't goin' to hurt you. Right at
the last it might hurt just for a second, but I'm goin' about it
slow and easy and you tell me whenever it starts a-hurtin'."

"All right, Billy," she said and helt out her hand. I remembered seein' my dad operate on a commercial fisherman
one time who had run a awful big splinter under his thumb-
nail, and I had watched my old man take it out. I figured
I could do the same thing for Miss Loofy, so I got out my
knife and began scratchin' her fingernail right over the tip of
that splinter—which was almost down to the half-moon. I
just taken the point of the knife and scratched real easy,
shavin' that nail. I didn't dare press down hard over that
splinter, but just took plenty of time and directly the nail
split open right over the end of the splinter—just exactly like
I wanted it to do—and the point of the splinter popped up.

"Now then, Miss Loofy," I said, "this next might hurt just
for a second, but there ain't nothin' to it and that splinter
will be out before you can bat your eyes. I'll just snatch it
right out through that hole and that's all there's to it."

"All right, Billy," she said. "I'm a-waitin'."

I got the edge of my knife blade under the end of that
splinter, pressed my thumb down on it and it came right out
clean.

"You just be careful of that nail for a few days and it'll
grow right on out in no time. Now let's me and you go back
to the boats. I've got me a bottle of turpentine in our boat
that I always keep handy to pour on a cut or when anybody
gets finned by a catfish. It'll sure take out the soreness and
keep away infection."

"All right," she said and then hollered, "Are you comin',
Tarley?"

"Never mind Tarley," I told her. "He's got a little business to tend to with that hog and he'll be along directly."

A lot of folks think the only time you can cut a hog is at a certain period of the moon, but when you got one of them mean old wild razorback boars fightin' to get loose and hatin' you with all his might, there ain't no time to set around and wait for the moon to change. I looked back and seen Tarl jump and run and I knowed he'd finished his job and was gettin' out of there. He'd turned that hog loose and it made a short dash for him, but then turned around and ran off.

"That gentleman will be travelin' in different circles from now on," Tarl said when he caught up with us. "Now he'll just lay around in the shade and do the rootin' for young pigs. If we can find him again in a few months, he ought to be fat and worth eatin'."

Miss Loofy pretended not to hear him and we walked back to the boats. Everybody was about ready to go home anyhow and we had plenty of fish.

That nor'west wind had blowed a lot of water out of the marsh and the creek was really gettin' low. Uncle Winton said he seen three flounders aground on one of them bars and Mr. Henry told him he thought that was pretty low water and Uncle admitted that if it had been any lower, he'd have said so. Anyhow, it were a hard fight gettin' out of that creek into a channel where we could run the motor and we was all just about give out when we got back to our landin'. But we had a real fine mess of fish, as well as a sack of them good oysters that Gaynus had gathered up while we was fishin'. He didn't care nothin' about fishin', and pickin' up oysters was somethin' that didn't strain his brain too much.

There were a feller in the settlement who claimed to have knowed the Henrys before they moved here and he said there'd been a third brother who were even halfer-witted than Gaynus.

"What happened to him?" Ma asked.

"He died," the feller said.

"From what?" Ma asked.

"He never did say," the feller told us. "But he was a big feller and stronger in the body than either Goin or Gaynus."

Tarl just shook his head and said, "I'm sure glad I never met *him*."

"It's a wonder he ever growed up at all," the feller told us. "They say that when he was borned his mother had trouble teachin' him to suck!"

18 TARL & THE DOG THIEVES & MA'S THOUGHTS ON BULLS, ROOSTERS, PREACHERS & MIRACLES

Uncle Wint had a bunch of dogs and one Christmas he gave me and Tarl an old red hound named Preacher with near 'bout the longest ears I ever seen on a hound. A feller could tie 'em in a knot on the top of his head. Uncle Winton had named him Preacher because he said he had a great loud voice and when he got started he never knowed when to stop. He could follow the coldest trail of any of the hounds and Uncle Wint claimed that one day he had got on the back track of a big old buck and trailed it right back to where it was a fawn!

Anyhow, when old Preacher throwed up his head and sounded off on a deer track, you could just about bet that he'd jump that deer. It might take him a long time, but he would sure stay with it. He were Tarley's favorite among all the dogs we had.

There was a heap of game in the Hammock around our place—deer, turkeys, squirrels and a lot of them old black mallards and greenhead mallards in the ponds where they would come to get the live-oak acorns. Every year it seemed there would be a few more outside hunters come in—fellers we didn't know and didn't know nothin' about. And some of 'em was pretty rough-lookin' fellers.

Among all us folks in the Hammock there was a pretty common rule about deer huntin'. If I killed a deer ahead of your dogs, I'd keep the head and horns and half the meat. If you didn't come get the meat, I'd take it to you the next mornin'. Sometimes your dogs would stay at my place if they was real tired, but generally they'd go home.

Old Preacher would run a deer all day if nobody shot it, but he'd generally quit and go home when night fell. Very often a deer would take to the Gulf marsh when it got tired of running, and most dogs would give up when they hit the water and saw grass. But Preacher would usually run right on till dark—briars, saw palmettos, saw grass or whatever.

One day we put him on the track of an awful big buck on the upper end of Gun Barrel Creek and that deer didn't circle at all, just lit out north toward Suwanee. There was four dogs in the race and three of 'em come stragglin' back that evenin'. But not old Preacher. So next mornin' me and Tarley saddled up and rode north. We would listen and blow our horns and stop by at every huntin' camp. Around noon we came to where two fellers had pitched a tent by a little pond on the edge of Gator Slough. They had a fire goin' and was a-cookin' dinner in a couple of dutch ovens. We reined up our horses and Tarley asked 'em, "You fellers seen anything of an old red hound? He run a deer off up this way yesterday evenin'."

One of the fellers didn't answer, but the other one looked up from the fire and said, "Nope . . . ain't seen no dog at all." Then he looked at the other feller and the other feller looked at him. They sure was a rough-lookin' pair of crackers.

"What you cookin' there? It sure smells good," said Tarley. "Smells mighty like venison stew to me."

"Well, it ain't," said the first feller. "We ain't seen no venison and we ain't seen no dog."

Tarley looked at me and he sure was gettin' that fightin' look in his eyes. He just raised his huntin' horn to his lips and let out two or three light toots. When he did, old Preacher squalled out from a cedar thicket in back of the tent. He knowed Tarley's horn as far as he could hear it. We rode out there and found him tied and he had a plumb fit when he seen us. Tarley reached down and cut the rope with his huntin' knife. Then we rode back to the campfire and Tarley just stood up in his stirrups with his thirty-thirty and shot both kettles off the fire. Then he shot the coffeepot off the fire and rode around the tent and cut it to the ground, whackin' off every guy rope with his big huntin' knife. All this time neither one of them fellers opened his mouth. There was just somethin' about the way Tarl looked at you when he was fightin' mad that made you know he would kill you and would a little rather do it than not.

The buck that old Preacher had been a-runnin' was hangin' up not too far from where he'd been tied. Tarley throwed his rifle on the two fellers and made 'em show us where it was.

"What we do around here when a man kills a deer ahead of another man's dog," said Tarley, "is divide the meat. Since you lied about it and figured on stealin' my dog, I ought to take all the meat—and would if it weren't such a big buck. So I'll just take both hindquarters and back straps. And me and my brother Billy, here, will just set in the shade while you butcher 'em out!"

Each ham and back strap must have weighed close to fifty pounds. I took one and Tarley took the other and just before we rode off Tarley drew a bead on the boss of them antlers.

"Don't do it, Tarl!" I said. They was as pretty a set of horns as a feller would want to see—twelve points—and I just couldn't hardly stand to see 'em spoiled.

"You want to tote 'em?" Tarley asked me.

"I don't hardly see how I can tote 'em," I said, "not and this hindquarter too." I was ridin' a young horse that was just about half broke and he weren't too crazy about that bloody meat to start with.

"Then nobody totes 'em," said Tarley. And he busted that big buck's head wide open, splittin' them horns apart like you'd bust a coffee cup on a rock. Then Tarley said, "Come on, Preacher," and we rode off and I'll confess I was mighty scared. I could just feel a bullet takin' me between the shoulder blades, but I guess them fellers figured they didn't want no more truck with a wild man. And old Tarl was a wild one, all right, when he got mad.

"That was a shame to spoil that head," I said after a while.

"Yeah, I reckon so," said Tarley, "but, Billy, I just can't abide a thief. A feller can get mad and get in a fight and maybe even kill somebody, but a man who just deliberately sets out to take somethin' that belongs to somebody else is too low to live and them fellers was a-fixin' to steal old Preacher. The venison weren't important, but I wouldn't trade old Preacher for a deed to Georgia and it planted in cow peas!"

Our ma was a real Christian woman and from the time I can remember she had done her best to bring us boys up to do the right thing. Our old man had been kind of a hell-raiser as a young feller and I reckon that's where Tarley got his wild streak.

Dad hadn't ever been much for church-goin'. Ma tried to get him to go and once in a while she was able to. But she sort of gave up after the time he got up and made a little speech hisself. The old man always liked his liquor and one of his friends from Turkey Creek had brought him a fruit jar full of right fresh 'shine which he'd been samplin' pretty lively. Both of us boys went along that Sunday mornin' and I do remember what happened pretty plain. The preacher was a-preachin' about Daniel and the lion's den, and I remember his bearin' down pretty heavy on how Daniel wasn't scared of that big fierce lion—just him and that cat down in that pit and Daniel wasn't scared one particle.

"The power of the Lord was on that holy man of Israel and he wasn't scared of that big fierce lion!" the preacher said.

That's when my old man stood up and made his little speech. He was always the first one to take the part of the underdog in any kind of a squabble, and he said, "Maybe Daniel wasn't scared of that lion, but let me tell you somethin'. That lion wasn't a derned bit scared of Daniel neither!"

That almost broke up the meeting and it's one of the few times I can remember when Ma really hopped onto Dad.

"You ought to be ashamed of yourself, Jim," she said when we got home, "talkin' out like that in church. And I'll tell you somethin', right now. That lion *was* scared of Daniel and that fear was put in his heart by the presence of the Lord. Otherwise that lion would have eat him and you know it."

Well, the old man didn't answer nothin' to that because Ma was really roused up and I guess he figured the presence of the Lord was on her too! And I reckon it was.

Although Ma didn't always have a chance to get to church, which meant that we didn't have to go either, she was, like I said, a real Christian woman and she believed in what she called the old-time religion.

"Boys," she would say to us, "you're wicked by nature and so is all mankind. They curse and fight and murder and steal and there ain't ary man from the time he's a grown boy that ain't lusted after near about every good-lookin' gal he ever seen. Women ain't much better, if they'd be honest. But there's a heap of other sins beside man-woman sin and I don't know but what some of 'em might grieve the Lord more— like disbelief and malice and such as that. Up to just a few hundred years ago, most of mankind had harems or concubines or whatever and that's just the way it was. Look at nature. We got forty hens and three roosters. We got fifty or sixty range cows and two bulls. What would happen if it was the other way around? I'll tell you what would happen. There'd just be one big fight and then we'd be out of the cow and chicken business!

"Back in the old days it was plumb natural for a man to have a bunch of wives, and some of the great old Bible folks did. Like an old song my grandaddy used to sing:

> King David and King Solomon
> Lived long and merry lives—
> With many, many concubines
> And many, many wives.

> But when they both grew older
> And with no further qualms—
> King Solomon wrote the Proverbs
> And King David wrote the Psalms!

Of course, bigamy is a sin today, along with a whole lot of other things. But the good Lord forgave everybody's sins when He died on the cross, if folks would just believe it and appreciate it. Of course, folks don't like to believe that, because it don't leave 'em much room to crow about how good they are. Most of 'em has broke just about all the Commandments, if they'd just tell the truth. Reminds me of the story about the two fellers who rode plumb over to Dunnellon to a big Revival. The preacher really bore down on the Ten Commandments and the penalty of breakin' 'em and the Judgment Day and everything. Well, after the meetin' these fellers rode a long way and at last one of 'em said to the other, 'Ed, I don't ever remember makin' any graven images, do you?' "

I remember hearin' Mr. Nash Buckingham tell a story at a dog trial one time. That feller could sure tell a story! And this'n were about a man who went to a big costume dance wearin' a devil's suit. It were red and covered him all over and there was horns in the hood and a long tail with a dart on the end. The shoes was wood and split like hoofs and he were carryin' a pitchfork.

I disremember whether this all happened to Mr. Buckingham or to some friend of his, but I reckon it don't make no difference to the story. Whoever it were had a car with the top folded down and a big rainstorm come up on him on his way home from the dance. He stopped near a country church to put up the top, but it stuck and wouldn't work, so he grabbed his pitchfork and lit out for shelter. A prayer meetin' was goin' on and when he hit the vestibule them muddy wooden shoes slid him right on into the aisle. And there he stood! Just then there come a mighty crash of thunder and flash of lightnin' and when folks seen him standin' there with that pitchfork they began goin' out the windows and some even went out the belfry. In ten seconds that church was empty exceptin' for the old preacher, who held up his hand and said, "Well, Mr. Devil, you got here at last. But wait a minute! Stop right there! You know that deep down in my heart I've been with you all the time!"

Ma really liked a good story and could sure tell 'em, but she wouldn't stand for a dirty one—not even from Uncle Winton, her own brother. And she wouldn't permit no cussin' from him or Daddy or nobody else. I remember one time when Daddy dropped a big old iron skillet on his toe and went to hoppin' around, cussin'.

"You can just stop talkin' like that in front of the boys, Jim," she told him. "They're too young to hear cursin'."

"What are you talkin' about?" Daddy said. "Why, your own Bible tells about a feller named Job who cursed the day he was born!"

"That ain't what it means and you know it," Ma said and went out to the kitchen.

My old man had had one friend who was a wicked old feller and Ma never could stand him. He didn't have much use for religion and was always tellin' some yarn or joke about preachers. Some of 'em was so funny that even Ma had to laugh. They could even have been true. Like one he told about a new preacher in town who was on his way to the Sunday mornin' service, a-ridin' a big old gray mule. Over where Hinson's fence corner comes close to the road there was a little old boy about eight years old a-settin' on a stump with a twenty-two rifle watchin' for a fox squirrel.

"Son," the preacher said, "ain't you a-goin' to church this mornin'?"

"Hadn't figgered on it," the kid said. "Who's a-preachin'?"

"I am," the preacher told him.

The little boy looked him up and down for about five minutes and then kind of laughed and said, "Huh, if I was a-settin' to shoot a preacher, I wouldn't even snap at you!"

Another one he told liken to have tickled my dad to death. It was about a country preacher who was goin' by a field where a feller was hoein'. The preacher stopped his horse and hollered out, "Are you prepared to die?" Well, the feller stopped hoein' and looked around real careful to see if there was a rattlesnake close by and then hollered back, "Why?"

"The Judgment Day is a-comin'," the preacher said.

"When is it?"

"I don't know," the preacher said. "It could be tomorrow, it could be the next day."

"Well, don't tell my wife," the feller hollered. "She'll want to go both days!"

This was a story that Ma didn't like at all. She said it weren't only sacrilegious but that it throwed off on the womenfolks. Of course, there's some pretty rough and ignorant folks livin' way back in the Hammock and this same friend of Dad's liked to tell about some old woman who was cuttin' wood when the new country preacher rode by.

"Good mornin', madam," he said real polite-like. "Is your husband home?"

"Nope," said the old woman, slammin' her ax into a light'd knot so that the sparks flew. "He's off a-prowlin' around somewheres in the woods, a-leavin' me to do the work."

"Is he a God-fearin' man?" the preacher asked her.

"I reckon he is. He totes a rifle with him everywhere he goes, so he must be scared of somethin'."

"Ain't there ever been any preachers around here?" the preacher asked her.

"Derned if I know, Mister," she said. "Look in the smokehouse—if there's been ary one here, you'll find his hide. He skins everything he kills!"

Ma couldn't stand for that and she said so. "Maybe some of us crackers are pretty stupid," she said, "but not that stupid! And you can just stop tellin' such as that in front of my boys! I want 'em to respect preachers."

Along about that time there come a preacher feller to the settlement who had a mission in South America somewhere. I heard him tell Ma he was on a fun-raisin' tour and he had to raise a thousand dollars before the end of his physical year, which he said were July first. Well, from the amount of fun he raised around our territory, he sure wasn't comin' to the end of his physical year anytime soon, much less July first, although two Crystal River gals did leave town before that date.

Some of the church folks was took in by that feller, but he didn't fool Ma none, and she said he was a disgrace to the cloth—whatever that meant. Anyhow, she didn't give him nary a dime. I heard he didn't get two hundred dollars all told, but he sure cleaned up a lot of fried mullet and grits.

Uncle Wint had mistrusted him right from the start. "That feller's as smooth as a maiden's thigh," he said.

"I wish you wouldn't talk that way in front of the boys," Ma told him.

"Shucks," Uncle said. "Ain't nothin' the matter with the boys, is there? And I can't think of nothin' any smoother— not even that preacher."

Uncle didn't take much stock in religion or most preachers and that used to aggravate Ma a heap. When any kind of argument come up about religion, she would settle it by "the Book," meanin' her Bible. And she sure knowed her way around in it. What's more, she believed it, cover to cover.

"If it says a big fish swallered Jonah, that's what it means. A miracle? Course it's a miracle. But it ain't no more miracle than watchin' that sweet little ol' Melody have pups."

Melody was a young hound gyp hardly a year old and she'd just whelped eight pups. Ma had called me to come and watch and said, "Now that critter is havin' her first pup. She ain't had nobody to tell her what was happenin' or what to do about it. She ain't read no maternity books nor nothin', but you just watch, Billy, and you'll see one of the Lord's miracles."

Well, when the first pup come, Melody licked him some and then she chawed off the cord—real close up to his little belly—and licked it till it stopped bleedin'. Then she licked him dry and rolled him to one side in the pine-straw bed we'd fixed for her. About that time here come another one! They wasn't no bigger than a flyin' squirrel and their little old eyes was squinched tight shut. We watched till all eight was borned and then Ma said, "There you are, son. You just seen a miracle. How did that dog know what to do—and her on this earth herself hardly a year? The Book says Jonah was swallered by a big fish—whale, shark or whatever—and I believe it. It was a miracle, not a parable. A parable was

an imaginary story to show a picture of somethin', but a dad-
burned miracle is somethin' real that God done. Why, the
good Lord himself said, comparin' it to his own death and
resurrection, 'Even as Jonah *was* three days and three nights
in the belly of the whale.' He didn't say, 'Like the story about
Jonah' or 'Like the parable about Jonah.' He says Jonah *was*
in that whale's belly and come out alive. I don't know *how*
any more'n I know how Melody growed them pups in her
belly and brought 'em into the world and cared for 'em just
right. But Jonah in the whale ain't no more miracle than that.
I believe both of 'em. Both is easy for the Lord."

19 UNCLE WINT IN THE HOSPITAL, TARL & THE BUZZARD EGGS & SOME FACTS ABOUT SNAKES

For a long time Uncle went pretty heavy on the whiskey, and once he got hold of some 'shine that really poisoned him.

"Boys, I was some kind of sick," he told us. "I seen over the fence! Old Doc Joyner saved me with a dad-burned stomach pump and I'll never forget that as long as I live. He went to pokin' that tube down my neck and I went to swallerin' it like a biddy swallerin' an eelworm! All I could think of was that Doc told me the last time he used the dern thing had been on old lady Bowen, and I never did like any of them Bowenses, most specially the old lady! It seemed like I swallered fifty feet of that tube."

"Too bad that deal didn't come off while you was a-havin' all that trouble with the tapeworm," Tarley said. "Maybe Doc could have pumped him out of there."

"No," Uncle Wint said, "this was a long time before I got the tapeworm. And that liquor would have killed that tapeworm when the first drop hit him. It likened to have killed me. They carried me to the hospital in Tampa and I stayed there a solid damn week.

"They treated me pretty good in that hospital, but a feller had a hard time drinkin' that coffee and they'd come in at night and shine a light in my eyes and wake me up to see if I needed a sleepin' pill. And what made me maddest of all was a big old hatchet-faced night nurse who waked me up at five thirty in the mornin' to give me a bath. I told her that a feller didn't have time to get dirty that quick, but she said it was the rules and she done it for the convenience of the day nurse, who was most always busier. It might have been convenient for the day nurse, but it sure weren't convenient for me! Specially when I'd had a rough night and were just beginnin' to get some good rest.

"One day some of your Aunt Effie's kinfolk come to see me and left a bunch of them dead folks' lilies. I felt just like I were layin' in a funeral home. I couldn't stand that, so I told the nurse to get me my pants—that I was a-leavin' there. And I did. I went to my cow camp and didn't put a dern thing in my belly for two weeks but the hot, fresh milk of a pieded woods cow. And, by gollies, I overed it."

"Some of that hospital grub ain't the best in the world, they tell me," Tarley said.

"Hit sure ain't," Uncle Wint said. "They brought me stuff that would gag a turkey buzzard."

This really got me tickled, rememberin' the time Tarley tried to play a joke on Ma. We'd been deer huntin' and found a buzzard nest with a couple of eggs in it.

"Let's take 'em home and tell Ma they're turkey eggs," he said, "and get her to hatch 'em." So when we got home Tarley told her that he had a couple of wild turkey eggs and would she put 'em under a hen. This were the day before we left on a camp hunt to be gone a week. When we got back Tarley asked Ma if the turkey eggs had hatched and she said, "No, I didn't have nary hen a-settin', so I cooked 'em for you the last mornin' before you left."

Another time Tarl thought he'd be smart and play a little trick on Ma was when he found a mouse nest out in the barn with three little old blind, naked, pink baby mice. He carried 'em into the kitchen and told Ma he'd like 'em fried up for his supper. Ma didn't say nothin'—just give him a kind of a squinty-eyed look and put the mice in a paper bag.

We was havin' pork chops for supper that night, but when she set Tarl's plate down, there weren't no big, fine pork chop on it. Just three fried mice. Or what sure looked like it! Us boys had shot some doves that mornin' and when Ma picked 'em she saved them red feet. Then she took the hearts and gizzards and fried 'em up good and brown and fixed 'em on the plate. The hearts was heads, the gizzards was bodies, the feet was them pink doves' feet and she'd stuck pine needles in 'em for tails. It weren't what I would call a real tasty-lookin' dish and Tarl throwed it out to the dogs—much as he loved gizzards.

"Why didn't you eat them little fried mice, son?" Ma asked him. "They'd be just as good as turkey eggs!"

Speakin' of turkeys, Sheriff Charlie Dean over to Inverness told us about a time he heard a noise in their turkey roost one night and grabbed a shotgun and a light and run out to see if it was a bobcat or a fox or what. He said he was a-wearin' a little short cotton nightshirt and when he stooped over to look into the turkey roost, a hound puppy that were loose in the yard stuck its cold, wet nose up against his bare behind. When it did, he fired both barrels into the turkeys and killed six of 'em! He had forgot all about the pup and thought a moccasin had bit him.

"That would be enough to scare a feller," Uncle Wint said when he heard about it. "Of course, I don't pay no mind to moccasins—just stomp 'em into the ground like I was a-settin' out 'tater vines." Yeah, I thought, that's how dern lies get scattered around the country. Take me, now, I'm scareder of a cottonmouth moccasin than I am of a diamond-back. A moccasin is meaner than a rattler, and even if his poison ain't quite so bad, you wouldn't catch me stompin' one and I don't believe Uncle Winton ever did neither.

A cottonmouth gets his name from the way the inside of his mouth looks when he opens it wide. He'll rare back and open that mouth almost to a straight angle. A feller can see the skin over the fangs in his upper jaw, and his whole mouth

looks white as cotton. When he's rared back like that, there
ain't no way for him to see you, and I've had one to strike at
me when I was ten feet away. A snake hears through his
tongue, they tell me, so I reckon he picks up the vibrations of
a feller's footsteps. Whatever it is, a big cottonmouth moccasin is a real ornery customer.

Of course, a big diamondback ain't no baby's play-pretty
neither, but he mostly don't strike wild. He'll just stay cocked
and ready. He gets in a coil so as to be able to protect all of
his body and when he's coiled he can strike maybe half his
length. When he gets mad he'll rare up and draw back in a
S coil and then he can strike even farther—maybe even two
thirds of his length.

Sometimes when a big diamondback gets real mad, like
when dogs has been around him, he'll not only sing his rattles
but will give a sort of a blowin', hissin' growl. It's the awfulest
sound I ever heered and gives me goose bumps just thinkin'
about it.

The biggest diamondback I ever seen was one old man
Steve Kirkland killed over on Blackwater. Steve were about
two ax handles long hisself and he couldn't clear that snake's
head off the ground when he helt it up by the tail. We figured
it must have been about seven and a half feet and as big
around as Mose Baldree's arm. And if you'd ever seen old
Mose Baldree you'll know that were a big snake.

Most city folks think that a rattlesnake always gives a
warnin' rattle, but this ain't so. If you step on one while he's
sleepin', he'll pop it to you right now. Mostly he'll rattle when
he gets mad, but not always, so it pays to watch where you
put your feet when you're in rattlesnake country. Don't
never step over a log. Step up on it and look on the other side.

Another thing, a lot of folks think that you can tell a
rattlesnake's age by the number of his rattles. There ain't
nothin' to that neither, because he grows a new rattle every
time he sheds his skin, and he sheds his skin every time he
eats a full meal—like a rabbit, for instance. While he's
sheddin' his skin he's near 'bout blind, because he sheds his
old skin even to the coverin' over the eyes. And durin' the
time he is sheddin' and half blind he's real touchy. When he

gets through sheddin' he's got a new rattle, but that don't mean nothin' because he might have twelve or thirteen and then bust off half of 'em in the brush or in a fight maybe. So you can't tell nothin' about his age by the number of his rattles.

What they call a button at the end of the rattles ain't nothin' but where a new rattle is startin' to grow. Makes me think of what old man Jenkins said when Tarley asked him how many young-uns he had. "Seven and a button," Mr. Jenkins told him, lookin' as pleased as a blind hog findin' an acorn tree.

Sometimes big old male diamondbacks will put on a regular wrestlin' match over their territory until one gives out and crawls away. There ain't many fellers seen this, but me and Tarley watched it one mornin' for a long time. Them two big snakes would rare up their heads three feet off the ground and sort of lock necks and try to push each other over. One would fall, but he'd rare back up and here they'd go again.

I don't guess many folks believed us when we told 'em about this, but it happened just like I said. There was a young feller named Ross Allen startin' what he called a reptile institute way over east at Silver Springs. He come over to our neck of the woods once a-huntin' snakes and when I told him about them snakes wrestlin', he said that they was male snakes fightin' over the territory. Whatever it was, we sure seen it and I was glad to find one feller that didn't look at me like I was crazy when I told about it. This feller Allen sure knowed more about snakes than any two men I ever seen.

It's funny the ideas folks have about snakes. Most everybody thinks that a rattlesnake hates to get his rattles wet and that when he does have to swim he holds his rattles up to keep 'em dry. He does sort of hold his rattles turned up when he's swimmin', but it ain't because he's tryin' to keep 'em dry. That feller Ross Allen told me that he once timed a big rattlesnake that laid stretched out underwater for forty-five minutes in one of his pens where he could watch it.

I've seen a heap of rattlers in the water—in the creeks and rivers—and one time me and Tarley killed one a mile off-shore in the Gulf. I reckon it had started to swim the Pass and the tide carried it out. It was floatin' along just as happy as a tree toad in a thunderstorm and we couldn't figure why a kingfish or a big grouper or a shark hadn't already grabbed it.

A lot of folks think that a cottonmouth moccasin can't bite you while he's underwater—that he has to stick his head out of water first. There ain't nothin' to that story neither. You'd better never step on a moccasin underwater or you'll find out. I purely hate them ugly devils and I've had two or three mighty close squeaks with 'em.

Once when I was fishin' I'd caught three or four little old freshwater trout—what Yankees call black bass—and had 'em tied to my belt on a string. I was standin' in water almost waist deep, on the edge of a pond, and directly I felt somethin' sort of pullin' at my stringer. A cottonmouth five feet long and big as your arm was tryin' to swaller one of my trout. I come out of that pond so fast I knocked dust out of it!

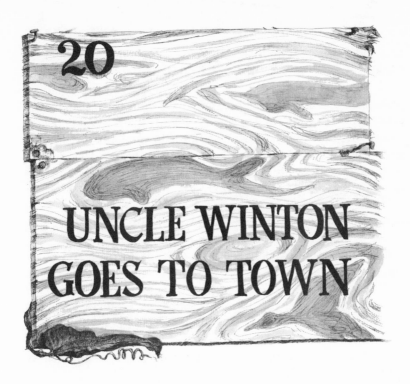

UNCLE WINTON GOES TO TOWN

Before Uncle Winton got so many things the matter with him he made a trip up north to visit his and Ma's sister, Aunt Rosa Belle Jenkins, up in Chicago. Aunt Rosa Belle had married a fast-talkin' Yankee salesman when she were pretty young, and had about nine young-uns. Her husband had lost one job after another and, from what she wrote Ma, their livin' conditions was pretty rough. Well, Uncle Wint had sold a big chunk of land and had a roll of money big enough to burn a wet mule. So he decided to stay in one of them big fancy hotels right smack dab in the center of town. You should of heered him tell about that trip when he got back.

"Boys," he said, "that's the derndest place I were ever in. I got me a room in the tower of the hotel and it were forty-three stories high. I hardly dared get within six feet of the window and it were some sight, lookin' out at all them lights at night. I never seen so many people in my life. Even at midnight it looked like court week in Ocala, and in the day-time you just walked out the whirlin' door, turned right or left and started takin' little short steps tryin' to find a place to walk.

"I near 'bout quit smokin' on that trip because I had so many pockets I couldn't find my papers and tobacco half the time. I had pockets in my shirt, pockets in my vest, pockets in my suit coat and pockets in a big old overcoat I had to buy. And when I did manage to roll a smoke, before I could lick it some scaper would ram into me and knock out all the tobacco. After a day on them streets, a-lookin' in them stores and all, my eyes was bugged out so far they bent the bows of my glasses, and after three days in that place I were as weak in the knees as a young whoopin' crane.

"Your Aunt Rosa Belle carried me out to a big museum where they had just about every kind of stuffed varmint you ever seen or heered of. Them big museums spend a heap of money sendin' out expeditions to collect all kinds of varmints from all over the world. I heered somebody say they was lookin' for something called the abdominal snowman. And there was another bunch of fellers over there somewhere after a giant panderer.

"I went at a dog trot all day in one building and them marble floors just about ruined my feet. But it were worth it. I seen tigers that had long hair on 'em and come from Siberia. Some fellers was gettin' up a expedition to go over after some more of 'em, and I got to see a couple of real live ones out at the zoo in Lincoln Park. They was the prettiest things I ever laid my eyes on. Their hair weren't so long because it ain't quite as cold in Chicago as Siberia, but they was the biggest cats I ever seen. The keeper told me that the old boar weighed around six hundred pounds. There were a shelf in their cage that were a good six feet off the floor and one of them cats would just look up there and be there— quick as lightnin' and near 'bout as light and easy as a flyin' squirrel.

"One of them tigers yawned, and I'll swear he had big old yellow tushes long as your finger. I thought about them fellers goin' over to Siberia huntin', and I'll tell you right now I wouldn't want to fool with one of them tigers without an eight-gauge shotgun loaded with gill-net leads and dog chains!

Because if one of them cats ever got to you he'd skin a place on you!"

Accordin' to Uncle Wint, a man could see near 'bout every kind of live varmint in that Lincoln Park.

"Boys," he said, "they had a whole house full of the derndest monkeys you ever seen in your natural life. There were one big old feller near 'bout as big as a man and just the color of a ripe tangerine. He had orangy-red hair about a foot long all over him, chin whiskers like old man Frank Butler, and were the ugliest thing I ever laid my eyes on. I stood and looked at that ape for the longest while and I thought to myself that I'd give a pretty to be settin' up in a mangrove bush out in the Gulf marsh and see old Jingles run up on this big old red monkey in one of his coon traps— caught by just a couple of toes!"

Uncle Winton got so tickled just thinkin' about it that he could hardly go on talkin'. Jingles were the nickname of a little old feller who done a lot of trappin' for coons, minks and otters and who just about lived in the marsh. He were a real excitable little feller and I could just picture him takin' off through that marsh grass. He sure would have made a new trail!

"There was several black apes just as big as the red one," Uncle said, "and one of 'em were a-settin' flat on the floor of his cage with his arms reached up over his head, holdin' to the bars. He'd just set there with a faraway look in his eyes, kind of pursin' up his lips like he were a-fixin' to spit. Directly he looked at me and I told him, 'You're the second ugliest thing I ever seen and I've got a first cousin, Jim Lewis, down in Gulf Hammock that looks just like you!'

"Well, he *had* been a-fixin' to spit, all right, because when I said that, he spit all over me. It were Sunday afternoon and there were a big crowd of people around and everybody went to laughin' at me. For just a second or two I got pretty mad.

" 'I've got a good will to kill you,' I told him. 'I've killed a man for less than such as that!'

"Well, by grannies, when I said that, derned if he didn't spit on me again! Everybody laughed and he made such a funny face that I had to laugh myself.

" 'O.K., brother,' I told him, 'think nothin' of it. I guess you've seen old Jim yourself and I don't blame you a bit in the world!'

"While I was in Chicago," Uncle Wint went on, "we went to a fancy restaurant and really put on a feed. They had some pretty good rations in that town, but I sure am glad to get back home to some hot biscuits. Why, that bread they have up there has got such a hard crust they cut it with a hacksaw and then don't cut it plumb through—it takes two fellers to pull a piece from the loaf. And them rolls! Why, you couldn't bust one in a concrete mixer. And that were back in the days when I had my own teeth too."

"How did you like livin' in that hotel?" Tarley asked him.

"It beat anything I have ever in my life ever saw," said Uncle Wint. "The door to the room were hollow and you'd open it from the inside and chunk your dirty clothes in and phone 'em about it downstairs. Two days later you'd open the inside cover of the door and there'd be your clothes, washed and ironed and packed in a box. And you hadn't seen nobody or nothin'!"

"How was the bed?" I asked him. "I'll bet there were a mattress two feet thick."

"The bed was good—real good," Uncle told me. "It were the sheets that worried me. You can believe it or not, but I tore a label off of them sheets every night for the first three nights. I don't mean clean sheets, I mean brand-new sheets. Why, I'd sooner sleep between a couple of dry deer hides!

"Aunt Rosa Belle come to see me one Sunday mornin' at the hotel and, just for the hell of it, I had ordered my breakfast sent up, just like some dad-burned millionaire. Well, sir, the waiter wheeled the table into the room, covered over with silver dishes with tops on. 'You see that,' I told Rosa Belle, 'that's just a sample of what goes on here. You want somethin' to eat, or somethin' to drink, or somethin' to read, just ring a bell. And then, by gollies, once a week they ring *your* bell!'

"Near the hotel was a fancy German eatin' place they called a rat cellar. You went downstairs to a big room with a lot of tables with checkerboard tablecloths, candles burnin' and three pudgy fellers in knee britches marchin' around beatin' on a drum, blowin' a horn and workin' a squeeze box. I mean that place were jumpin'. The air were so strong with beer smell that you could almost drink it."

"That ought to have suited you just fine," Aunt Effie told him.

"Well, I never was too crazy about beer and you know it," Uncle said. "Anyhow, the lady I was with done the orderin' and she sure picked some good eatin'. We had—"

"What lady was you with?" Aunt Effie interrupted him.

"A young lady from that doctor's office and she sure was nice and offered to show me around," Uncle said.

"I'll bet she did," Aunt Effie said.

"Why can't you just let me tell about that eatin' place?" Uncle said. "And if you want to raise hell, do it after the folks go home. Anyhow, the lady ordered up a lot of stuff with some strange-soundin' names but mighty good taste and the sauerkraut was the best I ever eat. To drink she ordered somethin' called leap-frog milk. It didn't look or taste like much of anything, but I was thirsty and she kept fillin' my glass. And I'll guaran-dam-tee that was a well-named drink. I felt like hoppin' all over Chicago."

"And probably did," Aunt Effie said.

One of the reasons Uncle Wint went to Chicago were to see some big specialist doctor because of all the pains he'd been havin' for so long. He thought there were somethin' real bad wrong, but there weren't.

"I'll bet he told you it weren't nothin' in the world but that rotgut moonshine," said Aunt Effie.

"No, ma'am," Uncle told her, "he X-rayed me and do you know what were the trouble? If you remember, I use to go to a lot of them country dances when I were a young bucko. I'd dance with them fancy town gals and bite the earbobs off'n their ears and swaller 'em! Well, that's all in the world that's been the matter with me all this time. I had a double handful of them earbobs in my belly—red and green and blue and pearl and gold ones."

"I wonder how that tapeworm found his way around in all them things," said Tarley.

"I don't know," Uncle said, "but there ain't but one way to get rid of 'em and that's just keep dissolvin' 'em little by little." And he pulled the cob stopper out of his jug.

"Well, just be sure it's little by little," Aunt Effie told him.

"Naturally," Uncle said. "I wouldn't want to do away with 'em all at once. Now I just take a little snort and each time I do I think about a different set of 'em and where they come from. There was them pretty pearly ones come off a great big old fat gal from down around Homosassa somewhere—Nora somethin' or other. She were so fat she had to back up to a door to knock, and I'll declare I can't figger out how in the world I ever managed to get to them earbobs while we was a-dancin'!"

"You're just a long-necked old buzzard like all them Eppses —that's how come it," Aunt Effie said, "and if you'd of wanted Nora, why didn't you marry her?"

"Who said I wanted Nora?" Uncle answered. "There's a heap of difference between wantin' a woman for a life partner and just wantin' to snap off her earbobs at a dance."

"Yeah—you never tried snappin' off *my* earbobs," Aunt Effie told him.

"Of course not," Uncle said. "These here teeth cost me a hundred and fifty dollars and it's all I can do to chew sausage—much less snap 'em on gold or silver."

"You know perfectly well what I'm talkin' about," Aunt Effie told him, "and you're just dodgin' the issue."

Me and Tarl seen that Aunt Effie were gettin' mad enough for one of her fits, so we left out from there. Ma had always told us to get out of the way when Aunt Effie started gettin' mad.

"When Effie Epps gets mad she has forty fits a minute and every one of 'em lasts a hour," Ma said. "There ain't nobody in the world can handle her but your Uncle Winton and he does it by saddlin' a horse and disappearin' for three days!"

Ma said that sometimes Uncle Wint and Aunt Effie reminded her of the time when they were all at a big frolic over at the Whiddenses' place and everybody was dancin' up a storm.

"Your Uncle Winton was a big old gawky kid of sixteen,"

Ma said, "and he didn't know nothin' about dancin'. I don't reckon he'd even seen much dancin' before and he just stood there and watched with his eyes bugged out like a fiddler crab's. Directly Effie come over to him and asked him if he would like to dance with her. He'd been moonin' around over her for a couple of months and she knew it. Well, he turned two or three shades of red and looked at the ceilin' and looked at the floor. Then he said, 'I don't know how to dance, but I sure would like to hold you while you do!' She just turned around and walked off.

"Along about then a real pretty little old gal from across the river come up to him and said, 'Mr. Epps, wouldn't you like to dance with me?' Well, whether it was the 'Mister' that done it or whether he was just mad from the way Effie had left him, I'll never know. But I want to tell you he grabbed that little old gal and they went to cuttin' a flutter! When Effie seen *that*, it didn't take her long to figure that she'd done dropped her candy and she'd better be a-pickin' it up. She was a jealous filly even then.

"The minute the music stopped, she went over and grabbed Winton's arm and said, 'I thought you didn't know how to dance.' 'I didn't,' your uncle said, 'but I'm gettin' on to it right fast!' "

I got tickled thinkin' about it. I don't know what dance Uncle and the pretty little blond had been doin', but it put me in mind of a story folks told about Rantsy Webb when he was courtin' Kitty Riggs. Old man Riggs was awful strict, so one night when she went off with Rantsy the old man follered 'em to the Oddfellows Hall and went upstairs to where they was a-dancin'. Accordin' to the story, Rantsy and Kitty was doin' a dance they called the Black Bottom and old man Riggs taken one look at 'em, ran out on the floor and grabbed Rantsy by the neck and dragged him downstairs and liken to have beat him to death. Old man Riggs was deaf and just couldn't hear the music!

Anyhow, Uncle Winton and Aunt Effie had managed to get crossways the very first time they met and seemed like they just stayed that way. Ma said they reminded her of old man Eph Drawdy and his old lady, who lived out from Weeki-

Wachee. He was blind and she was deaf, but he wouldn't tell her what he heard and she wouldn't tell him what she saw!

I remember one time me and Tarl was over to Uncle Winton's when him and Aunt Effie was havin' one of their go-'rounds. I don't know what started it, but she hollered out, "Winton Epps, if you ever do that again, I'm a-goin' to turn you every way but loose!"

"Now you just listen to me, woman," Uncle told her. "I didn't eat no breakfast this mornin' and I didn't eat no dinner at noon and you just fool with me a little bit more, by grannies, and I won't eat nothin' for supper neither!"

I couldn't see where that were gainin' him very much, but derned if she didn't quiet down. I never seen poutin' do no good before, but it sure worked that time.

Uncle used to come over to our house when Aunt Effie got on a tear and tell Ma all about it.

"When Effie gets on one of them streaks, the best thing a feller can do is just to get away from there and stay away. She taken one of them spells at a school meetin' just last week and a teacher lady told her she was a ptarmigan."

"How do you spell that?" I asked him.

"How do I know?" Uncle said. "But that's what she called her."

"A ptarmigan's a bird," Tarley said.

"Well, Effie's a bird, all right," Uncle told him.

"A ptarmigan's a white grouse," Tarl said.

"That's *exactly* what she is," Uncle said.

Anyhow, Tarl got the dictionary and tried to explain it all to Uncle Winton—about there being another word somethin' like it that meant a cranky woman.

"But the bird word," Tarl said, "is spelt with a 'p' and the 'p' is silent."

"Yeah," Uncle said, "I know that story too and I just don't want to hear no more about it."

It was hard to tell if Uncle Winton was really scared of Aunt Effie or just didn't like arguments. Like most fellers, he talked pretty big when he was away from home, and I remember one time when we went huntin' after him and Aunt Effie had had a big ruckus. When we started home that evenin' Uncle said, "If that woman don't have my supper ready, I'm a-goin' to give her a fit. And if she does, I ain't a-goin' to eat a dang bite of it!" Then he got a bottle out of his saddlebag and took a long snort to make himself believe it.

We didn't have a deer to dress out, so I left Uncle at the old bridge across Snake Creek and rode on home. I reckon he didn't find no supper ready at his house because he disappeared for three days and when he finally come to our house Ma took one look at him and said, "Don't open your eyes no further, Winton, or you'll bleed to death!"

I never seen Uncle in such shape before or since. He had the shakes and Ma had to give him a shot of her hid-away brandy. I guess he figured he was goin' to die because he got real repentant and even asked Ma to pray for him.

"I'll pray with you, Winton," Ma said, "but you've got to do some of it yourself."

Well, Uncle began prayin' about how weak he was and how far short he'd fell of being a good Christian and what a sight he'd made of himself in the eyes of his nephews and a lot more stuff like that until at last Ma said, "Just tell God you're drunk, Winton."

That must have shook him up because he got up off his knees and went walkin' out of there without lookin' back or sayin' ary word. It must have shamed him a heap because he didn't even come over to go huntin' with us boys for a long time.

21 BOBCATS, FOXES & SOME FOLKS' IDEAS OF FITTIN' FOOD

When me and Tarley first began gettin' together some hounds of our own, we done a lot of coon huntin'. A feller could get a pretty good price for a coon hide back in them days. But a coon don't give a bunch of dogs nearly so good a race as a fox or a wildcat. Our cats down here are long and lean and I've knowed one to run five or six hours ahead of the same pack of hounds that would catch or tree or hole a gray fox in thirty minutes—that is if the fox tried to run the open woods. Sometimes a smart old fox will get into a thick scrub and dodge 'round and 'round, and then it takes the dogs longer to put him down a hole or tree him. But a fox don't dare dodge so close or run in such tight circles as a wildcat for fear one of the dogs might see him and catch him. Most any hound will make short work of a fox all by himself, but a wildcat is somethin' else again.

Our Florida cats, like I said, are long and lanky and even a old boar cat won't weigh much over twenty-five pounds. Me and Tarley killed one that went thirty and they said that my Grandaddy Driggers killed one fifty-pounder down in the

Big Cypress—but I guess that's like most grandaddy stories. And there sure ain't nobody left around to say he didn't. Toward the end of his life, poor old Grandaddy's memory went bad and he got to rememberin' things that never happened. Maybe that's the way it were about the fifty-pound cat.

There were a feller from over around Leesburg who had a pack of ten or fifteen Walker and July hounds that was wild-cat specialists. Along with 'em he had a great big old frizzly-faced, kinky-coated black-and-tan dog named Sandy that were what they called a Airydale. He were a ugly, box-headed scaper and didn't look like he'd be much good for nothin' but to keep cold grits from spoilin'. Once in a while the feller from Leesburg would bring his dogs over to the Hammock and camp for a week or so down below Log Landing on the river. There was a heap of wildcats in the scrubs and bay heads and flatwoods along the edge of the Hammock, and all of us who had any good cat-runnin' dogs would join up with this feller and sometimes we'd have twenty or more dogs in the race. On a frosty mornin' they'd make the woods ring so the needles was a-fallin' off the pine trees. I'll never forget old man Kelly Runnels sayin', "Just listen at them dogs! I sure am glad I didn't ride my horse this mornin'— I'd of beat him to death with my hat!"

The big old frizzly-faced Airydale were good for about two hours on a cold mornin' and less when it were hot. He couldn't smell a cold trail, but when the hounds would jump a cat, old Sandy would fall in and stay with 'em till he gave out—or got too hot. Then he'd find him a swampy place and lay down in the water to cool off. When he got his wind back he'd cock up them little short ears, tip his head to one side and listen. When he located the race he'd get back in and go for another half hour. When he gave out, he'd cool off again and fly back at it when he got his wind.

But what I want to get on your mind is that if he ever set eyes on the fox or cat, that critter just had a bad day! Old Sandy would go to yippin' and put on a spurt of speed and the fox or cat had to take to a tree right now or he were a caught son-of-a-gun. And what I mean, it didn't take old

Sandy long to finish either one. He'd kill the biggest kind of a cat in five minutes, and he didn't want no help from them hounds while he were a-doin' it. He'd go right in and get that cat by the back of the neck and go to backin' up, shakin' it just as hard as he could—and that were plenty hard. Whenever he got that neck holt, church were out! I guess he'd learnt never to let a wildcat get underneath him where it could get leverage with its back legs. A big old cat can cut a dog's guts out if he ain't careful. After he'd killed the cat, old Sandy would lay down on it and look around at the other dogs. If one started up to sniff the dead cat, he'd just wrinkle one lip a little and that were enough. That were his cat and if they didn't believe it, they soon found out.

I believe this big old Airydale could of whipped any other two or three dogs I ever seen, but he weren't bad to fight, and he didn't permit no other dogs to fight around the camp. If they started to fight, he'd bust into 'em, knock 'em loose and then walk around stiff-legged, kickin' dirt and raisin' his leg on every post, stump or tree. He were sure the boss dog of the outfit.

Of course there was a heap of deer in the Hammock and most any hound would rather run a deer than anything else —specially young dogs—and a lot of these here high-bred Walkers and Triggs and Julys and Birdsongs and such as that never knew when to quit and they'd run a deer plumb out of the county. This often happened when some outsider would come in, like the feller from Leesburg. He were always havin' to hunt lost dogs—sometimes as far north as Cedar Key.

When he really wanted to go deer huntin' he'd just take that old Airydale, tie a turkey bell on his collar and turn him loose. That dern dog would go a-dashin' back and forth and when you heard that bell go to tinklin' real fast, you'd better cock your gun because old Sandy had jumped a deer— or were just about to. He wouldn't run too long, maybe fifteen or twenty minutes and then he'd be right back huntin' another one. When you seen that little stub tail go into a blur and heered that bell go into a whir, you could look for business to pick up.

The flatwoods back of Log Landing was full of quail, and a man could take his shotgun and old Sandy and get him a mess of birds in no time. All you had to do were to watch his tail and listen to the bell and keep up with him, 'cause he didn't point 'em when he found 'em. Sometimes he'd pause and crouch for a second or two, but just enough to get set for a good jump. He'd try his best to catch one when they flushed and you could hear his teeth click fifty yards. I believe that dern dog were crazier about huntin'—any kind of huntin'—than any dog I ever seen.

Gray foxes was plentiful in the sand hills east of where we lived and of course they was hard on quail. There were always a squabble goin' on between the bird hunters and the fox hunters over whether or not a fox done more harm than good. The fox hunters claimed that a fox lived mainly on woods mice and rats, and the bird hunters claimed he preferred quail eggs and young birds. It's pretty slim pickin's out in them sand hills, though, and I guess a devilish fox is glad to eat anything he can find, including gophers.

A lot of folks from up north, where they have nothing but red foxes, don't believe that one of our grays can climb a tree. But he sure can! He'll go thirty feet up a straight pine trunk as good as ary house cat. I don't think they climb very much, though, unless they have to. Once in a while the dogs will catch one, but mostly he'll take a tree or pop down a gopher hole.

I always have a lot of trouble explainin' gophers to Yankees. Some Yankees tell me that up in their country a gopher is a ground squirrel and lives in a hole about as big as a hoe handle. They say he's sort of yellowish and got little spotted stripes on his back. Other Yankees call a gopher a pocket gopher and describe him different. Well, down here a gopher is a land-livin' turtle who digs a hole big as a stovepipe. Foxes, rabbits, skunks and rattlesnakes all use them gopher holes—and sometimes even a wildcat.

Rattlesnakes love to den up in gopher holes come October and November and they seem to get along all right with the gopher. And other varmints such as foxes and rabbits use 'em to get away from dogs. Me and Tarley even killed three or four wildcats that went down old gopher holes when the dogs got to crowdin' 'em.

A feller wouldn't hardly believe how deep and long some of them gopher holes are less'n he tried diggin' one out. We use to catch a lot of foxes alive to sell to some huntin' clubs upcountry and we'd take our shovels when we went to the sand hills. We dug out a heap of foxes and it's a miracle we never found a snake.

When the dogs put a fox down a gopher hole we'd tie our horses and go to diggin', and I'll give you my word, we dug holes deep enough and wide enough to bury a Model A. When we'd get down to where we could see the fox or hear him growlin', Tarley would take our fox-catchin' stick and lay down in the hole while I helt his legs to keep him from slidin'. This catchin' stick were a forked stick with a couple of rawhide thongs tied across the forks—just like you'd draw a line across the top of a Y. The stick were about two feet long with each fork about four or five inches long. He'd poke this down at the fox's mouth and it would latch on to them rawhide thongs. Tarley would twist the stick and Mr. Fox would come on out with a rawhide thong back of his tushes and over his nose. Tarl would draw that varmint up to where he could grab it by the back of the neck and we'd drop it in a crokus sack.

A funny thing were that we never found either a gopher or a snake. I know dern well that we put many a fox in a hole that sure didn't have time to check and see who else were down there!

There's some place in Florida, they tell me, where little old owls live right down in the hole with the gophers and rattlesnakes. It may be so, but I ain't never seen it. I feel about that like Tarley did when I told him about the bullfrog I caught one night. That frog covered the whole bottom of a ten-quart pail and were all puffed up in the belly from some-thin' he'd eat. I cut him open and found a whole rat in his belly. Now, I don't know whether he caught that rat alive while it were swimmin', or whether he found it dead, or what. But it sure were in his belly and I told Tarl about it.

"Well, I'll be dogged," he said. "You wouldn't have believed that, Billy, if you hadn't seen it with your own eyes, would you?"

"No, sir!" I told him. "I sure wouldn't."

"Well," Tarley said, "that's just how I am about it!"

And I feel the same way about them underground owls. But whether or not he believed my frog story, it were so. And that devilish frog were so big me and another feller eat his front legs as well as his hind legs, which was as big as the drumsticks of a big rooster. I will admit, though, I had to keep my mind off of that rat while I were a-chewin'! I had a special reason for this. One time when we was a-huntin' way back in the Hammock, near the Gulf marsh, I come into camp starvin' hungry. Everybody else had come in, eat dinner and gone back to the woods turkey huntin'. All but Tarley, that is. He hadn't been feelin' too good that mornin', so he just set around camp.

"Anything to eat?" I asked him.

"Yeah," he said, "there's some grits left in the pot and one squirrel in the fryin' pan."

One of the fellers had brought in a few loaves of store-bought white bread, but we called it "wasp nest" and didn't like it much. It were half air bubbles. I warmed up the grits and the squirrel and cleaned 'em up and mopped up the gravy with a slice of that sorry light bread. Then Tarley said, "You know, that were the funniest dern squirrel I ever did see. I shot him on the woodpile back of camp and there weren't a single hair on his tail!"

Well, it taken me a second or two to understand just what he were a-tellin' me, but when I did, I jumped him. He were then three inches higher and a lot heavier than me, but I fought him to a standstill for five minutes. It's terrible for two brothers to fight like we done and it's a wonder somebody didn't get killed. Tarley whipped me so bad I couldn't get around for two days, but he knowed he'd been in a fight and he finally apologized about the rat.

This happened the second day in camp and nobody had killed a deer, a turkey, a wild hog or a duck. There was always plenty of squirrels, though—and they're mighty good eatin'! They're just ordinary gray squirrels—what we call cat squirrels down here. I guess they get that name from the funny meowin'-like noise they make when they get real aggravated. If a cat squirrel spots a hawk or a owl or a snake or a hunter, he'll bark and bark for quite a spell and then he'll settle down and make that funny noise like a cat meowin'.

Our fox squirrels are two or three times as big as cat squirrels and you find 'em more out in the piney woods. They're sort of yellowish brown and darker brown or black around the face. Both cat squirrels and fox squirrels is mighty good eatin'—specially when made into a purloo with rice. When we'd fry cat squirrels, we'd fry the heads too. There is a good chunk of meat on each jaw and the brains are the sweetest meat you near 'bout ever tasted. Folks eats calves' brains—so why not squirrels' brains?

Some feller were tellin' me about a old lady at a sandwich stand over in Miami. She asked the waitress what were real good that day and the gal said, "We got a special on beef tongue."

"Oh, murder!" the old lady said. "I couldn't eat nothing that come out of a animal's mouth. Bring me an egg sandwich!"

A feller has to keep his mind off a lot of things if he wants to enjoy his food. A chicken ain't the cleanest thing I ever seen, and I love ham and bacon but I don't study about the hog kneelin' around in the slop! And take oysters, now. There ain't no way you can fix 'em that I don't like 'em—raw, fried, stewed, roasted in the shell or what Ma called "scalloped"—fixed up with crackers and milk. I believe you could roll a dad-burn oyster in sand and fry him in crankcase oil and I'd like him. But when you look at the dern thing a-layin' in his shell, you wonder how the feller felt who first tried one. He sure must have been some kind of hungry!

One time when Uncle Winton were tellin' about his Chicago trip, he said he stopped in at a picture show and they showed a movie of a bunch of fuzzy-haired fellers with ear-bobs and bones run through their noses and totin' big spears. He said they was cannibals—that they ate people.

"Great day in the mornin'!" Tarley said. "I couldn't do that under *no* conditions. Could you, Billy?"

"I don't reckon so," I told him, "but that time I got lost up on Otter Creek and laid out a couple of days and nights, I got hungry enough to eat a raw dog!"

"That might be," Tarley said, "but I'll bet you wasn't hungry enough to eat *somebody*! I just don't believe I could do that at all—under *no* circumstances."

Then he thought a long time and sort of shook his head and said again, "I don't believe I could ever eat a man. Now, if I was plumb starvin' to death I *might* eat a woman. But I'll be derned if I could eat a man!"

I got to thinkin' about gnawin' on one of Uncle Winton's tough old arms, comparin' it with one of our neighbor gal's soft little arms, plump and smooth as a little old quail ham. There sure would be a heap of difference if it come right down to where a feller had to do such a terrible thing!

During our huntin' me and Tarley has tried just about everything! A dern possum's too greasy, but a coon's pretty good. And one time when we was a-cookin' up a big bobcat for the dogs, it smelled so good I tried a piece of it. It tasted good, sort of like veal. Uncle Wint says panther tastes the same way. I never did try a fox, and most hounds don't like one either, even if it's cooked. But a bobcat's right good —if you can keep your mind off it.

Speakin' of bobcats, the Knight boys over on the river done a lot of trappin' and was always gettin' a big old bobcat in their coon traps. For a long time coons would bring three or four dollars a hide, but a cat were only worth about a dollar. Mostly folks didn't even bother to skin one—just killed it and left it there, figurin' it were good riddance. A big old cat will kill a fawn deer and he's real rough on turkeys. I don't believe there is anything in this world meaner than a fresh-caught wildcat—or bobcat, if you'd rather call him that. He's got four razor blades on each foot, and when he slaps out, somethin' gets cut.

I heered that the Knight boys really fixed up a carload of fellers from over on the east coast somewhere who was camped near their place. They was strangers and it weren't long before folks around there began missin' a few things. Everybody thought the newcomers was stealin', so they give 'em a test. The way I heered the story, the Knight boys caught 'em a great big old he cat and crammed him into a old trunk and set it out alongside the road where these east-coast fellers would come along on their way to town from their camp. They had one of the first closed cars to come into our country, and when they first showed up, one of the commercial fishermen on the river were tellin' Tarley about it and said, "They got a shiny new car with a glass cabin on it!"

Well, pretty soon some Negroes who was chippin' turpentine in the flatwoods come along and started to stop, but the Knight boys jumped out from behind the bushes and told 'em to get goin'! Then old man Simpson come along and they told him not to stop. After while the east-coast fellers come along in their Model A—four or five of 'em. And when they seen that trunk, they stopped, two jumped out and ran and got the trunk and ran back to the car. Then they took off. It were a real cold day and all the windows was rolled up. The car went about a hundred yards down the road and ran into the ditch and all the doors flew open and the cat was the first one out!

Accordin' to the story, Doc Joyner took one hundred and six stitches in them fellers, all told, and had to use bag string on the last two. Anyhow, that's the story, and if it really happened, I sure am glad I weren't in that car! I wonder what would have happened if they'd been harnessed like a feller has to be in one of these here modern cars—a belly cinch, a breast strap and everything but a crupper!

22 MOSTLY ABOUT DEER DOGS & DEER HUNTERS— YANKEE-STYLE & CRACKER-STYLE &

When a feller wanted to travel through the Hammock at night, he could use dead cabbage-palm fans. The ground is covered with 'em and you can't hardly walk thirty steps without steppin' on one. They're real brittle and dry and burn like paper. You just pick one up by the stem, light the fan and it'll make a fine torch for a right good ways. Just before it burns out, you pick up another one, light it and go on. There ain't much danger of startin' a woods fire unless there's been a long dry spell. There ain't much undergrowth to catch fire in the Hammock and the ground is pretty soggy. And most always there's a good dew falls at night, so when we're through with a torch we just chunk it down.

We get most of our kindlin' wood out in the flatwoods, just pickin' up light'd snags and knots. When lightnin' kills a pine tree, the sap wood rots off, leavin' the heart, which is full of turpentine and turns hard as iron. Weather, termites nor nothin' else has much effect on it. There's light'd fence-posts in our country that has been in the ground fifty years. The more turpentine gum there is in a light'd knot, the "fatter" it is, and a feller can take a chunk of fat light'd and it'll catch afire almost like gasoline and fry and sizzle like bacon cookin'! A light'd knot weathers to a soft gray color, but when you split it open it's yellow—almost orange if it's real fat—and looks almost like rock candy. And it smells near 'bout good enough to eat.

I remember a Yankee feller who was huntin' with us boys once and went out to collect up some wood for the campfire. He must of tripped over a cord of light'd layin' around on the ground, but he cut down three little green pine saplin's the size of your arm, and cut 'em in lengths and toted 'em in. When he got through, he had pine gum all over his clothes and hair and hands and you couldn't of burnt that wood in a blast furnace. Three pieces of it would have put out Hell. We explained it to him and put him to cuttin' up a great big old light'd log about ten feet long and a foot thick. The ax would ring and sparks would fly when he'd hit it, and he really went to work on it. I guess his feelin's was hurt and he wanted to show us how he could use a ax. I watched him a while and directly I said, "If I was you, Mister, I think I'd go at that job kind of gradual—like a house cat eatin' a grindstone. Not all at once." Just the chips from that log would sizzle and fry and blaze up. It were some kind of fat.

I reckon I'd be just as ignorant about firewood and kindlin' up in Yankee country as this feller were down here. I hear lots of Florida-cracker fishin' and huntin' guides laughin' about how ignorant their Yankee sportsmen are, but I always tell 'em, "Maybe you boys are mighty smart and they're plumb ignorant, but I don't see any of you fellers goin' up to New York or Chicago or somewheres and hirin' *them* to show *you* around!"

It seems like to me that if a feller would just try out the other feller's way of doin' things, before spoutin' off, maybe there'd be a heap fewer fights in the world. Me and Tarl has guided Yankees on deer-huntin' trips down here who started out by makin' us fightin' mad. Seems like most Yankee deer hunters and a lot of deer-story writers ain't got much use for our way of huntin' and they don't mind sayin' so. Up where they come from they say that anybody who'd deliberately chase a deer with dogs is just a mean, sorry, no-good scoun'el who'd step on little kittens' feet, push little chickens into the water and pull up young corn.

They get their sport out of walkin' around still-huntin' and shootin' an unsuspectin' buck while he's in the middle of his lunch or tryin' to pick him a good place to sleep. Us boys have killed quite a few deer that way too—just chancin' up on 'em when we was turkey huntin'—but it don't compare for sport with the excitement of hearin' them hounds squall out on a hot trail, maybe go out of hearin' for an hour or two and then come back in full cry. Boy, when you hear that music your hackles raise up and your heart goes to thumpin' and you're strainin' your eyes to see that old buck fannin' the palmettos. If you've guessed right and got in the right place and hold the gun right, you'll roll him over at the top of one of them long, high jumps and have a thrill you'll never forget. And when some of them know-it-all up-north hunters get a taste of this excitement they sing a different tune.

But not all of 'em. Me and Tarl guided one Yankee who missed the biggest kind of a buck up near Blue Sink. It were a long walk from camp to Blue Sink, but when a feller got there he had one of the best stands in the Hammock. All along the east side of the Sink was a ridge of big oaks and hickories without much undergrowth, so a feller could see a good gunshot in any direction. Of course, I'm talkin' about shotgun range and not no high-powered rifle distances. Blue Sink is really a shotgun stand, but this Yankee wouldn't use nothin' but his rifle—a thirty-two special Winchester, lever action, which he claimed had killed a heap of deer.

Anyhow, this buck run the whole length of that open glade with Prophet and Ranger and old Blue just a-cryin' after him, and the Yankee shot three times and never cut a hair. On top of that he wasted the best chance he had. He'd already put two bullets into the trunks of big oak trees, but then he waited for the deer to come into a good openin' and I'll be derned if he didn't jack out the last shell from the barrel and snap on the deer. He'd only had four shells in the gun to start with and he throwed away the best chance he had!

I was the first to get to him after the shootin' and he done a lot of explainin'. The most part of his song were that he just didn't care for our style of deer huntin'. He had to walk too far and the deer run too fast. He said he was used to huntin' at a game preserve someplace where a man could just set down in a nice blind and the deer would come up to eat and a feller could pick out the one he wanted and shoot it. And he wouldn't have to listen to a bunch of dern dogs barkin'!

Of course, right now I'm doin' just exactly what I criticize other fellers for doin'—that is, downgradin' the other man's way. If a feller wants to shoot a buck while he's eatin' supper or walkin' home with his gal friend, that's his business. Me, I like to bust 'em while they're travelin' high, wide and handsome. But I reckon we all like the woods and we all like venison steaks, or else we wouldn't be out there.

And all us crackers have to have our coffee in the mornin' before we go huntin', but I talked with a feller once who'd been down in South America on a big hunt and he said everybody down there drunk tea—some kind made from the leaves of a wild tree. They called it "ma tea," as I remember. This feller said they all drank it mornin', noon and night and just couldn't get along without it. He said it was a stimulant and a medicine and a food and that some feller lived on it and nothin' else for forty days. Either that or forty fellers lived on it for one day. I don't remember which. Anyhow, different folks has different ways of doin' things and, like I said, the world would be better off if we done things the way we wanted to and let other folks do it their way—eatin', drinkin' or deer huntin'!

The ideal deer dog for our country is a hound that'll run a hour or two and then come back and hunt for another deer. If a dog just keeps on runnin' a deer, the deer'll go to the Gulf marsh and that's the end of it—with maybe a lost dog or a 'gator-caught dog in the bargain.

Fellers huntin' out in the sand hills and down in the prairie country and Everglades like to take a young hound and train him to be what they call a slow-trail dog. They'll put a rope on him and lead him across a fresh deer track and when he wants to run and give tongue on it, they'll switch him across the nose and hold him back—but they'll keep a-walkin' on after the deer. After while they get him so he'll trail a deer without barkin' or tryin' to run, just walkin' along a-waggin' his tail.

The hunters will flank along to each side of him and when he begins to get excited at the edge of a thicket or bay head and starts really switchin' his tail, they'll get ready to shoot because that deer ain't far off and will get up and go any second. If you shoot the deer and hit it, one of them dogs will take the blood trail and foller it full cry just like any runnin' hound. But if you tell him to wait, he'll start slow-trailin' again without sayin' a word. It all depends on how bad hit you think the deer is and what you figure will be the best way to git him. It sure takes a heap of patience and know-how to train a good slow-trail dog.

Uncle Winton had the best slow-trailer I ever seen. It would even trail up a covey of quail. It wouldn't point, but would just stand there lookin' back and waggin' its tail like it were sayin', "What you waitin' for?" Me'n Tarl use to get us a mess of birds now and then, but Uncle Wint never would go. He'd say, "I believe God Almighty put women here to pet and birds to sing, so I don't beat women or shoot little birds."

Of all the fellers who hunted with us, I don't reckon anybody loved to hear the hounds run better than Jingles. He wasn't much for stayin' on a deer stand but always wanted to do the drivin', and he was right nimble in the woods. If anybody could stay with them dogs on foot, he could, and it weren't often they went out of hearin' on Jingles. Sometimes an old buck would go clear up to Hickory Ford or plumb out to the Gulf marsh, but Jingles most always stayed in hearin', and a heap of times when the deer doubled back Jingles would be waitin' for him. Then he'd have to do a lot of horn blowin' and waitin' cause he weren't very strong and couldn't tote ary sizable deer by himself.

Like I said, he really weren't very well, and when he got down and in the hospital, me and Tarl went to see him. He almost hadn't made it through the night, and when we set down by his bed he whispered, "They went out of hearin' on me last night, Tarl . . . but they come back." They went out of hearin' on him again the next night and didn't come back, and we sure missed seein' him around the Hammock.

While we was on one hunt we had a visit from Pappy Easton. He was a little old wizened-up feller with a long, scraggly beard who had a camp about two miles from there. He wasn't skeered of nobody or nothin', and when he was drinkin', just about everybody was skeered of him.

He'd come into a camp, get a can of tomatoes from the grub box, pick up a rifle—his or anybody else's—throw the can just as high as he could and bust it so that tomatoes showered down on whoever was standin' underneath. I've seen a few trick shots, and my brother Tarl is a extra good rifle shot with his own rifle, but I never could figure how old Pappy Easton could just pick up any old rifle and near 'bout never miss. But he sure could! Furthermore, it weren't a good idea to squawk, even if the tomatoes fell on you, because old man Easton had killed several fellers in his life and was right ornery when he was drinkin'. It was after supper when he come into our camp and we was a-settin' around the fire talkin'.

"You got a gun that'll shoot, Billy?" he asked me.

"I sure do," I told him.

"Where is it?"

"Yonder in the corner by the chimney—a forty-four forty."

"That ought to make 'em splatter," the old man said. And it sure did. He didn't bust 'em right over the fire, though, so nobody got messed up. We asked Pappy if he'd have somethin' to eat, but he said that he'd rather have somethin' to drink. So we gave it to him. He was huntin' a lost dog and after he'd had two or three more snorts, along with what he was already carryin', he got pretty wobbly.

"Tarl," he said, "looks to me like you're goin' to have to tote me home."

"All right," Tarley told him. "Let's go."

The old man didn't weigh much more than two straw hats and Tarl set him up on his shoulders, just like he would have a young-un. There was a pretty good old log road from our camp back to the Easton place, but it rambled around a lot and Pappy said they'd take a short cut. Tarl told me about it the next day.

"That old scoun'el had to take a short cut through the hammock—said it would save us a half a mile and that he knowed every tree and we wouldn't get lost. That was some trip! The old man would say, 'Son, you ain't got no more idea of where you're goin' than a weevil in a biscuit.' Then he'd reach over and pull my right ear and say, 'Bear to your right,' like he was drivin' a mule. After a while I told him, 'Pappy, I'm give out. I can't tote you no more. Can't you walk some?'

" 'Set me down, Tarley boy,' he said, 'and I'll see if I can make it over to that cabbage without lettin' my centerboard down.' Well, he made it with a little tackin', so after while I got him home. Lucky there was plenty of cabbage fans to see by, but I stayed in the old road comin' back and made better time. That old man sure gives me a pain where I ride horseback."

THE KNOW-IT-ALL FELLER

One summer a feller moved into the old Riggs place whose name was Blank. I ain't tryin' to hide nothin'—the feller's name actually was Blank. He come from up in Ohio somewhere—seems like it was Chilly Coffee or somethin—and he used to get into some awful arguments with Uncle Winton. He'd argue about anything, that feller would, and he knowed right smart about a heap of different things, specially sports. Uncle Winton loved just about any kind of sport and he kept up pretty good with what were goin' on by readin' about it in the *Tampa Tribune*.

Mister Blank had traveled a lot, to hear him tell it, and been to the Chicago Coliseum and Yankee Stadium and Madison Square Garden and places like that. He claimed that he'd saw some of the top stars in action, but sometimes he'd get sort of mixed up, seemed like to me. Like when he said he'd saw so many great football players—the four hunch-backs of Notre Dame and some feller called the "Gallopin' Goat" who ran the wrong way with the football.

Uncle Winton called him on that and said he'd read about

that feller and his name were Grange and folks called him a
ghost and not a goat, and when he got that football he went
to town with it and he sure knowed which way was town.

"Well," Mr. Blank said, "maybe you're right. But there *was*
a feller who ran the wrong way."

"Maybe he were just turned around and excited," Uncle
said. "Like my nephews was the night they went fire-huntin'
and shot my goats."

"I guess that was it," Mr. Blank said.

One of the things that Uncle and Mr. Blank argued about
most was baseball. Uncle Winton was a American League
fan and Mr. Blank thought there was nobody like them old-
time National Leaguers, particularly the Chicago Cubs. And
he were always talkin' about Johnny Kling and Mortified
Brown and Joe Tinker and Frank Chance and a lot of fellers
whose names I can't remember.

"They was good ones, all right," Uncle admitted. "And one
of the best ones was old Dazzy Vance, who pitched for Brook-
lyn. I know that feller—he's got a hotel down a couple of
rivers below us. Old Bernie Neis and Jimmy Foxx and Babe
Ruth used to come up there fishin' and I set around the fireplace one night with 'em and listened at 'em swappin' yarns.
Old Dazzy topped 'em all with a story about a catfish. He
said he went fishin' one cold January mornin'. There was a
white frost and it was so cold by the time he got his skiff
anchored in the pothole where he wanted to fish that he just
had to take a little nip."

"That's sure understandable," Mr. Blank told him.

"I'd of done it myself," Uncle said. "Well, old Dazz claimed
he was so sorry for the fiddler crab he was usin' for bait that
he helt it up to the bottle and let it lick around the neck.

" 'Then that old fiddler didn't wait to be cast,' Dazzy said.
'It just helt up that big claw and jumped overboard and swam
around lookin' for a fish! The first thing it seen was a catfish
and it made a dash at it and scooped it out like you'd scoop
out a baked Irish potato.

" 'Naturally, that catfish couldn't submerge with its in-
nards scooped out, so it just took off down the Homosassa
River, skitterin' along on top of the water. About noon it was

sighted by a Coast Guard cutter off of Boca Grande Pass and late that evenin' it was reported in Florida Bay, headin' for the Atlantic and lookin' for sympathetic catfish. It didn't find none and a fisherman seen it goin' under the bridge at Islamorada about midnight.

" 'Nothin' more was heard of it for three and a half days and then it was sighted travelin' fast around the Cape of Good Hope, still right on top of the water. It was headed east across the Indian Ocean and nobody seen it for four days more. Then an Australian fishin' boat reported it between there and New Zealand on a northeast course and it had slowed down to what they estimated to be about fifty miles an hour. Nobody knows how it got through the Panama Canal, but just a few days ago it was reported in the Gulf of Mexico and this morning a mullet fisherman sighted it off of Cedar Key. Accordin' to the best way we can figure, it's due to dock in the Homosassa River around five o'clock this evenin'!' "

"A feller couldn't always believe them ballplayers," Mr. Blank said. "Especially them old Rebel hillbilly boys."

Uncle bristled up at that. " Just let me tell you something, Mister. Them old southern boys make up a mighty big percentage of both leagues and the greatest one that ever wore spikes was Ty Cobb, the Georgia Peach."

"I can't argue about that," Mr. Blank said. "He done it all—hit, field and run the bases. And he stayed at the top year after year after year. He was like one of them Airedale dogs that they claim can do anything any other dog can do and then whip the other dog."

"Old Ty would sure fight," Uncle said. "That old cracker boy would fight a buzz saw."

"Tell me," Mr. Blank said, "while we're talking about that feller from Georgia, what do you mean by 'cracker boy'?"

"Well, back in the old days most of the early settlers had cattle and they drove 'em with cow whips which they could pop like a pistol shot. I reckon that's where we get the name Georgia crackers and Florida crackers. But we was talkin' about ballplayers and I'll just make you a little bet that

there's more great ballplayers come from the south than anywhere else."

"Could be," Mr. Blank said. "I ain't as sure about baseball players as I am about fighters and wrestlers. I can sure tell you crackers a few things about them." He went on to say he'd saw the heavyweight wrestlin' champion Strangler Lewis try for two hours to clamp a headlock on the old Nabisco, whoever he was. He said old Nabisco had his head shaved and would just roll up his neck muscles past his ears and it were just like a blacksnake tryin' to get a hold on a china egg.

"Or tryin' to grab a big soft-shell turtle by the neck to keep it from snatchin' its head back into its shell," Tarl said. "It just can't be done."

Then Mr. Blank told about a wrestler named Stecher who mostly used his legs. He'd get the other feller between them legs and just squeeze till his eyes bugged out and he'd give up. "I seen him wrestle a feller named Daviscourt in Madison Square Garden one time and he kept trying to work them legs closer and closer, and when he did, old Daviscourt would jerk a hair or two out of Stecher's thigh and he would jump and holler like a branded bull.

"The fastest wrestler I ever saw and the best built of 'em all was a Greek named Jimmy Londos," Mr. Blank went on. "I saw him wrestle a big fat Turk one hot night in Chicago and both of 'em was wringin' wet. The perspiration was just rollin' off 'em like sweat. After while Londos picked up that Turk, all three hundred pounds of him, and whirled him around a few times and then throwed him out of the ring— or tried to anyhow. The Turk caught on the top rope and hung there, and some feller in the balcony hollered out, 'That's right, Jeemy, hang him out to dry!'"

"That Turk had done got his tallow hot," Tarl said. "A feller can't do much when he's carryin' around a lot of hot tallow."

"Oh, I don't know about that," Mr. Blank said. "There was a fighter called Two-tone Tunney that was built just like a beer barrel and had a left uppercut that would nearly

take a feller's head off. In fact, he mighty near got to be a
world champion with that same uppercut. It started right
from the floor and everybody in Yankee Stadium seen it
comin' but the champ, Joe Louis."

"You're all mixed up," Uncle told him. "That feller was a
Eyetalian named Tony Galento. I read all about him."

"Vas you dere, Charlie?" Mr. Blank said. "*I* was!"

This aggravated Uncle Wint because he were a real fight
fan and did know a heap about them old-time fighters. "Maybe
so," he said, "but you sure never seen Tunney fight Joe Louis
because he never did. I'm beginnin' to believe you ain't seen
as many fights as I have."

Uncle Wint used to go plumb down to Tampa to see some
fights and he almost went over to Havana to see that big feller
Willard fight Jack Johnson. The time he went to Chicago he
just missed a big fight, but I forget now who was fightin'.
Anyhow, him and Mr. Blank really butted heads when it come
to who was the greatest heavyweight champion. Mr. Blank
liked Jim Jeffries, but Uncle Wint's favorite was Bob Fitzsimmons, a powerful-hittin' feller with sort of spindly legs
and most of his weight up in his shoulders and arms, which
is the way Uncle himself were built. They hassled a while and
at last Mr. Blank told him, "Epps, no wonder you like that
freckle-faced, spindle-shanked feller. You're built just like
him and, come to think of it, you ought to be a wonderful
singer—you've got legs like a mockingbird! And speaking of
birds, I hear you've been doing a lot of bragging about that
big red fighting rooster."

Uncle Winton loved all kinds of fights, even chicken fights,
and he did have some right good fightin' cocks of his own,
and he said, "Well, I *was* braggin' up to a few days ago. Ain't
nothin' ever whipped that rooster before, but he flew over
into an old Muscovy drake's pen last week and made a big
mistake. He crowed a couple of times and then he jumped up
and popped his spurs to that drake and that drake didn't do
nothin' but just grab him by his neck feathers and beat him
nearly to death with its wings. Then it turnt him loose and
that rooster got back into his own pen as soon as he was able

and I don't believe he'll ever be fit for nothin' but the pot. That old Muscovy sure took the fight out of him."

"I saw somethin' like that happen when I was in the Navy," Mr. Blank said. "I was on a battleship and we stopped off for a few days in Shanghai. Them Chinamen are great on cockfights and some of the officials that come aboard our ship seen our mascot, which was a bald eagle, and asked what it was. Our officers told 'em it was an American fighting cock and they got up a fight between the Chinese champion and our mascot. Some of them Chinese game cocks was real big birds and their champion was specially big, so there wasn't as much difference in size as you might think. Our old eagle's wings was clipped so he couldn't fly, and when they pitted 'em, the rooster flew up and hit the eagle a pretty good clip with his spurs."

"What happened then?" Uncle asked him.

"When the rooster sailed into him the second time, the eagle just reached out, grabbed him in the breast with his claws, pulled him up and bit his head off. Then he dropped him and just looked around and batted his eyes and that's all there was to it. Well, those Chinamen had lost their money and their champion and the ballgame was over. They claimed that biting wasn't fair and you never heard such jabbering in your life."

"It'd take a dern Yankee to tell a tale like that," Uncle said. "Anyhow, my rooster might as well of had his head bit off, far as any future fightin' is concerned."

"When you cook him, I want his cape," Mr. Blank said.

"What are you talkin' about?" Uncle asked him.

"His neck feathers. His cape. I want to tie up some trout flies out of them beautiful red hackles."

Uncle Wint give Mr. Blank a funny look and then cut his eyes over at me. About a month before, Mr. Blank had offered me a dollar to get him three or four pretty feathers out of that red rooster's neck. "It won't hurt that chicken just to pull three or four feathers out of his neck," he'd told me. "He'll grow 'em right back and nobody need know about it." So we went over to Uncle Winton's one day when he was away and caught that big red rooster and snatched some feathers out of his neck. Aunt Effie saw me and told Uncle, but I never did tell why I done it or who the feathers was for.

"So you're the feller who hires a boy to go pick a man's chickens while they're alive," Uncle said. "But I reckon that's just what you might expect from a dad-burned Yankee. You know, Yankees is like piles. If they come down and then go back they ain't too bad. It's the ones that come down and stay down that cause the trouble."

"Well," Mr. Blank said, "I've come down and I'm going to stay down—even among mean-talking people who begrudge their neighbors a couple of chicken feathers. And I had sense enough to come to Florida, but if you hadn't been born here I doubt if you'd have had sense enough to come."

"I weren't borned here," Uncle told him. "My daddy were a North Carolina mountain man and he brought his family here when we was all young-uns—breast young-uns, hip young-uns, lap young-uns and yard young-uns. Me and my sister Froney Driggers had sense enough to stay here. The rest of 'em scattered."

"Then you're really a Yankee too," Mr. Blank said.

That really got Uncle Wint's dandruff up. "If my daddy had heered you say that, he'd of shot you. Why, our folks was some of the last ones to give up. Just last summer I heered there were a feller trout fishin' over on the Nantahaly and one of our cousins come a-bustin' down the side of the mountain through the rhododendrons. He had a long beard and a long-barreled old musket and he throwed it down and hollered, 'I don't care what Lee does. I'm through!' "

"I don't believe that," Mr. Blank said. "Why, he'd of had to be over a hundred years old."

"Sure," Uncle told him. "All of the Eppses lived to be over a hundred. Why, Mother helped Grandma with the milkin' till she was a hundred and six."

"No wonder you people was hard to whip," Mr. Blank said. "And let me tell you another thing. I don't appreciate what you said about piles. Piles ain't nothin' to joke about. I had a operation for 'em one time and for ten days it felt just like I was passin' a bunch of old broke-up Christmas-tree ornaments."

"That makes me shudder to think about," Uncle said. "In fact, I just ain't goin' to think about it or talk about it no more. And I'm sorry for what I said about Yankees."

"We ain't all bad," Mr. Blank said.

"I know that," Uncle told him, "but me and my family knows one that is."

"Who's that?" Mr. Blank asked.

"Oh, a certain feller," Uncle said. "If he ever comes back here, I'll guaran-dam-tee to show him to you. But he may not be very pretty to look at. And if I ain't around, my nephews will show him to you—if they ain't off fishin' and huntin' somewhere."

"Yeah, I know them two boys are just like a couple of Indians—always on the river or in the woods," Mr. Blank said and went on home. If he knowed what Uncle was talkin' about, he sure didn't let on.

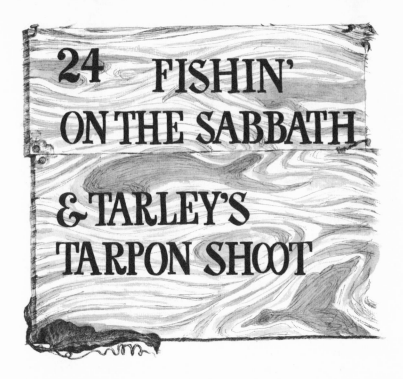

24 FISHIN' ON THE SABBATH & TARLEY'S TARPON SHOOT

I like to fish the best in the world, but Tarley would never spend much time at it—even after he had met up with Loofy Henry and we went on the picnic.

"I'll sit in the shade and tie a shoat by the leg and let him run off and pull him back and let him run off and pull him back," he always used to say, or "I'll tie a string to the limb of a tree and pull it down and let it fly back and pull it down and let it fly back—but I won't fish!"

I guess he got that way from just gettin' too much fishin' the year that he spent down on Shell Island commercial-fishin'.

"Billy," he told me, "that's the hardest life a feller can live. I stayed so tired I didn't have a evil thought for three months. I mean pullin' them heavy old wet nets is cold, back-breakin' work. And I handled fish and eat fish and smelt fish till it plumb sickened me on the devilish things!"

Well, I'm glad that didn't happen to me the time I went with the commercial fishermen, because I purely love to catch fish and eat 'em—specially saltwater fish like sea trout and redfish. A sea trout is pretty and mighty good eatin', but he can't fight like a redfish. A derned old redfish starts out easy, but when he sees the boat or finds out he's in trouble, he's a pistol ball. And when you git him he makes the best chowder you ever put in your mouth.

A freshwater trout, or bass, as the Yankees call it, is sort of sweet-tastin' meat and I don't like it compared with a mangrove snapper or a fresh mullet broiled over some buttonwood coals. But I sure do love to catch them big-mouthed scapers, and there was a old feller, whose name I've forgot, who had a piece of a rowboat in a pond way back in his pasture. He was a funny old feller, but him and Ma went to the same church and he told me I could fish in his pond. Tarley wouldn't go with me, so I got me a man from the turpentine-still quarters to go along and row the boat. I disremember his name, but he was so black charcoal would have left a white mark on him. He was plumb blue . . . and come to think of it, that was what folks called him—"Blue." And he sure could handle a boat.

I never thought nothin' about it bein' Sunday afternoon till I got out to old man Mathewson's—that were his name, I remember now—and when I got there the old feller come out on the porch and said, "No, Billy, I don't permit no fishin' in my lake on Sunday."

"We come a long way," I told him. "Couldn't we fish just a little while?"

"Nope," he told us. "If fishin' on Sunday is wrong, fishin' just a little while is just as wrong!"

Well, it seemed to me like I'd read where the Lord Himself had fished on Sunday or some of His people had, but I couldn't be sure without talkin' to Ma. So I just asked old man Mathewson if he knowed anybody else had a boat in the lake.

"Nope," he told us again, "and if I knowed about ary other boat, it would be just as wrong for me to tell you!"

Well, I seen we wasn't gettin' nowhere, so I turned the old Lizzie around and started back toward Dunnellon.

"Maybe we could find a boat up around Dunnellon some-where," I told Blue.

"I don't know," he said. "They's a heap of Christians up around Dunnellon too! But maybe Auntie Rhodes would rent us her little old boat down on the river—if one of her boys ain't got it and gone with it."

Old Auntie Rhodes was just fixin' to leave for evenin' church when we got to her house and I mean she was some kind of dressed up—a big white hat and a white blouse and a white skirt and white shoes and stockings. When we got out of her hearin', Blue started laughin' and said, "I'll be dogged if she ain't a sight! That old black face a-shinin' out of all that white—looks like a fly in a pan of sweet milk!"

I thought this was a real case of the pot callin' the kettle black, but I didn't say nothin'. Well, we fished for an hour before dark, almost down to the backwater, but didn't catch ary fish. On the way home I asked Blue where he learnt to handle the oars so good and he said, "I worked ten years for Colonel Baxter and we fished near 'bout every day. He was a natch'l sport."

"Where is he now and how come you ain't still workin' for him?"

"He left out two years ago on a big huntin' trip over to Indochina or Outdo' China or somewhere over there and never did come back."

Them black folks has got a way of puttin' things now and then that just tells the whole story. Like Aunt Effie's washwoman sayin' to Ma, "You know, Mrs. Epps sho' is sometimesy." Nothin' could describe Aunt Effie better'n that.

But I reckon the best one I ever heered was over to Inverness. There were a old crippled feller who had a shoeshine stand in the barber shop just up the street a short piece from that old red brick courthouse. You looked out the window right at the courthouse clock and the old shoeshine feller had been in that same place for forty years. One day a feller asked him if he knew where Mr. Charlie Dean lived.

"Course I know," he said. "He's the high sheriff. Course I know where he lives. I know where everybody lives. I been right here lookin' at that courthouse for forty-two years." Then he heaved a big sigh and shook his head and said, "I just wish

I had as much money as I know where that courthouse is!"

Folks say that one time a stranger asked this same old feller if he knowed where the Church of God was at.

"Let's see now," the old feller said, scratchin' his head. "Down two blocks on the right is Mr. Thaxton's church and over on East Main is Mr. Jared's church and then there's Mr. Brokaw's church on E Street. You know, I just don't believe God's got a church here!"

When I got home after the fishin' trip with Blue, I told Ma about what had happened with old man Mathewson and asked her if the Lord done any fishin' on Sunday. Seemed to me like He did, or at least told His disciples to put out their nets. But Ma said that there weren't no such thing as Sunday till after the Lord died.

"Sunday's the first day of the week and us Christians re-member it as the day Jesus rose from the dead," she told me. "This day ain't got no more connection with that old Jewish Sabbath Day than Christmas has with the Fourth of July. There was a heap of things a Jewish feller couldn't do or had to do on the Sabbath Day, which were the seventh day when the Almighty rested after makin' all things.

"There ain't no Commandment about the first day when the Lord rose, except maybe where the Book says not to forsake gatherin' together in His remembrance and that's why I'm always after you and Tarley to go to church."

Well, I'd always noticed that the sun comes up just as bright and the birds sing just as loud and the varmints all went about their business just the same on Sunday as they done on any other day. So I reckon Ma was right. I joked her a little about it one time and said I'd go to church in the mornin' with her if she'd go a-fishin' with me in the evenin'.

She said, "Billy, if we was off somewhere where there didn't nobody know us, I'd go with you in a second. Trouble is that there's a whole heap of folks around here that would just love to see Froney Driggers 'breakin' the Sabbath,' as they call it. The Book says, 'If meat causes my brother to stumble, I'll eat no meat.' You may remember Aunt Julie quotin' that to me."

"I see what you mean," I told her. "But did you ever stop

to think that maybe your *not* eatin' some meat might cause your *son* to stumble?"

"Son," she told me, "I'll go a-fishin' with you next Sunday evenin' if the Lord lets me live." And we went. We hid the fishin' tackle till we got to the Gulf, and nobody seen us, but we never caught a dad-burn thing! But it were nice on the water and Ma said we should be thankful for the pretty day the Lord had made.

Even though my brother Tarl didn't care nothin' about fishin', he liked boats and were a mighty good man on the water. One time he hired on as mate with a feller who took parties out in the Gulf a-fishin' and he told some awful tales about that trip. They had a thirty-foot cruiser pullin' two skiffs, and plenty of rations and water for a week. They had a Negro cook named Sam Hundley and they left him aboard the big boat every day while they'd go fishin' in the skiffs. One day when they got back, the cook were so excited he couldn't hardly talk.

"While y'all was gone," he told 'em, "I finished cleanin' up my dishes and set down on the back deck yonder to rest. They was one of them great big old hammer-nose sharks chasin' mullets back in a little cove and I could see the whole length of him. He were a vygrus-lookin' sump'n. He had a great big old high backfin like one of them pompouses. His eyes was way out on the ends of his hammer and it was four feet between 'em if it was a inch.

"Well, he got to chasin' them mullets and first news he knowed the tide had done gone out and left him. There was high, dry land all around that little cove! And do you know what that scoun'el done? He started goin' 'round and 'round and 'round in that little pocket just like you'd set up in a bathtub and rock back and to until you got all the water goin' with you. Well, he seen what water he needed to cross that sand bar and he taken it with him! When he went across there was three feet of water over that sand bar, and after he'd passed, it was plumb high and dry again!"

They had a real bad blow on that trip, but that old cook didn't pay it no mind—said it were a gentle breeze to a hurricane he'd been in one time on a big ship. He said, "Why, that whole ship was a-poppin' and a-squeakin' like a new saddle. One time she heeled over to where you could get right out on the keel and clean fish. When one of them seas would break over her bow, you could of swum a mule across the deck, and when she dropped down in the stern, you could of just set there and washed your hands. I mean that whole ocean wasn't nothin' but just high and low places. Why, back home that same wind blew three wells up out of the ground, blew the stove up the stovepipe, blew the kitchen out the window and mixed the days of the week up so bad that Sunday didn't come till Tuesday night!"

As well as tellin' some big yarns, that cook could sure throw together some good rations, 'cordin' to Tarley, and when he asked the old feller where he learnt to cook like that, he said, "New York, Chicago, Detroit, St. Louis. I was a dinin'-car chef's assistant." Uncle Winton said that really meant something because he'd eat in one of them dinin' cars on his trip to Chicago and the rations was really fittin'.

It was on that trip that Tarley done his first real drinkin' and he lost his job over it. He were always just on the edge of bein' wild and I guess the whiskey pushed him across. Anyhow, they had a couple of doctors from Chicago aboard and they was a-fishin' off the mouth of Crystal River. Bein' June, there was quite a few of them big silvery tarpon rollin' and feedin' in the Gulf. Both of them doctors had said they wanted to catch one to have mounted for their offices and it weren't long before one of 'em latched on to a tarpon weighin' about a hundred and twenty-five pounds and long as a man. When it picked up the bait, the doctor slammed on the brake of his reel and struck and the fish went six feet in the air.

It were about five o'clock in the evenin' and they'd all just had a toddy or two. Tarley weren't used to drinkin' and he said that whiskey made him feel so good that he just decided to help the doctor be sure of that fish! So he got his thirty-thirty out of the cabin and the next jump that fish made, old Tarl busted him wide open. The scales flew and the fish fell back in the water deader than a hammer. Tarley were near 'bout the fastest man I ever seen with a rifle, but even so, I doubt if he could of done what he done without the whiskey. Of course the doctor raised more sand about his ruined fish than the 'gator did when the pond went dry, and they paid Tarl off and put him ashore. And Ma gave Tarl another one of her long talks about the evils of alcohol and Miss Loofy wouldn't speak to him for a week. For a long time he didn't touch a drop.

25

MY TEMPTATION & THE LITTLE GAL IN THE PIERCE-ARROW

When the German Kaiser went on the prod and all Hell busted loose across the water, two or three boys from our settlement and up in the Hammock hid out. All kinds of stories was goin' around and one were about an old cracker boy from Otter Creek. Every time I heered it I got tickled thinkin' about the time Tarl hid under the porch out at the Yancy place. Anyhow, the story goes that this old cracker boy got a draft notice and didn't pay it no mind. At last a feller from the draft board went back into the Hammock to his cabin and found him.

"You didn't answer your draft notice," the feller said.

"What's that?" the cracker boy asked him.

"You're supposed to be in the Army."

"What army?"

"Our Army—the American Army," the feller told him. "We're fightin' a war."

"Yeah? Who we fightin'?"

"Germany."

"Never heered of it. Where's it at?"

"Across the ocean."

"Then what we fightin' 'em for?"

"There's a feller called the Kaiser over there who wants to rule the world."

"Then why don't somebody shoot him?"

"Why, you *can't* shoot him."

"How come?"

"He's in a armored car and he's got a guard of soldiers around him everywhere he goes. You just can't get a chance to shoot him."

The cracker boy thought it over awhile and then said, "But he's got to come out on the porch to pee *sometime*, don't he?"

As you might expect, Tarl went right over to Bronson and enlisted as soon as the U.S. got into the war. I can't tell much about what all he done and what happened to him because he just wouldn't talk about it when he come back. But he got some medals and almost won the heavyweight boxin' championship of the whole dad-burned Army. He had growed up and was some man—six three and two thirty and hard as a light'd knot. The way he could shoot and all, if we'd of had a thousand like him they'd of whipped the whole world.

Ma got a few letters from him and so did Loofy Henry and they'd get together and read 'em over to each other. Two or three times I got all stirred up listenin' to what my brother wrote and come mighty near runnin' off and enlistin' myself without nobody's permission. I were seventeen years old and counted myself a pretty good man. But somebody had to look after Ma and the stock and all, so I guess it had to be me.

One moonlight night after Loofy Henry had been over to our house for supper, I were carryin' her home in the buggy when all of a sudden, without no warnin', she leant over against me and put her head on my shoulder and said, "Oh, Billy, I'm just so lonesome and starved for some lovin' that I don't hardly know what to do."

"Well, I do!" I told her and jerked the reins back so quick that old Ginger stood up on her hind legs. There was a little old dim road that turned off right near where we was at that went through a pine-saplin' thicket and we stopped in it and I tied the mare. There weren't no weeds or nothin' under them young pines but a pure bed of pine straw and we walked back a little ways. My heart was knockin' on my ribs like a yallerhammer on a stump and the blood was poundin' in my ears. Loofy stretched out her arms to me and I gathered her in. She was a armful, all right—big and strong but smooth and soft too. When I kissed her, her face was hot and her lips was open.

I had been just about worshipin' that gal ever since I first seen her in the Henrys' wagon after the fight, but I wouldn't let myself think about her too much because she were my brother's gal and everybody knowed it and just took it for granted. She were two years older than me, but that didn't make no difference. Knowin' Tarl the way I did, I felt pretty sure he'd been makin' strong love to this gal, but this didn't make no difference either. All I knowed was that I loved her and wanted her right then more than anything in life.

When I started to do it, she tensed up and spoke. "Billy," she told me, "I can't do it. I want to and you're the sweetest one, but Tarley is over there a-fightin' for us all and we can't do it. We just can't do it. Oh, I'm so ashamed I could die."

"Loofy, honey," I said, "I love you and I always will. It ain't just heat, it's love that just goes all over me. But Tarl's my brother and you're right about not double-crossin' him, so I guess there ain't nothin' to do about it. Do you really love him?"

"I reckon I do," she said. "He's big and strong and reckless—much of a man—but I wish sometimes he had a little more gentleness. I know I'm a tomboy and all that and maybe he thinks I don't want no gentle lovin'. But I do, Billy, I'm a-starvin' for it." And she turned to me and put her arms around me again.

Well, I'll guaran-dam-tee that were almost too much for me, as my Uncle Winton would say. "We'd better get out of here," I said, "before I forget I've got a brother and every dern thing else."

So that's the way it were. Nothin' didn't happen, but it sure come close, and from that day on I knowed there weren't but one woman for me. If I'd of had any sense I'd have knowed it the day I taken the splinter out of her finger that time out on the marsh. Just to touch her made me shake and shiver like a baby bird. And when she walked into a room where I was at, it were like the sun poppin' through a cloud bank.

It were over a year before Tarl come home and I'd be a dern liar if I said I didn't do some sufferin' in the meantime. But both me'n Loofy "played it cool," as the kids say nowadays, although it sure weren't easy. But holdin' back my longin's weren't nothin' compared to what went on inside of me when my brother come home and took up where he had left off.

If anything, he had got a little more slap-dash-bang than he ever had been before and that is sayin' a heap. He was rough with everybody, even Loofy, and he worried Ma with a lot more talk about gettin' revenge for Dad's death. I reckon after you've shot a few fellers in a war you don't find it so hard to think about killin' folks. Loofy's brother Goin had been killed in Germany and so Loofy sympathized with Tarl about the revenge business and tried to understand him. But half the time when she'd put her arms around him, he'd just sort of push her off and that would purely kill my soul.

There ain't ary way for me to tell how it churned me up just to see them two together. I loved both of 'em, but my feelin's about Loofy was gettin' the best of me and I don't know what would have happened if things hadn't changed pretty quick.

One day when me and Tarl was up to the commissary there come a big shiny-red Pierce-Arrow car up to the gas pump. Everybody at the commissary had gone to dinner but old man Higgins and he was cuttin' some meat for a customer. Me and Tarl was sittin' on a bench out front and Tarl hollered to old man Higgins that he'd gas up the car.

Well, the gal drivin' that automobile were pretty and cute as a little speckled pointer puppy. She didn't look to be much over five foot tall and her hair were as dark and shiny as a wet otter. She had a box of candy settin' on the seat beside her and was eatin' a piece, and when Tarl finished gassin' up the car she asked directions about goin' to Tampa and they got to talkin'. Directly she passed the box of candy to

Tarl and when he took one she said, "Does your dog like candy?"

Old Barrister had followed our horses up to the commissary and was standin' there lookin' up at Tarl. He had real long ears and the saddest-lookin' eyes you ever seen from his bloodhound grandaddy. He'd been in a couple of pretty hard bear chases right recent and was poor as a snake. When he seen Tarl put that candy in his mouth he went to droolin'. And when old Barrister drooled through them big loose lips, he weren't foolin'.

So the gal asked again, "Will your dog eat candy?"

"Lady," Tarl told her, "that dog will eat gopher shells and he *loves* candy!"

"Can I give him a piece?"

"Better let me give it to him," Tarl said. "The old scoun'el will slobber all over you and your car both."

"Oh, please let me feed it to him," she said, payin' him no mind, and got out of the car. "I just love dogs and the old fellow looks so thin and tired."

"He ought to be," Tarl told her. "He run a bear seven hours in Chessawisky just yesterday."

"What?" the girl asked him. "You mean he chased a bear into a chest of whiskey?"

When she said that, Tarl went to laughin'. There's a river about twenty miles south of us where there's a lot of bad swamp and lots of bears. This river has a Indian name and it's spelt C-H-A-S-S-A-H-O-W-I-T-Z-K-A, but us folks just call it Chessawisky. Tarl explained it to her and told her that we was down there huntin' and the dogs got after a old boar bear that just wouldn't tree. He'd run and fight and run and fight but never hold long enough for one of us boys to get to him. Even our fightin' dogs couldn't stop him. There's a piece of country in there called the Devil's Pocket and if there's a worser place to get through I ain't never seen it. It's plumb hard on dogs and old Barrister sure showed the effects of his visit.

Well, that gal knelt down and petted that old hound and fed him some candy and taken her own frilly little handkerchief and cleaned out his eyes and wiped off his lips.

Then she throwed the handkerchief in the trash barrel and said, "He's a dear. What's his name?"

Tarl told her and then he told her about Rainey and the original old Barrister. "This Barrister is Barrister the third," he said.

Next thing I knowed, Tarl was settin' in the car with her eatin' candy. She were a pretty one, all right, and when she was kneelin' down to pet old Barrister, a feller could see that she had a beautiful little body.

Directly Tarl got out of the car and come over to me and said, "Billy, how about you takin' my horse home with you? Me'n this lady are goin' over to Dunnellon to eat—or maybe even Ocala."

There was sort of a dazed look on his face and he just didn't talk natural.

"Are you all right, brother?" I asked him.

"Uh-huh," he said. "But somethin' has happened. I'll tell you about it this evenin' when I get back."

So they drove off and I taken our groceries and the horses and old Barrister and went on back to Log Landing. Uncle Wint had brought Ma a mess of fresh conch peas and was just fixin' to leave, and when he seen me leadin' Tarl's horse he said, "What's happened—Tarl hurt?"

"No," I told him. "He ain't hurt and I don't know what happened, but he's done gone off in a big car with a gal and when he told me to bring his horse home he had a funny look on his face—just a-lookin' way off yonder like a dog a-breedin'."

"Where'd he go?" Uncle asked.

"Said he was goin' somewhere to eat—Dunnellon or Ocala maybe. Said he'd tell me about it this evenin'."

"Who were the gal?" Uncle asked.

"I don't know," I told him. "But she's a pretty one—a little bitty thing, but put together right and real easy to look at."

"Loofy Henry will scratch out her eyes," Uncle said, "and that old crazy Henry boy will get onto Tarley."

"Well," I said, "I'll let you know tomorrow—if and when Tarl comes home by then."

26
DOUBLE-BARRELED SHOTGUN WEDDING

Tarl didn't come home that night, and by noon the next day Ma was beginnin' to worry. To make matters worse, Loofy Henry drove over in their Lizzie and brought us a mess of fresh spareribs. She knowed that Tarl purely loved barbecued ribs. There weren't nothin' for Ma to do but to tell her Tarl weren't there, and it didn't take Loofy long to see that somethin' was really botherin' Ma.

Right about then that big shiny-red Pierce-Arrow rolled up to the yard gate and my brother got out. The same gal was drivin' and she just drove off without so much as a howdy-do. We was all standin' on the porch, Loofy still holdin' the kettle of spareribs, and Ma said, "Now, who was that and where was you at last night?"

When she said that, Loofy Henry set the kettle on the porch swing and started for the door.

"Wait a minute now," Tarl said. "I've got a lot to tell everybody."

"I reckon you have," Loofy said, "but I don't want to hear it."

"Well, you're a-goin' to hear it," Tarl told her and grabbed her and snatched her toward the dinin'-room door.

When he done that, it were just like somebody had poured a can of gasoline over me and I sailed into Tarl without hardly knowin' what I were doin'. There were a big old fork layin' on the dinin'-room table and somehow I managed to get Tarl off his feet and onto his back on that table and to get hold of that fork. I meant to put it into his heart, and I reckon I would have if Ma and Loofy hadn't of grabbed my arm and hung on. Of course, this were all that Tarl needed to get out from under me and he got to his feet and went to work on me. I believe he'd have killed me with just his fists and wouldn't have been long doin' it if it hadn't been for them two women. They scrambled and cried and got knocked down until Tarl seen I was whipped and that he was hittin' his own mother and his sweetheart.

I ain't too clear about what all did happen by then because Tarl had hit me some awful licks in the face and I felt pretty dizzy and sick. Before I passed out I do remember the main thing, which were that the name of the gal in the Pierce-Arrow were Morna McWirter and she were the daughter of the feller who had hired the guard who killed Daddy. Later on, after Loofy had gone home and Tarl had gone out somewhere, Ma told me the whole story.

"It's like I always told you boys, Billy. The Lord will repay just like the Book says. 'Vengeance is mine; I will repay, saith the Lord.' That feller McWirter who owned the property and fenced off the river has been dyin' of cancer for the past three years. He were a rich man, but his investments went bad and he wound up leavin' this here Hammock property to his daughter and that's about all. She told Tarl all this yesterday evenin' and that's how come he looked and acted so funny. He'd been just livin' for the day when he'd get his gunsights on McWirter and now he ain't got nothin' to aim at."

"What about the Georgia feller Speck Lukins, who got away

with the broke leg? Does the McWirter gal know anything about him? And did it take 'em all night to talk about it?"

"You'll have to ask Tarl about that," Ma told me. "He didn't say nothin' about it."

"I ain't askin' Tarl nothin' about nothin'," I told her. "I love that big old Henry gal more than he ever thought about lovin' her, and after the way he treated her and talked to her, he can go right straight to Hell!"

"Now, Billy," Ma said, "you're mighty near a grown man, but I won't put up with no talk such as that. Tarley is your brother and the Book says to love him. He ain't goin' to Hell if I can help, nor you either. As to Loofy Henry, she can make up her own mind, and from what I've seen of her, she'll sure do it!"

Tarl stayed away several days and never did get to eat them spareribs and I didn't neither. It were three or four days before I could chew anything solid. I had a pretty good idea where Tarl had gone, so I saddled a horse and rode back into Myrtle Island, where we had a little old camp on the edge of the big marsh. We'd go out there once in a while duck huntin' and I just figgered maybe that's where he would be. There ain't no use goin' into a whole lot of rigamarole about what happened, but we just set down and talked things over like we ought to of done in the first place.

"Are you in love with Loofy Henry, Billy?" Tarl asked me right off the bat.

"I reckon I am," I told him, "but if you think I done anything with her while you was overseas, you're plumb wrong. I wanted to, but I didn't."

"I believe you," Tarl said, "and I know how it is to get hit right between the eyes when you ain't expectin' it. That's what that little old McWirter gal has done to me. I'm sorry and I don't see no way I can ever explain it to Loofy. I sure am sorry."

"Well, I ain't," I said. "Loofy Henry is all I'll ever want in the way of a woman, and if she'll have me, I'll be just tickled to death and be in debt to Miss McWirter the rest of my life. She's a cute little trick, but Loofy Henry is worth two of her, by weight or any other way you want to measure."

"Now, wait a minute," Tarl said. "You don't know this little old McWirter gal, but she's all right. She's had a rough time takin' care of her daddy and she's down here lookin' after what he left her and she's asked me to help."

"Well, you just fly to it," I told him, "and the more you help her, the better it'll suit me."

In a few days I went over to the Henrys'. My face were still swoll up and I always will believe one of my face bones had been busted. Loofy made over me a heap and I guess that fight were the turnin' point as far as we was concerned. I know Ma didn't approve because I were only nineteen and younger than Loofy, but the green light were on and it weren't no time till we figgered we'd better be gettin' hitched and not be too long about it.

Old Tarl hadn't been wastin' no time neither and he told me one night, "Billy, me and Morna is goin' to get married. As a matter of fact, we *got* to get married."

"I'll tell you what," I told him, "both of us was brought up on that old double-barrel twelve-gauge of Daddy's, so why not let's us have a double-barrel shotgun wedding?" And that's just what we done.

Uncle Winton were best man for both of us and he had somehow or other dodged Aunt Effie long enough to get him a good glow. It seemed like everybody in the settlement were at the church—even old Gramma Henry. When the preacher asked if ary body had a reason why we shouldn't have got hitched, nary a soul said nothin' and so we was married. Everything went off smooth as frog hair except for Gramma Henry droppin' her uppers durin' the benediction.

A uncle of Morna McWirter had come down to give her away and I mean he were some dressed up. Like a lot of Yankee tourists, he were wearin' smoked glasses. I reckon he could see you, but you sure couldn't see his eyes to know what he were thinkin'—or even if he were lookin' at you.

"I like to look in a feller's eyes when I'm talkin' to him or when he's talkin' to me," Uncle Winton said. "But even then you can't always tell what he's really thinkin'. This Mr. McWirter taken off his glasses while he were talkin' to me

before the weddin' and he sure has a funny way of lookin' at
you. You can't tell if he don't like you, don't trust you, don't
believe you or don't even hear you. Best way I can describe it
is sort of like an old range bull lookin' at a bastard calf."

But in spite of lookin' at a feller sort of funny, this Mr.
Paul McWirter turned out to be a right nice person. He were
sort of a dude and real polite-talkin,' but he seemed to think
a heap of Morna and her best interests. The property her
father had left her covered about two thousand acres and included some of the best pasture and farmland in the county.
There was about two hundred head of pretty good beef cattle
and maybe a hundred hogs, most of 'em just runnin' loose in
the hammock like everybody else's.

Up to the north end of the McWirter land were some pretty
piney woods with some fine round timber. It fronted on a new
road that were bein' started to run down the west coast, and
Mr. Paul McWirter recommended that Morna and Tarl sell
some of that road frontage and use the money to build 'em a
house and stock some more cattle, so that's what they done.

They picked a place for the house in a grove of big live
oaks, back about a quarter from where the new road would
go. There were a pretty little spring bubblin' out of the lime
rocks and it didn't have no sulphur taste at all. Some spring-
water in this country smells and tastes pretty bad—like it
come right out of the bowels of the earth, as Uncle Wint says.

Of course their new house was real modern compared with
our old homeplace, which Dad had built out of cabbage logs.
And, in a way, I was sorry I couldn't give Loofy a brand-new
home to live in. But she was a good old cracker gal and had
growed up pretty much back in the woods herself, so she
seemed right happy.

We taken down two big sweet bay trees back in the hammock and had 'em sawed out and planed and you never seen
prettier wood panelin' in your life—sort of soft honey-colored
with dark chocolate watermarks makin' the prettiest kind of
patterns. It were even prettier than magnolia, and that's
sayin' something. This dressed up the old house a heap and
sure did catch the eye of ary Yankee visitor. We had enough

to finish off the big room and the dinin' room and we made enough money off of some hogs that fall to buy some new dishes and kitchen stuff.

Anyhow, Loofy liked it all, and her and Ma had always got along good, so everybody were just as happy as a tree toad in a thunderstorm. Me and Loofy had our own room and there were plenty of space to add on when the young-uns came.

27

WINTON ZEBULON EPPS

Uncle Winton and Aunt Effie hadn't never had no young-uns and Ma always said it were because Aunt Effie had a lot of female trouble. Anyhow, whatever it were had got worse and Aunt Effie had fell off till she didn't hardly weigh as much as a sack of meal. But it didn't affect her tongue any and it seemed like nothin' Uncle tried to do for her was right. There didn't seem to be nothin' the doctors could do for her neither and there was two of 'em come clear from Tampa. She died one night in her sleep about two weeks before huntin' season, so that Uncle had a little time to mourn.

After the funeral him and Ma went on over to Dunnellon to pick out a stone. Uncle had already wrote what he wanted to go on it:

> Euphemia Epps, beloved wife,
> Who now has left this mortal strife,
> She was a good, hard-workin' woman—
> What more to ask of any human?

Well, when the stone come back, derned if they hadn't
spelt Euphemia with a "n" so that Aunt Effie's name come
out "Enphemia." Ma had a wall-eyed fit, but Uncle Winton
didn't seem to mind very much. "Shucks," he said, "more'n
likely Effie might like to have somethin' to discuss."

After Aunt Effie was gone, Uncle Wint spent more and
more time at our house. He sure did enjoy Ma's cookin' and
most specially her chicken and dumplin's. She'd got in the
habit of cookin' this every Sunday and it was a pretty good
bet that Uncle would show up sometime between twelve and
one o'clock when Ma'd get home from church and would roll
out them dumplin's to drop in the pot. She'd have a big old
fat hen all stewed down so all she had to do was heat it up
and drop in them dumplin's. Uncle Wint was a right good
cook himself because he'd spent so much time in the woods.

"I can stir up some pretty fair country rations," he told
us, "but I get plumb sick of my own cookin'."

I can see how a feller would get awful sick of eatin' by
himself too. Uncle never let on that he was lonesome and
always said he had enough dogs to keep anybody company,
but he didn't need much excuse to come over to our place.

"Froney," he'd say, "me'n Effie hassled some, but I miss
her. I even miss the hasslin'."

"What you should do," Ma told him, "is look around after a
decent time and find you a good woman to marry."

"Maybe a one-eyed one will come in and I can slip up on
her blind side," Uncle said.

"Fiddlesticks!" Ma snapped at him. "You've got plenty of
money and you're still a pretty good man."

"I know it," Uncle said. "I was just funnin' about the one-
eyed woman. What I'm really lookin' for is a redheaded
Swedish widow about forty years old."

"You'd better pray the Lord you don't find her!" Ma said.
"You ain't that good a man."

Well, Uncle did find him a widow woman. She weren't redheaded and she weren't Swedish and she weren't forty. She
were a bouncy, black-haired sort of foreign-talkin' gal from
over toward Arcadia and she were just thirty-nine. In six
months Uncle looked like he'd been sent for and couldn't go

and got there and wouldn't do! That old gal dragged him to all the frolics and dances in the county and I'll bet he lost forty pounds. Even his mustaches looked droopier. It weren't long until he got him a lawyer and him and that hussy was divorced. Maybe I shouldn't call her a hussy—if she cheated on Uncle, there didn't nobody know it. It sure wouldn't have been safe!

Not long after that me and Uncle was up to the commissary one day and run into the widow Yarnigan—the gal who married John Yarnigan, who got snake-bit. She were about thirty, but plenty good-lookin', and everybody said she was real man-crazy. She sidled up to Uncle at the counter and said, "I'd be proud to have you stop in for a snort or two when you're out my way, Mr. Epps." And she batted her eyes and give him a look that would make most any man come a-runnin'.

"Oh, ma'am, I couldn't do that," Uncle told her, shaking his head real sad-like. "My parents wouldn't approve."

Mrs. Yarnigan stepped back and spluttered out, "Your parents?"

"Yes, ma'am," Uncle said. "Old Mother Nature and old Father Time!" Uncle had an answer for most everything.

In about a year Uncle went off to Tampa and stayed a while. When he got back he come over to our place and told Ma, "Well, Froney, I'm married again. This time I got me an old woman. Some folks just have to be shown!"

Uncle Wint's new wife were named Josephine, but didn't nobody call her nothin' but Jo. She were real pleasant and near 'bout as broad as she was tall—not quite as wide in the beam as Cousin Jenny, but mighty close. She'd been a blond, but had turned pretty gray and her hair was real nice and soft-lookin'. She were about the same age as Uncle and she'd been a widow for three years.

"My man went over to the east coast on a big construction job and got killed on a drudge," she told us. "I've been so lonesome I was ready to jump into the bay till I run into your uncle. He's a good man and I'm a-goin' to baby him like he ain't never been babied before—dogs and all." And, by grannies, that's just what that woman done. She baked cornbread for them hounds and fixed chicken and dumplin's for Uncle till even Ma scolded her for "alienation of affection."

It weren't long till Uncle Winton begun to grow a belly from all that good eatin'. One day he come over to see us and it looked like his britches would fall off. You couldn't even see his belt.

"If you don't cinch up them pants, Winton, you're goin' to lose 'em," Ma told him.

"I cinch 'em up forty times a day," Uncle said. "Then I let out my breath, take one step and they're down again."

"We used to have a horse that would do just like that when you'd saddle him," Tarl said. "He'd blow up against that bellyband and when he'd let out his breath you could slip your hat under it."

"You've got to do somethin' about that belly of yours, Winton," Ma said, "How are you goin' to get around in the woods?"

"Maybe I'll get me a job on a boat," Uncle said. "A feller couldn't never drown with a built-in life preserver. But I don't let it bother me. I just lay it up on the bed at night and crawl up by it and go to sleep."

"What does Jo think of that?" Ma asked.

"She ain't never said," Uncle told her and I guess she could tell from the way he said it that he didn't want to talk about it no more.

But Aunt Jo must have started sayin' somethin' right soon after that because Uncle began to slim down. Public huntin' season was comin' along about that time, when him and his cronies went on their big deer hunt up in the Hammock and usually Uncle done most of the drivin'. Me and Tarl didn't go on this hunt, which was a get-together for the old-timers. Uncle Wint would put the other old fellers on stands and take two or three dogs and hit the woods. Sometimes he went on foot, but most always he rode a horse, and steppin' up on a big horse ain't easy when a feller has a big belly to crease and lift.

I said "public huntin' season" because, like most of them old-time settlers, Uncle Wint had his own huntin' season, which was all the time. He didn't go on no big hunts, but just got him a deer or turkey or a mess of ducks or squirrels whenever he needed 'em.

When he come back from that week's hard huntin' with the old-timers he looked a whole lots better. He'd lost about fifteen pounds (most from around the middle) and he said he were feelin' extra good. Then he went out in the yard one day and reached up under a palm tree to prune off a dead fan. When he brought the handles of them prunin' shears together, he just laid his left wrist right into a nest of them little guinea wasps and about six of 'em popped it to him right on the veins of his wrist and one hit him right over the eye. All his life he'd been stung by wasps and bees and hornets and one time when he was bear huntin' he walked into a hole where a bear had dug out a yellow jackets' nest a few hours before and them jackets had put him in high gear. He'd robbed I don't know how many bee trees and been stung I don't know how many times, so I guess all that poison had just built up till the next dose knocked him out. He come in the house and set down and told Aunt Jo he felt dizzy and sick and then he began to turn white and numb around the mouth to where he couldn't talk. Then he just fell out of his chair and was gone. We couldn't hardly believe it, knowin' all the dangerous places he'd been in and the dangerous things that had happened to him, like his tapeworm and gettin' set afire by the doctors and poisoned by bad liquor. But that's the way life is, I reckon.

There was a friend of ours from up near Chiefland who'd come back from the Army after fightin' a year and a half in France, and his folks had a big homecomin' party for him. He said somethin' to one of the gals and she laughed and gave him a little push and he fell over the back of a chair and hurt himself inside somehow and died in two days. Now here was Uncle Winton, who'd been in all kinds of scrapes and been messin' with bears and panthers and alligators and rattlesnakes and horses and boats and bad bulls and bad boar hogs and bad crackers all his life, and winds up gettin' stung to death in his own yard.

Aunt Jo was sure tore up. I reckon she'd got right attached

to Uncle in the short time she'd lived with him. Anyhow, she sure took on and Ma tried to comfort her by saying, "I do believe Winton was happier with you than he was the whole rest of his life before. All of us know you was really good to him and from here on out you're one of the family."

When Ma and Aunt Jo was over making the arrangements at the funeral parlor, I had got to talkin' to a young feller who worked there and he told me some of the things that went on in their business. He said there was a feller actually bought a round-trip ticket for his wife's coffin up to Rome, Georgia, and back, because he said it would cost him a whole lot less to take her up there and let her folks see her than it would to have all of them come down to Florida and board on him for a week.

This same feller said that he knowed of a case where a couple of bodies got switched on purpose. Some hobo had been killed in a train wreck and was bein' shipped up to New York somewhere. A local cracker boy, who was a orphan and awful poor, had died in the same wreck.

"That old boy hadn't never had a chance to go nowhere," the undertaker said, "so they just sent him on up to New York instead of the other feller."

"What undertaker ever done such a thing as that?" I asked him.

"I ain't got no more idea about that than a wild hog has about Sunday," he said, but I'll bet a pretty he was the very one who done it!

I didn't say nothin' about all this to Ma or Aunt Jo on the way home because it didn't seem right to talk about anything funny at such a time. But I know dern well Uncle Wint would sure have got tickled over givin' that cracker boy a trip to New York.

Seemed like near 'bout everybody in the whole country come to the services when they buried Uncle Winton—some folks from as far away as Tampa and even Gainesville. He'd sure knowed a lot of people and had a heap of friends. All durin' the service folks was a-dabbin' at their eyes and I reckon they meant it, but I just didn't feel like cryin'. I knowed we would all miss Uncle Wint, but it didn't really seem to me like he was gone. Not then. But even the neighbors was cryin', so I done my best.

When I was just a little feller, my first pet was a little old baby coon and it had strangled itself with its chain. That had sure broke me up and for a long time just thinkin' about it would make me cry. So I squinched up my eyes and thought about that poor little old coon, but I just didn't make it. There'd been a heap of kids and a heap of coons in the last thirty years. But if Uncle Winton's soul were somewhere and knowed what was goin' on, I'm dern sure he could tell that nobody would miss him more than me.

It's funny what'll run through a feller's mind at the queerest times. You could see Uncle Winton's nose stickin' up out of the casket plumb back in the church and I couldn't help but think about the time he told Horace Johnson about the two-hundred-dollar offer he'd had for that nose and it was all I could do to keep from laughin' right out loud. I could almost hear Uncle say, "Be sure to get the cash, Billy!"

A couple of days after the funeral Ma and Loofy went over to help Aunt Jo go through Uncle Wint's stuff and asked me to drive them. While we was cleanin' out the dresser drawers we found a whole bundle of poems and what he called his epithets. I can even remember a few. There was one about a engineer, a railroad friend of his, that went:

> Here lies old Uncle Henry Runnels,
> He stuck his head out in the tunnels.
> One time he stuck it out too far
> And knocked the Pearly Gates ajar.

There was several about fellers he didn't like ten cents' worth in commissary trade and I wouldn't dare repeat those even if I could remember 'em. There was even one for Cousin Jenny, who he figured would be cremated like her old man:

> The last remains of Jenny Bradley;
> There must be some who mourn her sadly;
> So put her in the hourglass
> And let her help the time to pass.

Way down at the bottom of the pile there was one he had wrote for himself:

> Here lie the bones of Winton Epps,
> Who now has took his final steps,
> And as they moulder in this hole,
> May God have mercy on his soul.

When Ma read it, she didn't cry like I thought maybe she would. She just said, "Praise the Lord! My brother spoke almost the same words as the thief on the cross. Neither one of 'em ever done nothin' much to build any credit in Heaven, but Jesus said to that thief, 'Today thou shalt be with Me in Paradise,' just because he asked for mercy. That's the same as what Winton done and I know the Lord heered him." And she went to singin' her favorite song, "Yes, We'll Gather at the River."

There weren't no doubt in Ma's mind that she was a-goin' to see her brother again. I couldn't help but think of all the years she'd been a-preachin' at him when it seemed that he weren't payin' no more attention than a big 'gator does to raindrops. But he had, because there was a epitaph he had wrote for her. It were in a sealed envelope all to itself and when Ma read it she just set right down on the floor and cried like I never seen her cry—even when Daddy got killed. Uncle had wrote:

> Sophronia Driggers loved the Lord,
> And now has joined the Heavenly horde,
> Where she will sing her favorite song
> To have her kinfolks come along.

After while Ma stopped snifflin' and stood up and went to singin' another favorite:

> On the resurrection mornin'
> When the trump of God shall sound,
> We shall rise,
> Hallelujah, we shall rise.

And Aunt Jo sang out, "Amen, sister!"

Next day they went right over to order him a stone and

have it fixed just like he'd wrote. And Ma told me to save what he'd wrote for her and to be sure and put it on her stone when she went to be with the Lord. She never spoke of it as dyin', but just "goin' to be with the Lord," like goin' over to the neighbors' or up to the commissary.

We never did find nothin' for Aunt Jo and I guess her and Uncle Wint just hadn't been married long enough for him to think of her dead. She didn't say nothin', but it seemed like she kept a-lookin' through all his papers like maybe her feelin's was hurt at not bein' included.

After we got home Ma called me to one side and said, "Billy, I want you to read somethin' and then I'm a-goin' to tear it up and we'll forget we ever seen it." She passed the paper to me and this is what Uncle Wint had wrote about the young widow he'd married after Aunt Effie died:

> A widow I met in Arcadia
> Said, "Big boy, don't think I'm afradia,
> You're big and you're tough
> And I reckon you're rough
> But just wait till you see what I've madia."

> Well, I didn't wait long
> And she sure wasn't wrong,
> That curly-haired wench,
> Half Cuban, half French,
> Old Wint couldn't answer the gong!

Then she tore up that poem and burnt it in the fireplace. The rest of the poems and all she saved in a shoe box. I read most of 'em and I just somehow couldn't believe Uncle Wint had wrote 'em. He sure had some imagination and wrote about things you wouldn't believe he'd knowed about. I copied off two or three and learnt 'em by heart. They went:

> A big fat Turk with a harem
> Decided to go in and scare 'em—
> He bellered and roared
> Till the girls was all floored,
> And that's what we call harem-scarem!

And there was another about the Knights that tickled me. Uncle Winton always called rainy weather "family weather":

Old man Knight is long and lean;
His wife is short and fat and mean.
It takes a lot of rainy weather
For them two folks to get together!

Then there was one about Tarl and Loofy that I didn't like too well. Loofy hadn't been all that much of a hoyden (that's a name the schoolteacher had once give her and I looked it up). Anyhow, Uncle had wrote it a long time ago, when Tarl were crazy about Loofy:

I got two nephews, Tarley and Billy;
And Tarley's in love with a long-legged filly.
Her name's Loofy Henry and I'll tell you right now,
She'll outrun or outfight a razorback sow.

She'll outfish and outshoot the average man;
And purely outdo him however she can.
Any kids who are born to this four-fisted pair
Will have three rows of back teeth and two sets of hair!

Loofy had been a big, strong gal, all right, but near 'bout the best-lookin' female I ever seen. Like I said, her hair were the color of fresh-run cane syrup and her eyes was blue as the Gulf on a June mornin'. Whenever you seen her in a bathin' suit you seen a perfect woman if ever God made one. Even her feet was pretty, and that's sayin' somethin'. Of course, Uncle had knowed all that and he claimed to be a real judge of gal-flesh, but it seemed like all he could think of to write about had been how she could run, shoot or fight. Underneath, she were really sweet and gentle and I still get about half mad at old Uncle Wint whenever I think of that poem.

There was a whole lot more in that shoe box and Ma thought some of 'em was so good that she said she had half a mind to get somebody to put 'em in a book.

28

TARL'S VENGEANCE

In thinkin' back, it's funny what can happen when a feller gets married. Like when Tarl come over to the house one evenin', when we was plannin' a big hunt for the openin' of the deer season—*if* Morna would let him go.

"Howdy, Loofy," he said when he come into the kitchen, "you feelin' all right? You look kind of puny."

"If you had the green-pear quick-step and was nursin' a yearlin' young-un, you'd look puny too," Loofy told him, settin' the baby in his high chair. "Morna goin' to let you go on the hunt?"

"What do you mean 'let me go'?" Tarl snapped at her.

"I mean just what I say," Loofy told him. "Just like I always do. You ought to know that by now."

I horned in on the conversation about then because I seen there was storm signals flyin'. "Honey," I told Loofy, "if you do, you're the first woman who does. You know the old story about the difference between a politician and a lady?"

"Let's hear it," Loofy said.

"Well," I told her, "if a politician says 'yes' he means

'maybe'! If he says 'maybe' he means 'no' and if he says 'no' he's no politician. But when a lady says 'no' she means 'maybe' and if she says 'maybe' she means 'yes' and if she says 'yes' she's no lady."

Anyhow, the story broke the tension and everybody laughed and we started talkin' about the hunt. There wouldn't be no womenfolks on this hunt because Morna didn't want to go, Ma was ailin' and Loofy couldn't leave the kids. This baby were our seventh—all boys but one. Our oldest boy were nine and he was borned right on time after we was married—shotgun time. We missed one year for some reason or other. Tarl and Morna had just one kid, a girl, and she taken after her mother. When I were over to Tarl's farm one day I joked him about havin' just one gal child and me with six boys and he said, "Must be this well water or the soil."

"Nope," I told him. "It's the fertilizer!"

Back in the old days, Ma used to go on a hunt whenever she could get somebody to look after the stock and she sure made a difference in them camp rations. She just enjoyed bein' in the woods and didn't really care nothin' about doin' any shootin' herself—though she could handle a gun pretty good and weren't squeamish or nothin' about killin' game. Like when she'd bring down a gobbler.

"The Lord gave us all things richly to enjoy," she would say, quotin' her Bible, "and I mean I'm richly enjoyin' this here sliced wild-turkey breast, floured and fried."

She'd set on a log and look into the campfire coals and tell us about her young-gal days up in the mountains and how she met up with Daddy and how happy they was when we first come to the river and got the house built and all. Of course she had to quit talkin' about it after Morna McWirter come into the family. I don't see how she could keep from hatin' that gal, but she were a deep-down Christian and didn't believe in hatin' nobody.

"The Book says to love your enemies and do good to folks who treat you bad, so I'll try," she'd say. "And poor little old Morna didn't have no part in the ruckus. To tell the truth, her daddy didn't mean to bring about no such a terrible thing as happened. He just hired a reckless, no-good feller to guard the gate. Morna told me that her daddy never even seen Corson Lukins—hired him by mail."

"Do you believe that?" I asked Ma.

"I do if Morna says so," Ma said. "Tarl does."

"Sure he does," I said. "He'd believe a hog had wings if that little old gal was to say so."

"All right," Ma said. "That's the sort of confidence a feller ought to have in his wife. Don't you believe Loofy?"

"You ain't kiddin'," I told her. "You'd *better* believe Loofy. And while we're talkin', did you ever ask Morna if her or her daddy ever knowed Speck Lukins—or ever even seen him?"

"No, but I will," Ma said. "I hate to talk about it and I know she does, but I sure would like to know if that feller is still alive and where he is. He'd have to be pretty old by now. He wouldn't hardly show up now, do you reckon, after all this time?"

"If he's got ary bit of sense he won't," I said. "Uncle's gone, but Tarl will shoot him time he sees him."

"Can't Morna do nothin' with Tarl?" Ma asked.

This tickled me because that little black-haired heifer led my big, rough, tough brother around by the nose. "She can do ever'thing with Tarl *but* that," I said. "Ain't nobody or nothin' goin' to turn him aside from Speck Lukins." But I was wrong about that.

Our huntin' luck was poor on the trip we made the openin' of the season. Turkeys was scarce and even squirrels was hard to find. Our dogs couldn't seem to jump nothin' but does and yearlin's, so we didn't eat no venison. The Game and Fish folks had put in a buck law and us fellers all decided we'd go by that law and see if it done any good. Wouldn't hardly have made no difference, though, because I were the only one to lay eyes on a buck and he were a spindly little spikehorn that were too long a shot when I seen him sneakin'. There weren't no dogs after him. He were just slippin' along through the palmettos, keepin' his head low, and I seen him across a pond. We'd of had some tender meat if old Tarl had of been there with his rifle, but the deer were a good hundred steps away and I just had buckshot.

I think that were the first Thanksgivin' we ever had without a wild turkey and Ma sure hated it.

"Boys," she said, "I had my mouth fixed just right for a big old gobbler and now we got to eat pork."

"Never you mind, Ma," Tarl told her. "I'll get you one for Christmas I'll guaran-dam-tee."

"Just plain guarantee will suit me fine," Ma said. "Where you figurin' to get it? Billy said there weren't hardly no sign at all down in our end of the Hammock."

"There ain't," Tarl said. "I seen a little scratchin' around Blue Sink, but it weren't fresh. Reckon I'll have to go on up around Nuttall Rise somewhere. They tell me that country is just workin' alive with both deer and turkeys."

"Huh," Ma said. "Whenever anybody says 'they tell me' I want to know who 'they' is."

"Audrey Sloan. That's who," Tarl said. "Her and Jim was at the commissary yesterday evenin' on their way home from a huntin' trip up yonder with Jim's cousin. He said there were a sight of game of all kinds. He carried a couple of bird dogs up there with him and he said the flatwoods out from the swamp were full of birds. Said they was so thick the singles was gettin' up two and three at a time."

"Now, that's how dern lies get scattered around the country," Ma said. "When you goin' up there?"

"About four or five days before Christmas," Tarl said.

"You goin', Billy?" Ma asked me.

"Maybe," I said. "I ain't sure yet."

Well, I didn't get to go, but Tarl told me just what happened, so plain that it were just like I had been right there.

"Billy," he said, "what I'm goin' to tell you is the God's truth, every dern word of it, but I don't guess you'll believe it. I don't hardly believe it myself. I went up to Perry and looked up that cousin of Jim Sloan's and me'n him went in and made camp right near the Rise. That's a pretty place and it ain't far to where a feller can really catch a mess of big old shell-crackers—if he cared about fishin'. And there was deer and turkey sign everywhere. And bear sign. The tops of cabbages was mashed down where both bears and turkeys had been eatin' the berries and some of 'em had the tops tore out where bears had pulled the buds. And a buck had rubbed the bark off a saplin' right near camp. A real old snorter, from his tracks.

"Accordin' to Len Sloan, there weren't hardly any other hunters in the woods, but one bunch of fellers from outside somewhere was camped on the creek below the Rise a mile or two. He didn't know none of 'em, but they come from somewhere up on the Okefenokee. We heered their ax the first night in camp. It were frosty and still, and sound carried a long way. And we heered some lost hunter blowin' his horn way off toward the Gulf—three long notes over and over. At last somebody answered him—two long blows. I were glad because a feller wouldn't have suffered much comfort layin' out that night.

"We located two right sizable bunches of turkeys next day and I roosted one flock that evenin' in some tall pines just on the edge of the main swamp. They waited mighty late to fly up and it were pitch black when I got back to camp. Sloan's bunch had flew up into some big live oaks about a quarter south.

"We was up and gone next mornin' by five o'clock and the sky were just grayin' when I got myself hid good. A feller could hear an acorn fall a hundred yards away that mornin'. Some wood ducks went a-screamin' over and a couple of them little black-and-white fish ducks the Yankees call mergansers. Directly I let out a couple of yelps and listened.

"I got two answers—one I just could hear and one not over a hundred yards away. I waited a while and yelped again, kind of soft—'yeop, yeop . . . yeop . . . yeop.' Right away the closeter one answered and this time it didn't fool me. It weren't no turkey. Whoever it were, made a little bobble. He must of been usin' a cedar box and slate, and it sounded real good until he skidded that slate just a little bit.

" 'That'll do it,' I said to myself, but I'll be derned if the turkey didn't answer and keep comin'. It must of been walkin' when the hunter made the bobble. Near about always when you make a bobble the turkey says 'putt—putt—putt' and takes off. Anyhow, this big old gobbler walked on up into plain sight and he were somethin' to see. It weren't light enough yet to see all his colors, but I could see the size of him and his beard looked a foot long. Well, he were closeter to the other feller than he were to me, but I meant to try him pretty quick anyhow. So I slipped in some BB's 'stead of the seven-and-a-halfs. I'd rather shoot a turkey in the head or neck with fine shot whenever I can. It's surer than maybe just breakin' a wing with a buckshot or a BB. You remember Uncle Winton taught us that. But this was just too far for fine shot.

"Well, maybe the turkey heered me when I reloaded or maybe the other feller moved. Whatever happened, that dang gobbler putted, ran a few steps and took off. Man, he made a clatter gettin' into the air! For some reason he flew almost over the old herricane root where the other feller were hidin' and whoever it were showered down on him. *Ba-loom! Ba-loom!*

"That big old gobbler were hard hit and he come a-crashin' down way off in a palmetto thicket. But in a second or two he went flappin' and scramblin' off and by this time the hunter under the herricane root were after him. But the feller didn't go twenty steps till *he* fell! Then he done more scramblin' and thrashin' around than the turkey. When I seen he weren't goin' to get up I figgered somebody had to catch that crippled turkey, so I took off. I had to run pretty close to the other feller to keep the line the turkey had gone and it weren't till I got near about right up to him that I seen what a fix he were in. He had tore off a artificial leg in some bamboo briar vines and he couldn't get up. When he fell his gun had flew out of his hands and were a-layin' in the leaves thirty feet away.

"And then I seen who he were. There he laid, that speckled s.o.b. that had shot at my daddy so long ago. I started to raise my gun to shoot him right between the eyes.

" 'You're Speck Lukins, brother to Corse Lukins, ain't you?' I said.

" 'That's right and I am purely in one hell of a fix till I can find my leg and get it back on. Who are you?'

" 'You wouldn't know,' I told him. And that were the truth, Billy, because I didn't hardly know myself right then. Here I had been waitin' all these years to get my sights on that skunk, just livin' for the day, followin' false trails, layin' out on cold nights, and now when I had him under my gunsights,

I didn't want him. I just couldn't shoot him layin' there on the ground helpless, so I turned around and walked away."

I don't know whether I could of done that or not and I've thought about it a thousand times—wonderin' what would of happened if it had been me there instead of Tarl. A feller just don't know what he'll do until he's on the spot himself. But if old hot-headed Tarl could let him live, I guess I could of done the same. Anyhow, I'm glad I didn't have to decide.

Ma come into the room about then and Tarl told her the story just like he'd told it to me and she just went to cryin'.

"Praise God!" she said. "I'm just so glad and proud I don't hardly know what to do. I told you a long time ago that the Lord would repay."

I put in my oar about then, hatin' to see Ma cry. "What about that turkey?" I asked.

"You won't believe this either," Tarl said. "I didn't get ary turkey that day, and next mornin' were so cold that a feller just couldn't set still. So after I had waited till a hour after sun-up without hearin' or seein' the first sign of a turkey, I walked out in the low palmettos to find me some light'd knots to build a fire. There were a white frost all over everything and directly I tripped over somethin' that didn't feel like a light'd knot."

"Son," Ma said, "you ain't goin' to tell us it were a turkey?"

"Yes, ma'am," Tarl said. "A fine, fat gobbler. Frozen stiff. But he were a good half mile from where he'd been shot. Anyhow, he's in the ice house over to Dunnellon."

"God will provide!" Ma said. She had a Bible verse for near about everything.

So we had our Christmas turkey and Ma thanked the Lord for it and for the end of all her worryin' about the shootin'. The whole family was there and I know everybody was glad.

"Our Father in Heaven," she said, standin' at the head of the long table, "thank You for this food and for each other and this roof over our heads and an end to hatred and killin'. Bless Mr. Lukins and take any hatred out of his heart."

Everybody said "Amen," but I couldn't help thinkin' to myself that I were mighty glad Speck Lukins didn't know we was eatin' *his* turkey!

29

MA MOVES ACROSS THE RIVER

Anybody who thinks Florida don't never get cold in the winter-time ain't never laid out overnight in Gulf Hammock in January after a rain—when the wind goes around into the nor'west late in the evenin'. By midnight a brass monkey couldn't live—most especially if he was a-sleepin' on one of them coolin' boards. That's what I call them canvas Army cots. A feller is a heap better off sleepin' on the ground on a bed of palmetto fans. A couple of hound dogs in bed with you will help if you ain't got enough blankets or quilts, but even then a feller can near 'bout freeze on one of them winter nights. I reckon it's because the Hammock is such low ground—hardly more'n a foot above sea level—and the frost just settles in till it chills your bones.

I remember one time when we was camped a-deer-huntin' at the old Johnson place and me'n Tarl put our pallets down on the porch. It turnt off cold the first night we made camp and I'll tell you now that were a miserable night. Old Tarl had him a Navy sea bag he had got off of some sailor in the war, and he rolled up in his blankets and pushed down into that canvas bag as far as he could go. Next mornin' there were a white frost on everything and thin ice on the pond back of the camp. Kelly Runnels were first man up and when he got a fire goin' and some coffee makin' he went up on the porch and hollered, "Rise and shine, all you so-called deer hunters." And he grabbed the strap on the end of that sea bag and pulled on it. It were just like you'd pulled the peelin' off a banana—everything come off of Tarl and left him a-layin' there buck naked on them cold boards. You know what that scaper done? He stood up and stretched and yawned and then walked out into that pond, breakin' the skim ice, and sloshed water on himself.

"Ain't you goin' to take a bath, Kelly?" he said. And I still can't see how he could even move his jaws. But he wouldn't of let Kelly Runnels see him shiver if it'd killed him.

When we got home off that hunt Ma were bad off. She taken a heavy cold and it went on down into her lungs. But it weren't like in the old days when they didn't have none of them wonder drugs and if a feller got pneumonia he just had to tough it out. Ma run a high fever and were a sick some- body for a few days. Then her fever busted and the doctor said she had done passed the crisis. But she stayed puny for a long time and Loofy had to do everything in the house as well as look after the kids.

One day I were sittin' on the edge of Ma's bed, feedin' her some oyster soup, and she said, "Billy, I think I'll be movin' before long. This old place I'm livin' in is comin' apart."

At first I thought she were talkin' about our house, but she weren't. She were talkin' about her earthly body.

"It's only temp'rary quarters anyhow," she said. "Heaven is really home and I'm just a-waitin' for the *shout*. Folks say there ain't nothin' sure but death and taxes, but they're wrong. Taxes maybe, but not death."

"What do you mean by that?" I asked her.

"There's a place in the Book where it says that the Lord Himself shall descend from Heaven with a *shout* and the trumpet of God shall sound and the dead in Christ will rise first and then we who are alive will be caught up with them to meet the Lord in the air and be forever with Him. And it says, 'Comfort each other with these words.' Ain't that wonderful, Billy, to listen for that *shout*?"

"When will it be?" I asked her.

"Ain't nobody knows but our Father in Heaven," she said. "But we're told to watch and listen and that's a heap better'n just waitin' to die. Maybe He'll come today. I'd be sort of glad, far as I'm concerned, because, like I said, this old body is beginnin' to wear out."

"Soon as you get a little strength back, you'll chirk up," I told her.

"Maybe," she said. "You get down sick and you over it and after while you get down in the bed again with somethin' else and you over that. And time goes on and you're up and you're down and then one day, if the *shout* don't come first, you're down and you don't get up. But until then I'm listenin' for the *shout*."

Spring come and went and when summer come it were the longest and hottest I could ever remember, and the flies was the worst—all kinds of 'em. First was the yellow flies, the ones Yankees call deerflies. They started in May. They got spots on their wings and red-hot bills. They love to bite me on the knuckles and the place will swell up in ten minutes to where I can't hardly move my fingers. After the yellow flies come them bitin' houseflies. I reckon they're houseflies, but they'll light and bite before you can wink an eye.

Now, I got a way to kill them bullies and I'm a-goin' to tell you about it because it works. Whenever the fly lights on you or on the table near you, put your hand out and hold it steady about a foot high over him. Then look away and think about something else for a second. Then look back and hit him. You'll get him near 'bout every time and I think I know why. I knowed a feller once who had a pet monkey and that monkey could just reach out in the air and grab a housefly. You can't do that and I can't do that, but a dern monkey can. I think it's because his brain ain't all cluttered up with problems and the message goes through faster. He ain't thinkin' about mortgage payments or hog prices or divorce proceedin's. The track is clear for the brain signal.

But when *we* try to swat a fly, we got to do some plannin'

and probably move our hand just a tiny little bit so that devilish fly sees it move and checks out. But when we forget about him and look away and then look back and hit, we do it faster. That's my theory. Anyhow, it works. On any kind of bitin' flies. The best way to kill a skeeter, though, is just lay your finger on him. He don't feel no breeze comin' and he ain't got eyes like a fly, so the first thing he knows he's dead.

Ma stayed puny all summer and we fixed a couch out on the screen porch for her to lay on where maybe she'd pick up a little breeze off the river. The sand gnats was awful bad too, and seemed like they worried Ma more'n they ever had before.

One day when Tarl and Morna was over to see us, she asked us to set on the porch a spell so she could talk to us all together. I remember it were mighty still and muggy and hot and she couldn't hardly get her breath.

"All you children has heered me talk about Heaven as long as you can remember," she said. "Ain't that so?"

"It sure is," Tarl told her. "And on a day like this I reckon it would be a cool, shady glen high up in the mountains with nary a gnat or a yellow fly."

"Tell us where you think it is, Big Mamma," Loofy said. All the kids called Loofy "Mamma" and called Ma "Big Mamma" though Loofy were near about a head taller.

"Well," Ma said, "I'm goin' to tell y'all just what I believe about it. And like I used to tell your Uncle Winton, this is something you can't be wrong about. It's like if there was a feller who has a real wonderful, pleasant place up in the Smokies near Knoxville—high up where it's cool and there ain't no bugs. There's a lot of big hemlocks and firs and a beautiful little clear, cold brook full of big trout. And a view where a feller can see a hundred miles. The owner's got room for everybody and he prints a book tellin' all about this wonderful place and just how to get there.

" 'Shucks,' you may say, 'I don't believe there's no such place, so I won't read the book nor take no stock in it.' Well, that's your privilege because you're made with a will of your own.

"But if you say, 'That sounds like just where I want to go,

but I believe I'll take the Seaboard to Charleston 'stead of the Southern to Knoxville,' you'll never get there and you don't deserve to. So first of all, if you believe there's a Heaven, you've got to believe the only Book which tells you about it and how to get there."

"All right, Mother," Morna said. "How *do* you get there?"

"You got to get on the right train," Ma said. "And you got to have the right ticket."

"And what's your idea of the ticket?" Morna asked her.

"It ain't my idea at all," Ma said. "The Book names the ticket over and over and over again. It says, 'For God so loved the world that He gave His only begotten Son that whosoever believeth on Him shall not perish but have everlastin' life.' And it says, 'If thou shall confess with thy mouth Jesus as Lord and believe in thy heart that God has raised Him from the dead, thou shalt be saved.' The Lord Himself said, 'I am the Way, the Truth and the Life. No man cometh unto the Father but by me.' So Jesus is your ticket on that train. It won't do just to be a good passenger. Maybe there's a old crippled feller on board and you help him to the bathroom and there's a lady with two little old squirmy boys and you read 'em a funny book while she goes to get some lunch. But when the conductor comes through, it won't do you no good to tell him all that. He'll just say, 'That's fine. We're glad to have passengers like that, but I've got to have your ticket.' And you'd better produce it."

After a while Morna said, "What if I had my ticket and just sat there—didn't help anybody nor pay any attention to the needs of anybody? What about that?"

"Well," Ma said, "you'd get there, but you wouldn't have many friends and when the owner of the place sized you up you wouldn't draw one of the best cabins. Now I'm plumb tired, everybody, so let me lay down."

That were the most talkin' she done that whole summer and her breathin' got shorter and shorter all the time. After while she couldn't walk six steps without hasslin' so loud you could hear her in the next room and we all knowed we wouldn't have her long. One stormy night in September she slept away while the wind were whippin' the cabbage fans and moanin'

high in the pines. Wherever her soul went, it traveled fast to
the Lord. I'm as sure of that as I am that old Bull will fight
a bear. And I never forgot what she told us that evenin'
about Heaven. So I got my ticket. And I reckon Loofy did too.
Tarl didn't say nothin' much right then, but he sure thought
the world and all of our ma and what she said counted a
heap with him.

Morna didn't seem to take too well to that free-ticket idea.
Seemed like she would rather go on a "do-it-yourself" basis.
Her uncle, Paul McWirter, had paid off a note at the Dunnellon bank as a Christmas present to her and Tarl, and I told her
that this were what Jesus had done at the cross—paid off
a debt.

"All you can do is say, 'Thank you,'" I told her. "If you
was to go in there and try to pay some more, the bank people
would just say, 'It's done been paid.' Don't you remember Ma
singin' 'Jesus paid it all'?" I asked her.

"Yes, but I feel like I must do my part," she said.

"Your part is just to believe it and be thankful," I told
her, but I ain't sure she ever did.

"Leave her be, honey," Loofy told me. "Like that old blues
song says, 'You ain't no preacher, ain't no preacher's son.'"

"'But I can preach you a sermon till the preacher comes,'"
I said, finishin' out the song.

And that put me to thinkin' about all these things we'd
been talkin' about. I hadn't ever been able to believe that
people just come to a plumb stop when they died. Nobody
could tell me that the soul of a person like Ma weren't a-goin'
on and on to a reward somewhere. I ain't so sure but what
maybe old Bull and old Barrister might have a place. But
then I reckon if dogs had immortal souls, all animals would
have to have 'em and this would include cats. So, far as I'm
concerned, there ain't nothin' to it.

When we was all kids we used to say about some stuck-up
feller, "He thinks he's *it*." Well, that feller Jesus not only
thought He were It, but said He were It. If He weren't It, He
sure done a lot of braggin' and boastin' and you couldn't
believe nothin' He said. And if He *were* It, He were the Son
of God and, like Ma told Uncle Wint, you better believe it!

We went right over in a few days to Dunnellon to see about havin' a stone fixed for Ma with Uncle Wint's wordin' on it, and I printed it out for 'em so there wouldn't be no mistake like there had been on Aunt Effie's:

SOPHRONIA DRIGGERS LOVED THE LORD,
AND NOW HAS JOINED THE HEAVENLY HORDE,
WHERE SHE WILL SING HER FAVORITE SONG
TO HAVE HER KINFOLKS COME ALONG.

I hope Uncle Winton was there with that Heavenly horde waitin' for her, and down deep in my heart I think he were. He'd drank a heap of whiskey, all right, and done some fightin', and I reckon a lot of church folks thought he were purely a hell-raiser. I'll have to admit he'd been a sinner, but then who ain't been? As Ma used to say, "Underneath all them Baptist labels and Methodist labels or whatever, everybody's got a sinner label. It's what's in a man's heart that counts."

This here's been a long-drawn-out go-'round and I reckon I've done told a lot of things that didn't need to be told and maybe some things that ought not to be told. But I hope I ain't hurt nobody.

Me and Loofy are still goin' strong, in spite of all the kids and all their kids, and me and Tarl are goin' deer huntin' up in the Hammock the first of the season. It'll be in a jeep and not horseback and the Hammock won't look the same. Most of the big timber has been cut off and a feller can't hardly tell where he's at no more. Bottle Springs and Gun Barrel and Hickory Ford and a lot of the old places sure have changed.

We'll miss Uncle Wint and his long-blowin' horn and we'll miss little old Jingles and the other old-timers who used to go to camp with us. But there's still some turkeys and a few good bucks and lots of squirrels. The night wind will rustle the cabbage fans and the owls will hoot back in the swamp and me and old Tarl will have us a stomped-down good time . . . if nothin' don't happen!

HERE LIE THE BONES
OF
WINTON EPPS,

WHO NOW HAS TOOK
HIS FINAL STEPS,

AND AS THEY MOLDER
IN THIS HOLE,
MAY GOD HAVE
MERCY ON HIS SOUL.

JAMES

ENPHEMIA EPPS,
BELOVED WIFE,

WHO NOW HAS LEFT
THIS MORTAL STRIFE,

SHE WAS A GOOD,
HARD-WORKIN'
WOMAN—
WHAT MORE TO ASK
ANY HUMAN?

SOFRONIA
DRIGGERS
LOVED THE LORD,

AND NOW HAS JOINED
THE HEAVENLY HORDE.
THERE SHE WILL SING
HER FAVORITE SONG
AND HAVE HER KIN-
FOLKS COME
ALONG.

A NOTE ON THE TYPE

The text of this book was set on the Linotype in a face called Primer, designed by Rudolph Ruzicka, who was earlier responsible for the design of Fairfield and Fairfield Medium, Linotype faces whose virtues have for some time now been accorded wide recognition.

The complete range of sizes of Primer was first made available in 1954, although the pilot size of 12-point was ready as early as 1951. The design of the face makes general reference to Linotype Century—long a serviceable type, totally lacking in manner or frills of any kind—but brilliantly corrects its characterless quality.

This book was composed by The Haddon Craftsmen, Inc., Scranton, Pennsylvania; printed by The Murray Printing Company, Forge Village, Massachusetts; and bound by The Colonial Press, Inc., Clinton, Massachusetts.

Typography and binding design by Earl Tidwell